The Female of the Species

The Female of the Species
And Other Terror Tales

By Richard Davis

Selected & with an Introduction
By David A. Sutton

Shadow Publishing

The Female of the Species
And Other Terror Tales

SECOND EDITION 2017

The Female of the Species And Other Terror Tales
© 2012 by Patricia Davis
Cover image © 2017 by Peter Coleborn

The Female of the Species © 1964. Originally published in
And Graves Give Up Their Dead.
Elsie and Agnes © 1970. Originally published in *The Sixth Ghost Book.*
A Day Out © 1969. Originally published in *The Fifth Ghost Book.*
The Lady by the Stream © 1968. Originally published in *Tandem Horror 2.*
The Inmate © 1965. Originally published in the
The Sixth Pan Book of Horror Stories.
A Nice Cut off the Joint © 1964. Originally published in
No Such Thing as a Vampire.
Guy Fawkes Night © 1963. Originally published in
The Fourth Pan Book of Horror Stories.
The Time of Waiting © 1971. Originally published in
New Writings in Horror and the Supernatural 1.
The Sick Room © 1969. Originally published in *Tandem Horror 3.*
The Clump © 1978. Originally published in *A Chill to the Sunlight.*
The Nondescript © 1978. Originally published in
The Jon Pertwee Book of Monsters.
What We were looking for in Horror © 1967.
Originally published in *Twylight* No. 2.
An Interview with Richard Davis © 1969 by David A. Sutton.
Horror in Fiction © 1971 by David A. Sutton.

ISBN: 978-0-9539032-4-5

Shadow Publishing
david.sutton986@btinternet.com

For

~ Patricia Davis ~

Contents

RICHARD DAVIS
1935—2005

A T THE TIME I INTERVIEWED Richard for my small press magazine in 1969 (see 'An Interview with Richard Davis'), he was already an established short story writer, had compiled two anthologies for Tandem Books and the BBC series *Out of the Unknown*, for which he worked as assistant story editor, had been on air since 1965. Our paths had crossed in more ways than simply a mutual interest in horror fiction—we had both been hired by Sphere Books to edit annual anthologies, he *The Year's Best Horror* and me *New Writings in Horror & the Supernatural*.

Yet, some forty plus years later, Richard's fiction has largely been forgotten. Although not prolific, he was widely published in anthologies in England. Yet he never saw a collection of his tales published during his lifetime. Hence this book and its integration into a projected series under the collective tag, "Writers from the Shadows".

Richard Davis was born in 1935 in London, but it wasn't until he was in his late twenties that opportunities arose to find a career in the horror genre. His first published story appeared in *The Fourth Pan Book of Horror Stories* in 1963, pre-dating his work for the BBC.

Richard's stories often reflect their time, perhaps his own post-war experiences as a young man. The characters' dialogue, the descriptive details he uses, hark back to the sixties and earlier. 'A Day Out' is not just an amusing yet chilling ghost story, it is steeped in the seaside milieu of the fifties. 'The Sick Room' similarly, sets its scene in the post-war years, its "colour" reflected in the drab boarding house which provides its focus. Less redolent of place and time, 'Elsie and Agnes' is a neatly developed story on madness, and the title story uses its diary format to great effect in a tale that grows creepier as it progresses. In one way or another Richard's major theme was madness, but as he said himself: "It's okay for a character to do something *therefore* he's mad; but one mustn't allow him to do it *because* he's mad". The eleven stories here showcase Richard's own special take on horror and his post-war influences and locales.

Of course, Richard was also one of our most important anthologists, and he has left a significant body of work. As with most annual series, publishers inevitably fail to renew a contract after just a few volumes, or two, as in the case of Richard's first anthologies, *Tandem Horror 2* and *3*. (Volume 1 was edited by Charles Birkin). But then along came Sphere Books with a contract for *The Year's Best Horror Stories*, with the first volume appearing in 1971, and an American edition from DAW Books later the same year. That first volume featured some of the great names in horror fiction: Robert Bloch, Brian Lumley, Richard Matheson and Ramsey Campbell included. *The Year's Best Horror Stories* became, as the years rolled by, the major horror annual (until more recent times), under editors Gerald W. Page and then Karl Edward Wagner. However, a few complications occurred while Richard was still the incumbent editor. Volumes 2 and 3 appeared from Sphere in 1972 and 1973 (with writers such as Robert Aickman, Basil Copper and T. E. D. Klein featured). DAW Books then issued their volume II in 1974, but this was a selection of the stories from the second and third English volumes. Sphere must have declined to continue the series, since the DAW third edition (published in 1975) was a completely new anthology. In Britain this was republished as *The First Orbit Book of Horror Stories* (Orbit Books 1976. Incidentally, the only one in that series!). From my own experiences in compiling anthologies, I know how difficult it is to keep an annual going and Richard seems obviously to have had his share of bad luck here. However, Richard had spawned a series that became very successful for its U.S. publisher and new editors, running to twenty-two volumes... And in its way *The Year's Best Horror* was the harbinger of the current big-hitters, in the UK *Best New Horror* edited by Stephen Jones and in the USA, *The Best Horror of the Year* edited by Ellen Datlow, now both leading lights in the field of horror fiction.

Within two years Richard had started a new series, for younger readers, *Spectre*. From publisher Abelard-Schuman, these were issued in hardback and four volumes appeared from 1974-1977. Around the same period Armada Books published Richard's four *Armada Sci-Fi* anthologies for younger readers, 1975-77.

And in the late seventies he edited several one-off volumes. *Vincent Price Presents: The Price of Fear* (Everest 1976) collected eight stories from the Vincent Price BBC radio series. *The Jon Pertwee Book of Monsters* (Methuen Children's Books 1978) followed and in 1980, *Animal Ghosts*, from Hutchinson, also for younger readers.

But the series with the greatest longevity were the nine volumes published between 1973 and 1985, of the Abelard-Schuman/Hutchinson series for younger readers—*Space*. During its run many of the major science fiction authors were represented, Michael Moorcock, James Blish, Ray Bradbury, Brian W. Aldiss, John Wyndham and Anne McCaffrey amongst many others.

Richard had already moved to television by 1965, as assistant story editor for the BBC's *Out of the Unknown*. Created by Irene Shubik (also the originator of the Boris Karloff introduced *Out of This World*), there were four series produced, forty-nine episodes in all, the opening play being an adaptation of John Wyndham's 'No Place Like Earth', and continued with excellent dramatisations of Alan E. Nourse's 'The Counterfeit Man' and William Tenn's 'Time in Advance', just in the first series.

Richard went on to be hired as story editor for *Late Night Horror*. He selected all the material for this, using short stories by Richard Matheson, John Burke, Roald Dahl, Sir Arthur Conan Doyle, Robert Aickman and H. Russell Wakefield. The series was broadcast in April and May of 1968 and nowadays no master tapes or copies are known to exist. The BBC archive does not have any and it appears that no one else is owning up to having any copies. Perhaps in someone's loft... well you never know! The creepy music was done by the corporation's famous Radiophonic Workshop and there is a rare title sequence which can be seen on YouTube, which gives a flavour of, sadly, what we now can no longer ever see again.

Written and produced by Richard, the film *Viola* (1968) is based on his short story 'The Female of the Species'. Made with the help of The British Film Institute's Film Promotion Fund, as far as I am aware it was only even screened a couple of times, one time at the National Film Theatre. The film was made up entirely of still shots, with camera pans, zooms and dissolves. The dialogue is simply that of the main character reading his diary. Running to under one hour, the music is performed by Ravi Shankar (released as the album *Transmigration Macabre*) and Les Structures Sonores, an avant-garde group using metallic sheets, rods, multi-tone keyboards and crystal bows. I have not seen this film, but I am sure that Richard would have continued in film production had *Viola* been more widely screened. Michael J. Harris, in his review of the film in *Twylight*, said, "The use of stills emphasizes the inescapable domination of the cat; the inevitable conclusion of death; the suspension (in Jim's flat) of reality as known in the outside world. The tremendously mystical music by Ravi Shankar heightens the aura of intangible evil and witchcraft".

In 1976 Richard moved to Whitstable in Kent and met his future wife, Patricia. They lived together for a while in Blandford Forum in Dorset, where they married in 1984, finally settling down in Bournemouth. Sadly Patricia lost two children in childbirth. But Richard was a devoted and loving father to his step-son, David, whom Patricia had had by a previous marriage.

By the mid-1980s Richard's genre output had waned and he produced no new fiction or anthologies after 1985. During his retirement years he and Patricia travelled extensively all over the world. He died suddenly of an aneurism, at his home, in 2005. He was seventy years old. It is a pity that none of the young Turks of the burgeoning horror small press, which sprang up in the eighties and nineties, had chanced to see what a fine collection could have been published then. *The Female of the Species & Other Terror Tales* rectifies this oversight, as collected here for the first time are all of Richard's short stories, plus two rare articles and an interview from the 1970s.

David A. Sutton
February 2012

THE FEMALE OF THE SPECIES

April 22.

Well! At last I've taken the plunge. I've started to keep a diary.

Actually, I must be frank. It was on Viola's suggestion. She thought it would be something to occupy my time while she was away. So that I wouldn't miss her so much. As this is confidential, I suspect that she also thought it would help to keep me at home in the evenings. Whenever I go out I'm always tempted to spend too much money. She wants to curb my extravagance. She's perfectly right of course. She always is. I just don't seem able to keep money in my pocket. And at the end of the day what have I got to show for it?

Dear Viola! Her sole concern is for my welfare. That's the only reason she likes to know I'm at home. She's not jealous of me, I should hate to give that impression. She's far too sure of me for that.

So I will try to be a dutiful stay-at-home, and compile my diary. Who knows? Perhaps one day I might even write a book! An autobiography perhaps, or a best-selling novel. And then I'll sell the film rights, and make pots of money! Oh, well! On that happy note I'll conclude my first entry, have a whisky and soda, and go to bed.

April 23.

Mrs. Perkins is that legendary phenomenon, a "treasure." After a perfect dinner, I'm relaxing now in front of a roaring coal fire with a cigar in one hand, a whisky in the other, and my diary open before me; balanced—somewhat precariously it must be admitted—on my knee. I always prefer to be as comfortable as possible, whatever I'm doing, and in keeping with this policy I'm sitting in my armchair rather than at the writing-desk. Not for me the hard-backed, hard bottomed chair, cushionless and austere. And especially not after one of Mrs. Perkins' mammoth nosh-ups! More power to her elbow!

Viola, bless her heart, would have gone over my menu day-by-day with Mrs. Perkins, to make sure I didn't neglect myself while she was away. She knows perfectly well that left to my own resources I'd end up every night at the Dog and Duck with a pork pie and a pint of bitter. And you can't do a day's work on that.

How empty the house seems without her. I wonder what she's doing now. I must be careful what I write, because she'll want to see it when she gets back. But we don't have any secrets, Viola and I. In a really happy marriage you don't need any.

It was a funny idea of hers, to give me this diary. When I was a very small boy at school I tried keeping one. I did what most diary-keepers do: recorded my opinions of everyone who was unfortunate enough to cross my path. Needless to say, most of them were uncomplimentary. One day the diary vanished. I hunted high and low for it. Eventually I was sent for by the Headmaster, a formidable personage whose name I forget. The wretched thing had fallen into his hands, and he had spent the previous half hour reading what amounted to some very frank home-truths about himself. He was understandably incensed, despite the truth of the words before him, however badly spelt, and he gave me six of the best. I never discovered who the traitor was, but my enthusiasm for following in the footsteps of Samuel Pepys waned somewhat after that.

My opinion of that particular Headmaster remained constant, but gradually I came round to the idea of reopening my diary, and promised myself that should other circumstances permit, I would discipline myself into devoting, say, a half hour each day to it. However, the days went too quickly, and I never seemed to have the time to sit back and take stock of myself.

Viola and I have never been separated before for more than a couple of days at a time. That damn brother of hers is always in some trouble or other: though of course one should be charitable enough not to blame him for being ill. It's just that whenever he needs assistance, whether financial or medical, he simply sits down on his bottom and yells for Viola. He never tries to do anything for himself. How I hate that kind of person. Poor Viola just has to up and go. She hated to leave me, and promised to get back as soon as possible, poor dear; but blood is thicker than water, and all that. Pneumonia is a dodgy business, and should complications ensue she could be gone for several weeks.

If only Robin could find some nice girl to marry. The trouble is she'd be more like a wet-nurse than a wife. Granted that Viola is the only family he's got left, he still makes absolutely no effort to stand on his own two feet. In all his thirty-two years he's never made a success of anything, and I doubt if he ever will.

Oh dear, I simply can't let Viola read that. It will hurt her feelings dreadfully. She thinks I rather like Robin, and I am loath to disillusion her. Perhaps I shall have to keep this to myself after all. One has to be perfectly honest in a diary, otherwise there's no point in keeping one.

April 24.

Another excellent meal à la Perkins. I suppose I shall have to give her a larger present next Christmas, though God knows where the money's coming from. I'll have to ask Old Man Stanley for a rise: after all, the work I did on the Wilkinson contract should be worth something.

I wonder whether Viola has got over the disappointment she felt when I got the job with Stanley and Partners. She knew I'd been after it for months, but the competition was keen and I didn't have much hope. She was as surprised as I was when my acceptance finally came through. She was very quiet when I showed her the letter. Just went very pale and those queer green eyes of hers flashed.

After her parents were killed, she'd hoped I'd change my mind and go into the family business, but I told her as unequivocally as I could that while I was perfectly ready to advertise agricultural implements, I wouldn't agree to make them. She always had Robin, I said, although even at the time I recognized the lameness of my observation. Robin is hardly the man to head a big combine like Watson's.

Apart from my total disinterest in the process of farm tool manufacture, there was another very strong argument against my joining Watson's. I didn't want to be kept by my wife's family. She said that was nonsense, but I stuck to my guns.

Of course, I'm not fool enough to believe that it was my own personal magnetism which won me a job in one of the top advertising agencies in the country. It was because I went to them with the Watson contract neatly wrapped and labelled in my pocket.

Most of the best jobs are won by knowing the right people, so who am I to carp? I got the job, that was the main thing and it was up to me to prove my worth and to show Stanley he hadn't made a mistake. I had kicked my heels in one or two of the smaller agencies since coming out of the Army, so I knew a little about the business, and realized how much more I could learn if I played my cards right. Then out of the blue came the Wilkinson Frozen Foods thing. They're a small firm, trying to get in through a crack in the wall put up by the big monopolistic concerns, and Stanley supports the underdog. He agreed to take them on, and let me handle the details.

Viola saw my point eventually, and gave in. She realized I was right, and that I needed my self-respect, although I fear she laughed secretly at my high-sounding arguments. Perhaps I did strike a slightly ridiculous figure to someone as sophisticated as she is, but it was important to me.

I do wish Robin hadn't taken it into his stupid little head to go to Oslo It's bad enough to get pneumonia at home, and expect your sister to drop everything including her husband to look after you, but when you do it abroad everything is ten times worse. He pretended to go for some Farming Convention, but I suspect his real motives were less praiseworthy. Now poor Viola has to rush across Europe to nurse him and bring him home.

I really think to cheer myself up I will see Stanley first thing tomorrow morning.

April 25.

Wonder of wonders! Stanley has actually coughed up! I've got the rise I wanted. I take back every mean thought I ever had about him. He's the tops!

Not only that, but I had a letter from Viola this morning to say that Robin is much better and she hopes to be back in a few days. Robin insists on staying in Oslo, so she'll be flying back alone.

As soon as she gets back, we'll celebrate.

Tomorrow is Saturday. No more high-pressure salesmanship till Monday. God's in his heaven, all's right with the world. I think I'll go to Portobello Road tomorrow morning. Far too excited to write any more tonight.

April 26.

Whenever something has gone particularly well with me, I always try to mark the occasion by indulging in one of my pet vices, browsing round the antiques stalls in Portobello Road market. I suppose, like everyone else, I have visions of picking up some undreamt-of bargain for two bob, and retiring on the proceeds.

What I picked up this morning, however, was the last thing I expected. I had been there for just over an hour without striking gold, so to speak, and my feet were beginning to ache. It was one of those oppressively close and airless days one usually finds only in early autumn, without the slightest trace of the elation of spring, and I wanted suddenly to get away from all the pushing, shouting people. There was a hint of thunder in the air, and everything was vaguely menacing. My spirits suffered a momentary unaccountable deflation, and as it was too early for the pubs, I looked round desperately for somewhere to have coffee. I seemed to be in the middle of an almost impenetrable mass of jostling humanity, and although I did my best to keep in the mainstream of moving pedestrians, I was impeded continually by the clusters of onlookers collected round the various stalls. I have slight claustrophobic symptoms when surrounded by too dense a crowd, and now I began to feel the mental distress signals which act as a warning. They were accentuated by the increasing oppression in the atmosphere. I felt as if a storm were just about to break, both outside and in. I had to get out of the crowd, or bust.

I began to push my way through with arms and elbows, ignoring the angry asides of the people around me. As I did so, I noticed something darting between the legs of those directly in front. It was a tiny ginger kitten, in imminent danger of being squashed to death with every step it took. No one else appeared to have noticed it, and quickly I stopped and managed to grab hold of it by one of its hind paws.

It couldn't have been more than six or seven weeks old, and was obviously very frightened. As I lifted it the first peal of thunder shook the heavens, and several large drops of rain began to fall. I managed to fight my way to the shelter of the nearest shop-front, wrapping the little animal inside my raincoat to keep it as dry as possible.

The shower was short and sharp. After about fifteen minutes the rain eased slightly, although lightning still flashed intermittently. I came out of Portobello Road into Ladbroke Grove, still clutching the kitten, and by the Public Library I put it down on the pavement. There was a coffee bar of sorts on the opposite side of the road near the Underground Station, and I hadn't given up the idea of that coffee.

I found a table in the corner and ordered an Espresso. Having done so, I chanced to look down. There, sitting on the floor beside my chair looking up at me, was the ginger kitten. It must have followed me across the road and into the cafe without my seeing it. I picked it up to stroke it, and it began to purr loudly. When the waitress brought my coffee I asked her if she would be kind enough to find a saucer of milk.

Luckily she was the soft hearted sort of waitress who doesn't mind small animals, and with many ejaculations of "oohs" and "ahs" at its extreme loveliness, she fetched the milk. The kitten lapped it up eagerly and hungrily and then jumped on to my knee.

'What am I to do with you?' I said, fondling one of the silken ears. 'Why don't you run home to your owners? They'll be worried about you.'

The kitten purred contentedly.

When I left the cafe the kitten was still following me. I walked to the bus stop, and so did the kitten.

'Go on, shoo,' I said, waving it away. But the kitten continued to eye me steadily and unbelievingly.

As my bus turned the corner into Ladbroke Grove, I came to a rapid decision. The thing was so obviously lost and for some reason had formed an attachment to me, that I picked it up, put it inside my coat, and brought it home.

Mrs. Perkins was as surprised as I was by my action. But she was soon disarmed by the creature's winning ways. On Monday I'll put an advertisement in the local rag.

April 28.

I spent most of yesterday playing with my new acquisition. Mrs. Perkins assures me it is a "she" and that if I intend to keep her I must have her doctored. But I hate the idea of depriving any living creature of its sex if it can be avoided. I must speak to Viola about this.

Viola has always had a predilection for cats, and I'm sure when she sees it she will want to keep it. I do hope so, because I am completely captivated by it—or "her" as I must remember to say. On Saturday afternoon I bought her a ping-pong ball, and she seized upon it immediately, with all the frenzied delight of a child for its first toy.

One of the falsest myths handed down to posterity, and fostered continually by writers of macabre fiction, is the one which gives rise to the conception of all cats as in some way sinister. Nothing could be less the case with my little friend. As I write she is sitting on my bookcase staring at me owlishly. I suppose for appearance sake I must insert the advert, but I hope sincerely I get no replies.

I realize I have written at too great length of my little find: I must try to curb my enthusiasm. To make a good writer one must have self-discipline.

April 29.

Long telegram arrived this morning from Viola. Robin is so much better that she can't stay away from me a moment longer, and is flying home. I'm not to bother to meet her, as she has cabled Bill Jennings from the office to pick her up in the car.

This is wonderful news. I can't believe I'll be seeing my darling again so soon. These last few days have seemed like years. When she's away from me I feel only half alive. The house, too, is like the "Waste Land."

I do hope she'll like the kitten. It really is the most enchanting creature, and has settled down as if it had been born here. I'm afraid I put off phoning the local paper, but will do it tomorrow. I feel suddenly that I couldn't bear for anyone else to claim it: nonsense, of course, as we can always buy another. Must break off here as the phone is ringing.

May 3.

I haven't had the heart to write anything for the last few days. My whole world has crashed about my ears. Viola, my darling Viola, is dead. Plane crash. No survivors. It was all over in a minute. Somewhere over the Channel. I can't write about it at any length. I tremble all over. I'm not at all well.

May 5.

The funeral is over. Beforehand they flew me over the spot where the wreckage was found. What there was of her was quite unrecognizable, except for the hands, her beautiful hands, which by some miracle had remained unburnt. It was by her hands that I identified her.

Mrs. Perkins has agreed to remain with me for the time being, but of course she won't be living in. I shall be alone here at night. I haven't decided yet whether to stay on here indefinitely. The place is too full of memories.

I must think soon of returning to work. At the moment I feel too broken to concentrate on advertising copy, but they won't keep me on the payroll for ever. This diary is a sort of safety valve to me, although I can't write much at a time.

Robin phoned this afternoon. He wants me to go round to Watson's to collect some of Viola's stuff from her office. I know it is useless and futile to blame him for what happened, but I can't help it. Perhaps I shall see straighter in a few days.

May 11.

I went to Watson's today. It was as harrowing as I expected. Somehow I sensed the presence of Viola more acutely there than at home. I had the uncanny feeling that she was watching me as I collected and tidied round the office. I've brought quite a lot of stuff home.

Robin was there, and of course, received me as tactfully and correctly as possible. Relations have always been a trifle strained between us, a fact which I know is as much my fault as his. But he offered his condolences dutifully, and said all the right things. None the less, I felt he was merely playing a part.

He seems remarkably in command of the situation at Watson's. I might have to take back all I said about his unsuitability for an executive desk. With Viola's guiding arm removed, though, it remains to be seen. She was the one who dictated company policy. I shall watch developments with interest.

While I was there Bill Jennings came in to know if he could help. He's the Sales Manager of Watson's and was a great friend of Viola's. He had originally been detailed to meet her at the airport, and later phoned to tell me the news. He made a very touching little speech about his admiration for Viola, both as a business-woman, and also as a person. I could see he was affected deeply by the loss, and that his grief was as obviously real as Robin's was feigned. I suspect he was a little in love with her. I've asked him over for a drink tomorrow evening.

May 12.

Bill has just left me. I'm now surer than ever that he was in love with her. As he gazed round the room, and saw some of her things around, I thought at one point he was almost going to break down. I wonder in how many other men Viola inspired such feelings.

He admired my little cat, and this created a welcome diversion. She took to him immediately, and rubbed herself against his legs until he lifted her on to his lap. Normally she doesn't like strangers, ignoring them pointedly with a martyred air. She is growing too at a terrific rate, and I can almost see the difference day by day. I don't know the normal rate of growth in kittens, but I'm sure she exceeds it. Needless to say I forgot to phone in the advertisement, which is hardly surprising, and now I couldn't bear to be without her.

She seems scrupulously clean, even for a cat. She sits washing herself by the hour, and is remarkably delicate and dainty in her movements. The other day she walked right across the mantelpiece, which is littered with ornaments, without touching one. She lifted her paw over each obstacle with all the nicety and precision of a ballerina.

There! I spoke too soon. Bill's whisky glass has just gone flying. As Mrs. Perkins has gone home, I'll have to clean up the mess myself. Strangely though, the cat seems nowhere about. She must have dashed out of the room as soon as she realized what she'd done.

Odd, though, the door is shut. She must be hiding behind the bookcase.

(*Later.*) Funny thing. I went into the kitchen to fetch the cloth, and there was the cat finishing her supper. So she couldn't have been in here ten minutes ago. The glass couldn't have knocked itself over, and there wasn't a draught: all the windows are tight shut.

For some reason a thing like that troubles me disproportionately. I must still be in a state of shock. The best thing I can do is to go back to work. Bill said much the same.

But the thought of an endless vista of loneliness and emptiness stretching far into the future frightens me. If only we had had children—

It was Viola's idea not to have a family. She wanted to be free to carry on at Watson's for a few more years unimpeded, she said. Until Robin was sufficiently sure of himself to be able to step with confidence into his father's shoes. But last time I saw Robin he appeared to be in perfect control, both of himself and the firm. Exactly who has been fooling who?

There! What was that? One of my books has fallen off the shelf. It's fallen *forward* on to the floor—as if something had pushed it from behind...

May 13.

My first day back at work. I must say everyone was very kind and pleased to see me. I feel a little strange. It'll take me some time to get back in harness.

Paradoxically, now that Viola is dead, the house seems far fuller of her than when she was alive. When she went to Norway, the house was an empty shell. Now it's full of activity—there's a sort of continual humming below the surface. I'm sure the cat feels it too. She is becoming quite neurotic, and jumps at the slightest sound. This morning I found her in the kitchen, baring her fangs at a point just below the window. All I could see were the usual tiny motes of dust, dancing in the ray of a sunbeam.

One day, shortly before we were married, Viola and I made a frivolous pact that whoever died first should try to appear to the other. I suppose we wanted to prove the existence of an afterlife, and also that our love was stronger than death. In common with all lovers we were a treasure house of the banal. Strange to say, now I'm not at all sure that I want love to be proved immortal.

Now why should I write that? Surely we need that reassurance.

But the thought that Viola might have survived on some other plane of existence, and may even now be trying to contact me, all this doesn't ease my mind; somehow it rather appalls me.

May 14.

Second day at work. Everything that much easier than yesterday. Wilkinson Frozen Foods progressing favourably. Stanley seems glad to see me back.

Robin phoned me about some business on the Watson contract. During the course of conversation he said one curious thing. It seems that he never asked Viola to fly out to Oslo to nurse him: it was Viola's idea, and she had cabled him to say she was coming. No, unfortunately, he hadn't kept the telegram. Yes, it was true he had written to say he was ill, but he was being looked after quite satisfactorily by the local doctor. It was also true that he had got very much worse later, and was very glad to see her, but he was worried that she had felt it necessary to leave her husband and home in London, and very possibly this worry had aggravated his condition. Although no complications had developed, his progress had not been as satisfactory as could have been hoped.

All this was very odd. Viola had told me exactly the opposite. According to her, Robin had cabled frantically for her help. Why should Robin lie so obviously and deliberately? I'm afraid I put the phone down somewhat precipitately.

The more I think about it, the more puzzled I become. Unfortunately, Viola hadn't kept her telegram either. In fact, I never saw it: I had taken her word for what it had said. It is unthinkable that she should lie. She never told a deliberate lie in her life.

May 15.

Woke up this morning with a splitting headache. I seemed to be struggling for air, and there was a tight feeling round my throat.

I find the evenings very close, and will sleep with all the windows wide open tonight.

I couldn't get the thought out of my mind that Viola had lied to me deliberately over her trip to Oslo. There must be an explana- tion. Either that, or Robin is playing some extraordinary game of his own to put me against Viola's memory. But why? After all, he was her brother. The whole problem has made me feel very unsettled.

There are still a lot of things in Viola's room which I must go through. Her dressing-table is still as she left it, and I can't yet bring myself to open her wardrobe and look through her clothes. There's also a small writing-desk up there which she kept locked.

Mercifully, the house seems to have quietened down. There are no more sudden noises or things getting dropped about or broken. The feeling of unrest has gone too. Probably I imagined it, but the cat seems to be happier as well.

She really is growing at an alarming rate. Just over two months old, and practically full grown. I must ask a vet whether this state of affairs is common. Certainly none of the cats I've ever kept or even heard of could match it by half.

I will go over Viola's things tomorrow.

May 16.

The second morning I've woken up with this wretched headache. All the windows of my room were wide open, but I still found myself literally gasping for air as if I were drowning. My throat, too, was aching, as if somebody had been fastened round it. If this continues I shall have to call in Doctor Garrett.

To make matters worse, I discovered something this evening which has given me a disagreeable shock.

I decided, when I came home from the office tonight, not to put off any longer what I knew had to be done.

I went through her wardrobe first, and then turned my attention to the little writing-desk. I couldn't find the key, so I had to break the lock. I thought she kept papers and letters inside, but what I saw made me step back involuntarily. A number of small cardboard boxes fell out as I opened it, the lid of one of which came off. The box was full of scraps of hair, nail parings, and a conglomeration of disgusting and idiotic rubbish. What was so frightening was that at first glance the whole mess was so absolutely pointless. I opened the other boxes, and with one exception they boasted similar contents. In one of these there was a dried toad, in another what looked like a small heart, probably of a stoat or a weasel. In a third there was—something so unmentionable and blasphemous that I cannot bring myself to write it.

One of the boxes, however, bigger than the others, contained tiny scraps of paper. I smoothed them out on the floor. They were charts and diagrams, full of meaningless signs and symbols. On one was a five pointed star, on another, one of eight points. As I was studying these I noticed the cat, who had crept in unobserved and had jumped up on to the dressing-table, among the perfumes and cosmetics. She was watching me intently. Then I noticed something else. The rug on which I was kneeling when I spread the rubbish out in front of me had been pushed slightly to one side, and I now saw traces of rubbed out chalk marks. I made out that to some extent the marks followed the diagrams, particularly the motif of the pentacle, which was repeated several times. As I was examining this, the cat jumped down to see what I was doing.

Replacing the rug, I saw that there were several books in the desk. After looking at their titles, I knew without a doubt what the whole ridiculous business meant. Viola had been dabbling in witchcraft.

I knew, of course, that she was interested in the occult, and she had often tried to induce me to read the books that she read. But I had no time for such nonsense, and thought her excessive tastes for such objects morbid and unhealthy. I had no idea, though, that she had gone as far as this. I had the most preposterous vision of Viola, now grown hideous, cackling revolting spells over a boiling cauldron. Could this Viola, crouched surreptitiously over a corner of the bedroom floor, drawing pentacles with a piece of chalk, and surrounded by the fossilized innards of insects and animals, be the same Viola who, elegant and sophisticated, presided over board meetings, and wined and dined influential colleagues and clients at the smartest restaurants in London?

One of the books caught my eye. It was slightly more dog-eared than the rest, and had obviously been read more often. It had to do with something called the transmigration of souls, whatever that was.

Now that Viola was dead, I suddenly had an overwhelming urge to find out what it was that had so fascinated her about all this. I wanted to share every aspect of her life, however vicariously. I took the book and decided to read it, with as open a mind as I could muster.

May 17.

Began the book last night. It's too early to say, but I'm not vastly impressed by it. The cat watched me steadily all the while I was reading. She's taken to staying more and more by my side. She's so affectionate, bless her; a great comfort when Mrs. Perkins has gone in the evenings.

Talking of the cat reminds me. I've solved the mystery of my daily headaches. This morning I woke up again with the familiar feeling of suffocation, to find the cat lying on top of me. One paw was resting on each shoulder, and her head was somehow coiled round my neck. I'll have to stop her coming into my room at night.

I've decided to find out from Robin once and for all the truth about Viola and this Oslo business, and so I've asked him to dinner tomorrow evening.

May 18.

I locked the cat out of my room last night. But she mewed so pitifully outside the door, that I was hard put to it not to relent. Poor animal, her devotion to me is very touching, but quite unmerited. She has her own basket in the kitchen, where she always slept until a few days ago; but now for some reason she won't go near it. Cats are fickle creatures.

However, I woke up feeling far fresher, and all ready to tackle Robin.

He presented himself punctually at 7.30 and we had another of Mrs. Perkins' royal meals. Luckily her gastronomic standards have not slackened since Viola's death, and Robin was duly appreciative. The atmosphere between us was naturally tense at first, but I did my best to make him feel at ease. I didn't want to antagonize him by calling him a liar, but I was anxious to draw him out to hear his full version of what had happened. At first he was reluctant to talk about it.

'What's the good of raking up the past, Jim. Honestly, I don't want to talk about it.'

'Why not? What is there to hide?' I persisted.

He shrugged. 'Viola's dead, Jim. She was my sister, and your wife. Let's forget it, please.'

'But I don't understand. What is there to forget?' 'You asked me a question. If I answer it, you'll only be hurt and angry.'

I promised not to be hurt and angry.

There was a long pause, while Robin seemed to be turning over in his mind how best to say whatever it was he was going to say.

'All right. If you want the truth, you can have the truth. And then you'd better kick me out.'

'I'll be the judge of that, when I've heard this truth of yours.'

'Viola was an evil woman, Jim.'

For a moment I could hardly believe my ears. After a momentary urge to get up and strike the little bounder, I decided to let him finish this pretty speech.

'Go on.'

'I'm sorry. But it's true. She was—evil.'

'Evil? That's a very melodramatic word.'

'Perhaps it is. But I know no other way to describe her.'

'All right. In what way was she evil? Did she go round coshing old ladies?'

'For one thing she was possessive to an almost pathological degree. Even when she was a little girl she was jealous when Father gave more attention to Mother than to her. She could never bear to play second fiddle to anyone. When she was about ten she once told Mother that she hated her.'

'That's nothing. Lots of children say things like that in a fit of temper.'

'You weren't there, though, were you? Well, I was. She was deadly serious. She just stood there and said it quite calmly and quietly, and stared with her green eyes. You know how strange her eyes were. They seemed to bore right through you,'

I acknowledged that one of the things that had so fascinated me about Viola had been her eyes.

'Well, I can tell you she fairly sent shivers up my spine, and I was older than she was. Mother didn't say anything. She didn't slap her or scold her, she just went away and lay down on her bed, Later I heard her crying.'

It was a grim little picture Robin conjured up. But I determined to make light of it.

'Surely if she had had a damn good slap it would have been the best thing for her.'

Robin shook his head. 'It wasn't something you could mend with a slap. It went deeper than that.'

He paused again.

'Go on.'

'When Father and Mother were killed she transferred all her attention to me. She was determined that I should be head of Watson's, with her as a sort of power behind the throne. You may remember I rebelled a bit at first, and tried several other things—'

'I do.'

'—without making a go of anything very much. Then I began to realize she could be right, so I agreed to play along with her. I had never seen myself as a top pressure business executive, but the funny thing was I began to enjoy it. I really did.'

'With Viola behind the scenes to push you. Surely that wasn't such a bad thing? You made a success of yourself, didn't you? Viola was doing it for your good.'

'That's what I thought at first. I'd misjudged her. Then I realized that I was only a puppet. In reality it was Viola who made all the decisions. When I taxed her with it she just laughed in my face. She told me that I wasn't and never would be capable of running the show on my own. I needed her and always would.'

'You're exaggerating.'

'I'm surprised that you, of all people, should say that.'

'Me?'

'Yes, you. She dominated you every bit as much as she did me.'

'Now look here, Robin—'

'Jim, let's put our cards on the table, and stop fencing for once. Viola's one aim was to possess the soul of every man she met, utterly, completely, and exclusively.'

'Oh, come off it!'

'It's true, Jim. I told you when you heard the truth you'd want to kick me out.'

He bent down to fondle the cat, which was rubbing itself sensuously against his trouser-leg.

'I don't want to kick you out,' I said magnanimously. 'I just think you're labouring under some kind of delusion.'

'Look, Jim. I wanted to get married twice in my life.

'Each time Viola got to the girl and warned her off.'

'Warned her off? How?'

Robin shrugged. 'I don't know the full story. They just didn't want to see me anymore. When I asked for reasons, they wouldn't talk about it.'

'Just supposing it was Viola—which I doubt—why didn't you tell her to go to hell?'

'Because—to be perfectly frank, I was frightened of her.'

'Frightened of her,' I repeated stupidly.

'Although I was two years older than Viola, I was frightened of her. In some way I was helpless before her, like a bird and a snake. Her will—'

'Yes, she had great will-power,' I interrupted, trying to get the whole thing back into proportion.

'It was more than that. It was a positive force. And it was a force for evil. Damn and blast!'

This savage exclamation dissipated somewhat the effect of his melodramatic words. The cat had torn a long gash through his right trouser-leg and the sides of the material showed red. I sprang up.

'Robin, that looks awful. I've got bandages in the bathroom. What a thing to happen!'

It was a very nasty wound. The blood was flowing freely, and when I tried to tie the bandage I found that the edges of the soaked cloth were sticking to the flesh.

'You'd better call in at Hammersmith Hospital,' I said. 'This looks quite deep. I'll drive you there if you can trust me at the wheel of your car.'

He was obviously in pain, and after I'd attempted a very inexpert job of staunching the blood, I decided to get him there as soon as possible.

While we were in the hall, and I was fumbling for the front door key as usual, something shot past my legs and into the garden. I decided to give the animal the thrashing of its life when I got back.

The doctor pronounced the wound not as serious as at first seemed the case, and afterwards I drove Robin to his flat.

He was a little white about the gills, but more from shock than anything else. When I was leaving he pressed my arm.

'Thanks, Jim. Listen, I'm sorry for what I said. I had no right to talk as I did.'

'But you meant what you said.'

'Yes, I'm afraid I did. And—'

'Well?'

'Get out of that house, Jim. Get right away.'

'What on earth—?'

'Viola's will was very strong. Believe me. It was very strong indeed...'

And on that cryptic note I left him.

I could see he was very shaken, so I thought it wiser not to ask any more questions. But all the way home I thought about what he'd said, and couldn't make up my mind about him. I still can't. Is he merely a young man of weak character with a very unpleasant bee in his bonnet, or is there really something in his ramblings?

If one accepted his story at its face value, and Viola had really dominated him as much as he said, then of course she would have grabbed at the chance of flying out to Norway after him. But surely she had never tried to dominate me in that way? Robin had said that she had, but how would he know?

Of course it was true that she had wanted me to spend as much of my time with her as I could when I wasn't working. After we were married I had tended to lose touch with my own friends and contemporaries: still, I had accepted that state of affairs as universal and inevitable. Surely it was only natural for a man and woman in love to be sufficient unto themselves, that's how I'd always looked at it.

Now I realized that in a hundred little ways Viola had discouraged me from having any interests distinct and apart from herself, or into which she couldn't enter. There was always some reason why it wasn't convenient to have anyone to dinner, unless she'd asked them, and if I wanted to go out in the evening for a drink on my own she would always tell me I spent too much money. Why, even when she went on her Norwegian trip, she had given me this very diary to keep me in at night, playing on some old childish fancy of mine.

A diary, this very diary. And it had worked!

May 19.

It's strange how one's feelings change towards a pet if the pet has shown itself capable of some sudden unexpected ferocity. You don't feel any less affection for it, but this affection becomes tinged with something else, a slight fear perhaps, or even a subtle respect. You find yourself becoming less patronizing towards it; less conscious of it as a piece of property, and more as a separate living being which you cannot own to the extent you supposed. You find yourself subconsciously studying its moods, wondering whether or not it really wants to be petted and patted; you don't just pet and pat it willy-nilly!

All this is merely a preamble to my confession that after all I took no disciplinary action whatever against my cat. Instead I recognized that in one evening and certainly prematurely she had thrown away every last vestige of kitten-hood, and emerged into fully-fledged adult cat-hood. And she is barely three months old!

When I returned from Robin's she was nowhere to be seen. I went out into the garden, intending to beat the living daylights out of her, as the saying is, but she remained hidden. There wasn't much to be gained from scrabbling about in the grass in the pitch-dark, where she had the advantage of sight and I hadn't, so I came in and went to bed.

Soon, however, I heard the familiar mewing and scratching outside the bedroom door. I had had a special cat-door fitted to the bottom of the front door, and after waiting until my mole-like search had ended she must have followed me in, in the superior way cats have.

'Go away,' I called, 'I'm not letting you in.'

But the mewing persisted. And then an odd thing happened. Even now I'm totally unable to explain it. I somehow felt my brain invaded, as if something outside myself were putting thoughts into it deliberately. I felt constrained to get up and let the damned animal in. The urge was so strong it was almost a compulsion. The cat immediately .jumped up on to the bed, and no amount of entreaty or threats on my part would induce her to get off, and to sleep on the floor as I intended. Eventually she made herself comfortable on top of my dressing-gown, which was lying across the bottom of the bed. But this morning when I awoke she was in the same attitude of almost human embrace as formerly. When I looked in the shaving mirror I noticed her claw-marks on my neck.

Today I thought more and more about what Robin said. It's true that Viola was possessive. I must face that indisputable fact. To think I've spent whole days doing nothing, seeing no one, just play-ing with the cat. What sort of an existence is that for a man of my age and capability? Before I know it I shall become a spinsterish neurotic. I must rebuild my life, catch up on all my friends before it's too late. Tonight I shall go out and get drunk.

May 20.

Last night I went out and got drunk. When I came in I saw Viola sitting in my armchair in front of the bedroom window. I state it like that, baldly, because that was the way it happened to me. Without any warning. I just pushed open the bedroom door and—there she was. She was facing me, her eyes looking into mine, and smiling. If only the room would keep still, I thought, I could focus on you properly. But the room didn't keep still. I was the one stationary object in a madly reeling universe. The fumes of the beer and whisky I had drunk threatened to rise up and engulf me like the waves of a noisome sea. I blinked, and put my hands out to steady myself. When I looked again it wasn't Viola, of course, it was the cat. She was sitting on the window sill gazing at me steadily, with her green eyes. I found myself yelling at her, 'For God's sake get out of here,' and this time she stayed out of my way all night.

This morning, even amidst the throbbing agony of the world's worst hangover, the hallucination remained remarkably vivid. It has stayed with me the whole day. I decided, when eventually I plucked up enough courage to get out of bed, that it wouldn't be fair either to me or Stanley & Partners to go into the office today. So I stayed at home, and ploughed on through Viola's book.

Once or twice throughout the day I've had the same odd sensation I had two nights ago, that some outside agency is putting thoughts into my brain. And each thought is in some way connected with the cat. To give an example, round about three o'clock in the afternoon while reading the book, there protruded between me and the printed page a sudden distinct picture of a saucer of milk! I looked up and there was the cat. 'Are you thirsty then?' I murmured. I got up, without quite knowing why, and fetched a saucer of milk from the kitchen. The cat lapped it up to the last drop, and then ambled slowly out of the room. I returned to the book, and the empty saucer was left in the middle of the floor, as a sort of mute testimonial to this odd little episode.

If I were to write down what really appeared to happen, and somebody found this diary, I should feel they were quite justified in packing me off to the nearest asylum!

May 21.

Today I had a bonfire in the garden, where I burnt all of Viola's detestable paraphernalia. The cat sat on the wall watching me, and as I threw the last of the cardboard boxes on top of the pile, she came to the edge of the wall and spat at me. This marks the begin-ning of a new stage in our relationship; if she does it again, I shall either give her away or if no one will take her, I'll have her destroyed.

Had another day off from work.

May 22.

A letter arrived this morning from Robin urging me to take his advice and leave this house, but he wouldn't say why. He also advised me to have the cat destroyed as it wasn't safe.

May 23.

I meant to go to work today, but somehow I couldn't bring myself to get up. I told Mrs. Perkins I felt under the weather, and she remarked that I hadn't been looking well for some days. She brought me trays of food in bed, and I finished Viola's book.

It's difficult for me to criticize the book objectively, because I cannot for one moment accept the pseudo-mystical tenets employed. Briefly, the theory of transmigration lays down that at the moment of death the soul passes into some other "corporeal substance", or body, and carries on from there. The number of different domiciles which the soul occupies is limited only by the state of grace in which it finds itself, and in many cases the choice is very much a deliberate, conscious process. The belief is widespread in certain Eastern cults today, and has turned up again and again throughout recorded history, with various minor modifications. The author mentions that at the time of Julius Caesar's conquest of Gaul it was common among the Druids, and Horace touches on it in one of his Odes.

The difference, I understand, between this process and the far more widely held belief in reincarnation is that in the former case the change is practically instantaneous, and the incorporeal spirit can take over an already extant body, whereas in the latter the soul has to go through all the stages of being actually born again, and can remain for an indefinite length of time in a state of limbo, or suspension between this world and the next.

And that was the book Viola was reading a few days before she died.

May 24.

I can't shake off this unpleasant feeling of lethargy. Everything is too much trouble. It seems to be increasing.

The cat leaves me alone now very seldom. She seems to have got over her little outbreak of hostility, and now follows me around more closely than ever. Could she be spying on me?

Now what put a thought like that into my head? My mind seems more than ever to have been invaded by something outside myself, and I feel as if I have lost control over my own mental processes. This morning the oddest sentence came into my head. I found myself thinking, if only I could get over this ridiculous urge to go out and kill a bird. But I've never had any urge to kill a bird or anything else!

I had an awful nightmare last night. Something came into my room, and when I put on the light, I saw that it was half-cat, half-woman. From the waist up Viola's body had been grafted on to that of the cat. I woke up in a cold sweat.

I suppose I had been thinking too much of Viola's wretched book. I must consult Doctor Garrett, or buy a nerve tonic, or something.

May 25.

I can no longer keep the cat out of my room. Although I lock the door, it seems to get in just the same. Again this morning it was lying on top of me, but I couldn't account for the auditory hallucination. It was with my right ear alone that I heard a low humming, like a woman crooning. Although I barely heard it, and then only on the tail-end of a dream, I knew that it was Viola's voice. I couldn't help the horror with which I pushed the thing off the bed. For the voice, or whatever it was, was coming out of the cat's mouth.

She hopped on to the window-sill and sat looking at me unblinkingly and mockingly.

I've taken the diary and am writing it in bed. All day long the cat has been outside the door, scratching, scratching, scratching to get in.

(Later.) I had to get up and let her in. I couldn't stand the noise any longer.

Immediately she jumped back on to the bed again and tried to resume her former position. Before I realized what was happening, she had kissed me on the lips. It was not the lick of an animal, it was the kiss of a woman, and I cannot convey the disgust and nausea I felt, as I threw the thing from me across the room, and rubbed my face all over with a handkerchief. For in that kiss I recognized all the exquisite longing, all the unspent passion of a woman crying out for long-denied love, and I knew beyond a shadow of doubt that that woman was my dead wife, Viola.

May 26.

Looking over my last entry in the light of a new day, my first impulse was to tear out the complete page. Should this book ever fall into other hands than mine, my words would almost certainly be misunderstood, and I don't want to end my days in a madhouse!

But perhaps if I set down my darkest thoughts on paper, I might be able in this way to rationalize them and ultimately to dismiss them.

What if the arguments laid down in Viola's book are correct? What if Viola and the cat are the same—what? Soul? Spirit? Entity? This thing, whatever it is, hating to loose hold of life, clinging to her earthly haunts—hadn't I felt her presence that day at Watson's? Then the night of Bill Jennings' visit, when those strange disturbances began; pointless, senseless happenings like broken whisky glasses, dropped books; that strange feeling of hidden activity—She returned here, a spirit disembodied, earthbound, not knowing how to channel her energies, purposeless, only knowing she had to cling on to me. Yes, me. She had to cling on to me at all costs. She wanted to possess me dead as she had possessed me living. But how? And then the cat appeared, conveniently, and she had her solution.

I feel as if my brain were bursting.

June 5.
I have been ill for the last few days. The doctor has just left me. I am pronounced out of danger. But he's wrong. He doesn't understand. None of them understands. I'm not out of danger at all.

The cat has been with me practically all the time. Whenever I told Mrs. Perkins to take her away she always found her way back. Whenever I woke up from sleep, there she was, either on the chair, or the mantelpiece, or the windowsill, looking at me, and smiling. Oh yes, she can smile now, Like Viola used to.

Perhaps she told Mrs. Perkins to bring her back. She talks now, you see. Quite often. Not just inside my head. That was bad enough of course. But now it's ten thousand times worse. She talks quite normally and openly. In Viola's voice.

The first time it happened was just after I'd finished my last entry. I said my brain was bursting, do you remember? Then I heard Viola say, quite clearly and distinctly, 'It's all right my dearest. Just a little longer. Be patient. It's hard at first, but soon I'll be with you. I'll be as you knew me. And we'll be together again. For always.'

I looked up, and there was the cat, her eyes gleaming. But they weren't her eyes any more, d'you see. They were Viola's.

Then she came and talked to me again. Many times. It was odd that Mrs. Perkins didn't notice anything. You know how cats move their heads: in a kind of jerky way? Well, she doesn't move hers like that anymore. She moves it up and down and from side to side, smoothly and easily, like a human. I feel as if I am on the brink of some tremendous revelation.

June 6.
It has suddenly occurred to me, quite out of the blue, that I never christened you. I shall have to call you Viola, won't I, my pretty pussy-cat. Viola, because that is your name.

June 7.
I noticed today for the first time that her colour has changed slightly. She's lost the ginger colour she always had. Her fur is more a shade of copper-blonde, like Viola's hair. I crept up on her when she wasn't looking this evening, to find her practising walking on her hind paws only. I wonder what the Zoological Society would make of that!

Was that a knock on the door? Mrs. Perkins went home half an hour ago.

(Later.) I said I was on the brink of a revelation, did I? Oh God, it's come at last. The ultimate blasphemy. The physical change.

Half an hour ago I broke off because there was a knock on the door. A human knock. Then the handle turned, the door opened, and Viola came in. But at the end of her paws, where the claws ought to be, there were hands. Human hands. The same hands I saw on the charred body in the wreckage. Can will-power, a sheer blind elemental force as it must be, can it really accomplish *this*?

She sits opposite to me now as I write. Scratching herself, like a cat does, but with her hands, each finger separate, moving up and down on her copper-blonde fur, and purring...

(Later.) What time is it, what day? I have lost all count of the hours...

Here is Mrs. Perkins...

(Later.) Is it possible Mrs. Perkins noticed nothing? She passed right by the chair where the thing sits, and absentmindedly patted it. She brought me breakfast, but I could eat nothing. It must be morning then, but I don't remember going to sleep last night. I can tell she is shocked at my appearance. Why doesn't she notice the horror? Has she noticed it already, and has it turned her brain?

I must kill it. Robin was right. I must leave this terrible house, but first I must kill this abomination, before it changes any more.

(Later.) I can't kill it. I can't kill my Viola. I would be a murderer. But if I can't kill it I must kill myself. Will that be an escape, if Viola is already dead? I call upon God in I Heaven to keep us apart.

But she's not dead. She's here with me now. There's an aspirin bottle in the bathroom cupboard.

(Later.) There now. I've taken the aspirin. All of them. There's a lovely feeling of drowsiness. Soon I won't be able to write any more. She tried to stop me taking the aspirin. Jumped on my back and tried to wrest the bottle from me. I can still hear the words she used, echoing round the room as if it were a vault. 'Damn you,' she said. 'God damn you!' The room is blurring and dancing before my eyes. I'm free of you, Viola.

Go to hell, Viola.

ELSIE AND AGNES

O N SUNDAY JUNE 3rd at two minutes to four precisely Elsie Sanders murdered her sister Agnes. She had been thinking of doing so for some time, so that the event when it occurred had attached to it a certain stylish inevitability. They were having their tea at the time and Agnes had just finished her third cup. She always drank more tea than Elsie; this was just one of the habits which had caused Elsie increasing irritation through the years. She had even tried making disparaging remarks about Agnes' bladder. But Agnes had continued to sit there, stolidly drinking her way through the pot, and it was invariably Elsie who could stand it no longer and had to leave the room first.

Not that it was only the tea that had caused Elsie's decision. For days Agnes had been getting harder and harder to live with, and had taken to making offensive and unnecessary remarks. Now everything she did seemed to grate on poor Elsie's tired suscepti- bilities. She had got up to pour herself a third cup—without, of course, asking if Elsie wanted another—and suddenly Elsie decided that enough was enough and that the moment of Agnes' demise could be postponed no longer. One thing you could always say about Elsie was that once her mind was made up it stayed that way; and so she got up carefully, tiptoed around behind Agnes' chair, and produced a skein of the beautiful blue wool she had kept originally for Tom's new birthday present pullover. It was all over in a jiffy: it almost seemed as if Agnes approved the swiftness and neatness of her action, for her head nodded as she lolled forward, slumping on to the floor before Elsie could stop her.

Almost as she hit the floor the clock on the mantelpiece struck four. At a quarter past Mrs. Watkins would be in to collect the tea things. That gave Elsie fifteen minutes to dispose of Agnes. She had it all worked out in her mind; how many times had she sat and thought about it, like they did in the detective novels which lined the bookshelf in her bedroom upstairs. It hadn't crystallized in her mind all at once, of course. At first it had just been a general wish that Agnes should no longer be there. There didn't seem, quite simply, to be any other way of getting rid of her. She was too old and unqualified to get a job and thus support herself, and there certainly wasn't enough money in the legacy that Tom's father had left them for the sisters to maintain separate establishments. And to cap it all, surely it wasn't just fancy that Agnes herself had begun to regard her sister a trifle oddly just lately. Perhaps she herself had the same idea? Well, Elsie must beat her to it.

The door from the drawing-room opened on to the hallway and immediately opposite was the door leading to the cellar. Luckily Mrs. Watkins in the kitchen was out of sight round the corner, and unless she chose to open the kitchen door before the clock struck the quarter-hour Elsie knew she had a safe fifteen minutes to get Agnes across the passage and down the steps. What she would do when Agnes was safely in the cellar required further thought. Still, first things first. She debated for a moment whether to take the head or the legs, and decided on the former. If she took the legs, and the head began to bump unduly on the stone steps going down, something would crack, and Elsie, who still felt faint at the sight of blood, didn't fancy cleaning all those steps. The prospect, indeed, quite sickened her.

Agnes was heavier than she expected, and Elsie felt a heart-stopping moment of discouragement. After all, she was already turned sixty, and although she kept herself hale and hearty and in good physical trim, the job in front of her would have daunted a woman half her age. Still, she'd never been one to give up, and if a job was worth doing at all it was worth doing well. Already she felt freer now that Agnes had departed. The momentary depression had given way to a sense of elation as she pulled up the head, which again seemed to nod with approval at what she was doing, as if Agnes herself was perfectly prepared to cooperate.

Once Elsie had a good grip, Agnes moved over the polished floor fairly easily. She was still overweight, of course, and Elsie thought of all the hundreds of times she had warned her about all that bread, and all those potatoes, and yes, those ridiculous chocolate steam puddings covered in rich sweet chocolate sauce that Agnes seemed to covet so greedily. Obesity was a word Elsie dreaded, as she devoured her starch-free diet, and Agnes, poor soul, was well on the way...

As the sisters reached the door Elsie saw out of the corner of her eye that Agnes' rocking-chair was still moving. The momentum of Agnes' fall must have given the thing an extra hard push. That was another thing that had irritated her, the way Agnes would insist on having a rocking-chair. It was so mid-Victorian, like lace caps and shawls, and Torn, dear Tom, laughed every time he saw it.

The cellar steps at last! Careful, now careful, this needs all my concentration. One—bump— two— bump— three. On the fourth step she had to stop to get her breath. Agnes was looking up at her, a puzzled expression on her face. She hadn't realized the eyes would be open. Supporting the head with one hand, she shut them quickly with the other. Again Agnes nodded approval. Bending her head round, Elsie noted with dismay that the steps seemed to go on interminably. At this rate her fifteen minutes would be up before Agnes was halfway down, and if Elsie wasn't back in the drawing-room Mrs. Watkins would come looking. The door at the top of the steps was open: Elsie had needed the light to negotiate the steps. She remembered once counting them; there were twenty-two. Come on, she told herself firmly, you can do it.

Four— bump—five—bump.

Every step was harder. She really hadn't thought it would be this difficult. Inwardly she cursed those chocolate puddings. I should have forbidden Mrs. Watkins to buy any. A woman of her age. Chocolate puddings indeed! It was sheer gluttony.

Six—bump— seven— bump— eight—

Gluttony was one of the seven deadly sins, wasn't it?

Agnes would surely be punished for that, she thought with a sudden satisfaction which gave her added strength.

Bump— nine— bump— ten—

Halfway! Or nearly... just another little rest. Elsie looked at her watch, cradling Agnes against her legs. Six minutes past. Not too bad. She might just do it...

Twelve— bump— bump— this must be fourteen... Dammit. I've lost count...

Yes, there'd be plenty of things Agnes would be punished for in the after-life. A sudden stab of hatred shot through her. Always nosing and poking and prying ... Only three more. Come on, old girl, come on, you can do it. Come on, come *on*...

Two more— bump— one more— bump—

The final bump. The one with the full stop. In her relief at her accomplishment Elsie forgot her caution and dropped her burden on the cellar floor. A moment later she remembered with a shock, and gingerly felt under Agnes' skull for any signs of dampness. No, it seemed to be all right, though the stone floor itself was cold and could well be damp from other causes. Still, it looked as if Agnes had a hard skull. One point in her favour, most decidedly.

Temporarily, she was safe. Mrs. Watkins would never come down into the cellar. Terrified of rats, she said. Rats, the very idea! Only Tom, when he visited his aunts for the odd weekend, would come down to make new encroachments on the dwindling wine cellar. Apart from that... Up in the drawing-room she would think of the next step. Just one final effort... Agnes sat propped against the wall, looking really quite contented, while Elsie sped up the stairs and into the drawing-room as the clock struck a quarter past four.

On the threshold she stopped involuntarily. The rockingchair was still moving! She went quickly across to steady it, and as she did so she discovered that her hands were shaking. It was absurd, but the teacup she held was rattling awkwardly when Mrs. Watkins came in a moment later.

She had decided what to tell Mrs. Watkins in case she asked about Agnes' sudden absence. The poor dear had been called away to London on sudden business about her dividends. Mrs. Watkins certainly wouldn't ask what dividends were— and in a day or two would be knocked down crossing Oxford Street in the rush hour.

'So careless about traffic. Living in the country of course she wasn't used to it.' And that would be that.

But Tom wasn't so easy. She couldn't fob him off. She toyed with the idea of telling him that Agnes had accidentally fallen down the cellar steps, and letting him be the one to find the body. But then he'd see the marks on her throat, and know poor Agnes had been strangled. And after all, she couldn't tell Mrs. Watkins one thing and Tom another. That would begin to look fishy. She suddenly realized that there were quite a lot of things to work out.

She watched Mrs. Watkins out of the corner of her eye as she collected the plates and cups and saucers. No questions? Really it was very odd, especially when you took into account the natural curiosity of the working classes.

'Miss Agnes has had to go to London on business, Mrs. Watkins, I don't know when she'll be back.'

'Oh—really ma'am?' She fancied that the woman looked vaguely startled.

'She might stay overnight. In fact she might stay for a few days.'

'That's nice.'

'Yes... I know it's unusual, but she said she wanted a change, and it's a long time since she's been to town.'

'Of course.' Mrs. Watkins looked distinctly ill at ease, as if it were she, and not Elsie, who had something to hide. Despite the incident of the chair, Elsie now felt quite confident.

'I dare say we can manage without her,' she said gaily.

'I expect so, ma'am.'

'Well I won't detain you, Mrs. Watkins. In fact, if you leave me something cold you can have an early night. I'll wash up myself.'

This would give her more time and freedom to work out something for Agnes.

'There's some of Tuesday's lamb left. I'll make you a salad.'

'That'll be fine.'

Was it only fancy that Mrs. Watkins gave her an odd look as she closed the door?

Left alone, she realized that the silly chair had upset her rather a lot. The woman couldn't suspect anything, not at this stage anyway, but she wasn't feeling as safe and secure as she thought she should feel. She forced herself to look at the chair again. It was perfectly still now. It must have been some sudden reverberation, a car passing along the road outside perhaps, or even something in the house itself. These old houses were full of creaks and thuds and odd disturbances. The pipes for instance. Sometimes they made the most alarming noises. Even Agnes had remarked upon it. Not that that would explain what for the briefest second she thought she'd seen—that shadow which had seemed to occupy the chair, and which was Agnes' shape and size...

Now although the chair was empty, she did see that the wool from Tom's pullover still lay where she had dropped it. In some ways Tom was like Harry, oddly enough. She still felt a slight pang of regret when she thought of Harry, although she'd tried so hard to force him out of her mind completely.

Harry was the son of a neighbouring farmer. The two families had been on visiting terms for many years but Elsie had felt no special attraction for him. Then, without warning, he suddenly found excuses to come to the house. Agnes had at first resented this invasion of privacy. Elsie, intuitively aware that she was the main attraction, began to feel shy and embarrassed. Harry at length asked her out to the local dance one Friday evening.

'You can't possibly go,' Agnes had stormed when Elsie had told her.

'Why ever not?'

'With Harry? A farmer's son? And besides, you're like brother and sister!'

'I don't see that that's got anything to do with it. I think you're just jealous he didn't ask you!'

Even now Elsie was surprised she'd had the courage to say that. Perhaps at that time the fear she'd begun to feel was still controllable.

'I wouldn't go with Harry if you paid me. I suppose you don't care if people talk.'

'People, what people? And what can they possibly say? And any-yway,' she had added with sudden weariness, 'what can it really matter?'

'People will say you're carrying on with him. Or don't you mind that?'

'No, I don't think I do. Harry's a very nice boy. You could do a lot worse. And anyway, who else is there?'

Agnes had grunted, 'I didn't know you were in such a hurry to get a man. Or is it just that you want to get away from me?'

Elsie did go to the dance with Harry. And Agnes didn't like it at all.

She continued seeing Harry sporadically for several months, without ever letting the relationship develop far beyond the good-night kiss. Agnes usually took good care to see that they weren't alone together for too long, if Harry visited her at home, so they had to go for long walks across the fields, and have picnics, and somehow these events weren't really as romantic in real life as they were cracked up to be in novels.

'I'm older than you are,' Agnes had said once, 'and I have to look after you. I don't think you're ready for marriage yet. Certainly not with Harry. He's entirely unsuitable.'

Certainly, as Elsie discovered with disappointment, Harry was far from being an ardent lover. She longed at times to beg him to assert himself, to sweep her off her feet—yes, she was still romantic enough for that. She would even have been prepared to elope with him if only he'd had the courage to ask her. She'd never guessed the real reason for his indecision.

Even now, so many years afterwards, with Harry dead for all she knew, she couldn't bear to think of it, to dwell on it for long. That awful day, the dreadful thing that had happened later.

She had come back from a shopping expedition to the village. It was a beautiful day, she remembered that. You always remember little things. It was the first really fine day of the season, and she'd managed to pick the first strawberries. With no psychic presentiment of disaster, no sinister foreboding, she'd pushed open the front door to find...

No, even now her mind shied away from it. She'd steadfastly refused to consider life in those terms; perhaps her starry-eyed and ostrich-like innocence had somehow kept Harry off, but that he should have been driven, even in desperation... that he and Agnes should have defiled and corrupted her own dear home, and done it so blatantly, so shamelessly, and after what Agnes had said... even after what Agnes had said... and when Harry had slunk shamefacedly away, Agnes had even stood up and faced her sister defiantly... And shame upon shame, defeat upon defeat, Elsie had merely crumpled in the face of that defiance, so that Agnes had won two victories instead of one...

That evening Elsie was a different person. The sickening shock, the stultifying sense of betrayal had passed, or at least she thought it had, and all that was left was a disgust, a loathing for her sister which frightened her by its irrationality. Agnes' attitude was that it was only natural, that these things happen, that nobody was to blame. She hadn't even the grace to be contrite, to be compassion-ate for Elsie's wounded sensibility, and the viper that Elsie nursed within her bosom stirred and hissed uneasily. It was true that she had never even seen herself with Harry on these terms; not in the sheer cold-bloodedness and mindlessness of what was going on. What should have happened after Harry's hundreds of kisses, which were seldom more than casual and which roused in her feelings which she was always careful not to define, was still for her bathed in a rosy romantic glow which effectively concealed any reality whatsoever. The sudden blinding knowledge of herself as well as of Agnes completely threw her off balance, and it was then, and only then, that the first wish for Agnes' absence obtruded itself.

Elsie had lain awake for most of the night deciding her own course of action. She knew that she and Agnes could no longer live together. And yet she loved her home, and failed to see why she should leave it. But would Agnes go either? Agnes was older and stronger than she was, and in a battle of wills would win every time. Elsie, though, was sure of one thing. She would never speak to Agnes ever again.

But only after she'd had this one thing out with her. She must do that, otherwise it would fester and embitter the rest of her life. She'd ask Agnes to go. It was Agnes who was in the wrong, after all. Perhaps she'd decided to marry Harry, although Elsie doubted it. But it was a possibility. And they deserved each other.

She took good care to avoid Agnes by not going down to break-fast until she knew Agnes had finished. When she finally opened the dining-room door it annoyed her to see that Agnes had managed to consume her normal meal, as if nothing had happened. The most Elsie could manage was a shaky cup of coffee, but she really meant to tackle Agnes, and she needed it.

After she had finished she saw Agnes dusting the stair carpet. The scene that followed wasn't clear any more. Most of it had gone, although Elsie was sure it was still buried, deep in her subconscious. Agnes, of course, had refused to leave, saying she had as much right to be there as Elsie, and if Elsie didn't like the arrangement she knew what she could do. Elsie, looking back, saw the two girls facing each other furiously, and heard a lot of meaningless shouting. She knew things had been said that could never be unsaid, although she forgot now exactly what they were. But the next moment she closed her eyes involuntarily. For she had seen one girl lurch forward down the stairs to lie, motionless, eyes staring upwards, at the bottom of the well.

The next few months dovetailed into one another. Doctors, grave-faced, came and went. During that time Elsie could hardly remember sleeping even once. The house was full of nurses, or seemed to be, of which Elsie, oddly, was one. Agnes couldn't be moved. There were numerous and serious complications, all stemming from one single and basic fact, which was a fractured spine. Agnes had slipped and fallen while cleaning the stairs. Elsie, hearing a scream, had run out from the dining-room where she was finishing a late breakfast, to see her sister lying unconscious. That was her story, and she stuck to it implacably throughout all the subsequent investigations. Surprisingly, perhaps, she felt no guilt at what had happened; she certainly had not pushed, nor attempted to push, Agnes. On that point she was quite sure. Agnes had simply lost her balance. True, they'd had a row, but people have rows every day, and you can't pin attempted murder on that. If Agnes recovered—and she debated this quite dispassionately and objectively— she doubted whether she wouldn't be quite as happy to keep the row, and the cause of it, to themselves as Elsie. After all, she had more to lose by its revelation.

Well, Agnes *did* recover, and her recovery, to Elsie, was little

46

short of miraculous, as she seemed entirely unscathed...

It was at this point that something made her turn round, and there was Agnes, smiling at her from the rocking-chair.

Elsie was lying in bed, a glass of brandy beside her on the aggressively scrubbed white bedside table. She couldn't stop shaking; almost, but not quite. She was perfectly aware that the thing had been a hallucination, but it was uncomfortably real, and she had never had a hallucination before. Five more minutes in bed, then she'd get up, go downstairs and back into the drawing-room to face the thing out. Of course, there'd be nothing there, she was quite sure of that.

She got up deliberately, slowly, not allowing herself to tremble more than she could help, and went carefully down the stairs. Of course, it was only her imagination that there was something behind her, pushing her... A moment later, when she opened the door of the drawing-room, her confidence was justified. There was nothing in the rocking chair.

Despite her relief, and her reassurance that she was not going mad, she still felt too shaken to do anything further about Agnes that night. Time enough in the morning.

Oddly enough, she had no bad dreams that night. She came down to breakfast the following morning rested and refreshed. It wasn't until she had finished her second piece of toast and marmalade, and had rung for Mrs. Watkins to clear away, that Agnes reappeared, this time in the chair facing her. Again she had the same cynical smile on her face and was watching Elsie intently.

Elsie looked away quickly, blinked a couple of times, and tried in vain to make her mind a complete blank. It was no good, she must have been thinking of Agnes subconsciously; now if she resolutely and categorically *stopped* thinking of Agnes, then Agnes would go away. At least, that was the theory, wasn't it? If she kept her eyes tight shut for a minute or so... She got up quickly and went to the window.

'You're not really there, and I refuse to talk to you.'

'Oh, but that's where you're wrong. I'm as much here now as I ever was.'

Elsie forced herself to face her sister. Agnes seemed so very much in command of the situation. For a moment there was a pause, while Elsie steeled herself to say what she knew must be said.

'But you're dead. I killed you.'

'A remarkably stupid and shortsighted thing to do, if I may say so.' Agnes sounded as if she were administering a reproof to a naughty child. 'It doesn't really solve anything, you know.'

'What do you mean?'

'I shall still be here, won't I?'

'But you *are* dead, aren't you?'

'Go and see.'

This time Agnes wouldn't go away or disappear. Distressingly, she had followed Elsie from the dining-room to the drawing-room and had giggled when Elsie had picked up the wool which had somehow found its way to the floor again. So Elsie *had* gone to see. Sure enough, there was Agnes' body where she had left it, looking very dead and unpleasant indeed. Flies had appeared from somewhere, and had begun to buzz round it. Rigor mortis had very obviously set in, and there was a new and distinct smell in the cellar. Elsie had looked up from a cursory and necessarily brief examination, and there was Agnes watching her from the top of the cellar steps.

She began to feel giddy. She could no longer trust the evidence of her own senses, or her surroundings, and imagined that she must be in a nightmare and that soon she would wake up. That was her first reaction. The second was how monstrously unfair and cruel of Agnes it was to haunt her like this. Hadn't she got enough on her mind already? Perhaps if she succeeded in disposing of the real Agnes, the ghost Agnes would go away too.

Elsie, now feeling very old, returned to the drawing-room. So did Agnes.

Perhaps if I ignore her, she thought, she'll go away. She'll see that her presence isn't having the desired effect—whatever the desired effect might be. She thought of all the traditional tales of hauntings and the reasons given.

'I'm not sorry I did it,' she said aloud. 'I don't have any conscience about it. I'd do it again quite happily.'

Should she try it again? The odd thing was that Agnes didn't look at all like a ghost. If she tried killing her again, would it work? Or would a third Agnes appear, then a fourth, and so on? The idea of the house crammed to overflowing with emanations of her dead sister suddenly presented itself with appalling vividness.

'How long do you..?'

'My stay is indefinite,' Agnes said.

'Even if I... if I..?'

'Even if you—dispose of me. How do you plan to do that, by the way? Have you thought? But even if you do, I shall still be here, so you'd better make the best of it.'

Elsie sprang to her feet in sudden anger. 'This is intolerable! Is this my punishment, or something? Do you mean to go on as if nothing had happened?'

'Nothing really has, you know.'

'But I killed you!' Elsie almost shouted, considerations of Mrs. Watkins for a moment forgotten.

'When you're in my position, you'll realize there's really no such thing as death.'

'D'you mean to say—do you mean to tell me that you don't feel any different?'

'I don't think so. A little light-headed perhaps. My neck's still sore, of course, where you pressed it, but on the whole... no, I don't think so.'

The door opened, and Mrs. Watkins came in. 'Would you like some coffee, ma'am?'

She seemed to look straight through Agnes.

'She can't see or hear me, you know,' Agnes said. 'Only you can see me. That much I know. I shouldn't ask her to bring an extra cup... I'll drink it out of yours.'

For the next few days Agnes never left her side. The haunting was horribly and ironically complete. In the old days she had gone out from time to time, if only to post a letter. Now the sisters were more together than ever. Elsie couldn't bring herself to re-enter the cellar. She knew that the longer she left it, the more danger there was for her; she knew that the task itself would prove more difficult and unpleasant, and she also knew that the chance of Tom's turning up for one of his frequent and periodic visits grew every day. But somehow, with Agnes so very definitely present it seemed so much more indecent to try and remove her earthly body even if, as was now painfully obvious, it was no longer required.

To make matters worse, Agnes reassumed her former role with redoubled fury. The stimulus of her forced ejection seemed to have increased her strength twofold. Her domination, her ceaseless prying, simply her unbearableness, were more marked than ever.

'You always were a fool, Elsie,' Agnes said once. 'I never told you before how much I despised you, because I wanted to spare your feelings, but killing me was the stupidest thing you could possibly have done.' And again... 'Your whole life has been useless, Elsie, d'you know that? What you did was merely the crowning futility, a fitting climax.' Elsie could merely bow her head and say nothing. Agnes had now begun to be explicitly rude and aggressive, an attitude she had thought beneath her previously, and hostility between the sisters was now no longer even thinly veiled. Yesterday she had locked the cellar door, in case Mrs. Watkins should take it into her head... All the time she was turning the key, Agnes was laughing at her, jeering at her from the drawing-room door. 'I can't go on,' she thought that night. 'I really can't. But what can I do?'

For she thought there was no escape, in this world or the next. And still Mrs. Watkins saw nothing.

Once she taxed her. 'Mrs. Watkins,' she began, as the latter peeled potatoes, 'do you never... feel anything about this house?'

'What sort of thing, ma'am?' Stolid, giving nothing away.

'Or hear anything? Voices. Other than mine.'

'I hear you talking to yourself, ma'am, but that ain't no business of mine.'

'Do you never... hear Miss Agnes?'

'Miss Agnes? Oh, ma'am, I don't want to talk about Miss Agnes! Please, let me get on with the lunch.'

'Then you *do* hear something. Come, Mrs. Watkins, please tell me.'

'You said Miss Agnes had gone to Town, ma'am, and I accepted it. Now, ma'am, please...'

And with all the force and obstinacy of the country woman, Mrs. Watkins was giving nothing away.

It wasn't even as if Agnes was happy in her revenge. She looked just as miserable as she'd always looked. So what was the point in it all?

'Wouldn't you be happier... wherever it is you go?' she said. 'After all, you haven't given yourself a chance to see what Heaven is really like.'

'Time enough for that,' Agnes said. 'I might wait until I can take you with me.'

So that was it! It was out at last! Funny she hadn't thought of it before!

Agnes wanted to drive her to suicide.

'So you want me to die. Will you be happy then?'

'An eye for an eye, so they say.'

'Will you leave me alone then or would we both have to haunt this awful house?'

'I really couldn't say. The matter is out of my hands.'

'But you want me dead.'

'I think it's you who would be happier dead. You're old, and useless. Why prolong it? Why go on, with what you've got on your conscience? Give Tom a chance to inherit this house. He's a good boy. You're only in his way.'

'But he doesn't... he doesn't want me to...'

'Of course he'll be upset. He's fond of you. But the old must give way to the young. And who else is there who needs you?'

'If it hadn't been for you... Harry...'

'Harry!' Agnes exploded with laughter. 'You'd never have married Harry in a thousand years! You were terrified of sex. He told me. It was pathetic.'

'So you... you...'

'I always wanted him. Yes, I admit it. I was jealous of you, but I needn't have worried; and anyway, he never came back, so much good it did me. Besides that's all ancient history now. There's only us left.'

'You want me to die,' she repeated slowly, and for a moment was silent.

'But first you must leave a note.'

'Yes?'

'Explaining why. And about the cellar. And me. How I wouldn't leave you alone. Otherwise poor Tom...'

'But they'll think...'

'Suicide while of unsound mind. A good solution.'

Now she had made up her mind she felt relieved. Perhaps Agnes would take pity on her and leave her alone— afterwards. Once her sin was expiated. An eye for an eye.

She dismissed Mrs. Watkins for the day, then went upstairs to the spare room, the one with the oak beam. Tom's wool wouldn't be strong enough, but she had a piece of rope that was normally used for tying trunks. The chair in the room wasn't high enough, but that high-backed Chippendale with the tapestried seat would do. She would fetch it. Agnes, watching her preparations, agreed. Once everything was ready, Agnes reminded her about the note.

'I'll dictate it to you,' she offered helpfully.

Elsie's last coherent thought—in this world anyway—was of Agnes. 'You *will* leave me alone?' she murmured. But she was gone before Agnes, standing in the doorway and smiling approval, could answer...

'I don't understand it, I don't understand it at all,' Tom said, holding up the note. 'What does it mean? Why should Aunt Elsie have done such a thing?'

Mrs. Watkins, coming in at her usual time the next morning, and finding that Miss Elsie's bed had not been slept in, had at length gone up to the spare room. Her screams bringing no help, she had rushed to the telephone and summoned Tom. Then she had found the suicide note. Now police and doctors were tramping about upstairs.

'Oh, Mr. Tom, I had no idea she was so ill. I knew she was depressed but...' Incoherently she plucked at her apron.

'Now, now, Mrs. Watkins, don't distress yourself. It's not your fault. You couldn't have done any more than you did.' Poor Aunt Elsie has been mad for years—we both knew that. But she was harmless and... I thought, reasonably happy.'

'They won't think that I...'

'Of course not. If it's anyone's fault, it's mine. I should have had her put away years ago. But I couldn't bear to uproot her from this house. And with you to look after her...'

'Oh, I know, Mr. Tom. And I didn't mind a bit, really I didn't. Occasionally she got on my nerves, gave me the willies she did, but

I tried to make allowances, poor lady. Towards the end she got worse though. She had such odd fancies. All about poor Miss Agnes.'

'It all stemmed from her sister's death,' Tom said.

'She thought Miss Agnes had gone to London, or something, but she was still here and... haunting her!'

'She was always here,' Tom said, 'ever since it happened. Poor Aunt Elsie.'

Tom felt no need to tell Mrs. Watkins the whole story. The note was indisputably in Elsie's handwriting and the verdict, if there were an inquest, would be suicide whilst of unsound mind. Straightforward. Cut and dried.

Unsound mind! The whole thing had happened so long ago, before Tom was born. His father had told him about it and had begged Tom always to keep an eye on his aunt, and look after her. Something about a boy friend it was, when the sisters had been young. Agnes had fallen downstairs after a quarrel, and broken her back. She had been very ill for a long time. Elsie had even helped to nurse her, but complications had set in and Agnes had died. The shock had been too much for Elsie, and ever since she had had strange fancies that Agnes was... still alive. Now, obviously, the whole thing had deteriorated into nightmare.

Tom unlocked the cellar door and went down the steps. Of course, there was nothing there. That was what a guilt complex did for you, he supposed, though he doubted whether Elsie really had pushed Agnes all those years ago. She wouldn't hurt a fly, really. Sadly, he went up to see about the arrangements for the funeral.

A DAY OUT

G HOST STORIES? Well, now, let me think. You want me to
tell you a ghost story, do you? Trouble is, I don't believe in
'em—and that really *is* the trouble, because I think I saw—and not
being able to really *believe* in it only makes the whole thing worse, if
you get my meaning.

The trouble with ghosts is that they've become hidebound. In a
rut, as you might say. All you writing chappies always put them in
old creaking houses, coming back to avenge their murder or
because they in turn murdered someone. And then usually only one
person sees them at a time. Well you know the sort of thing. My
ghost wasn't like that at all. But I'd better tell you straight.

Another? Well, if you insist. Not too much water with it this
time.

Well, as you know, I've never been one to stay in the same place
for too long at a time. Don't like putting down roots, it makes me
nervous. Footloose and fancy free, that's me. When I was a young
man a pal of mine who owned a small seaside amusement arcade
lent me his flat for the season if I would run it for him. He had other irons in the fire, and had to be in London. Well, it seemed like a
piece of cake to me, and apart from the little boys who tried to fiddle the machines—you know, bits of wire and bent pennies and
the like—things went fairly smoothly. I'd met this girl a few weeks
before I'd left London, at a dance I think it was, and she was a right
little dolly as they say today. I could have married her, no trouble
at all, and there aren't many you could say that about. Well, after
I'd been in this flat for a couple of weeks she phones me up and
asks if she can come down for the day to see me, and get some sea
air and so on. I say fine. I don't say there's this great big double bed

just ready and waiting to welcome a nice bit of crumpet. I don't say it, but already in my mind I'm preparing the big seduction scene. Always in London there's just no privacy. If it isn't landladies and all visitors out by ten, there's her family jamming up the works, and jam up the works they did, good and proper. You know that song, *And Her Mother Came Too?* Well, that was it. If I wanted to take her out, there was Mum and Dad, giving me the old third degree, hopping into the back of the car if they'd half a chance, even out to the pub for a free drink. There was no telly then you see, and they couldn't afford to run a car of their own so it was a treat for them. I mean you've got to see their side of it, haven't you, although it was pretty difficult for me then to make allowances like I can today. They were nice enough really, but I was young, the girl was a dolly, and sometimes it was just plain agony for me sitting in their front room drinking tea and making polite conversation, when what I really wanted was to...

So all this was going through my mind as she was on the other end of the line going on about train times and could I meet her and they'd bring sandwiches for lunch so I was not to go to any trouble. It was the use of the word "they" that first brought me up short.

'Who's they?' I said, but I knew the answer even before she said it.

'Well, I can't leave them behind, can I? I mean it wouldn't be fair, would it? You don't know what London's like in this heatwave, all hot and sticky, and there's you in your lovely flat on the seafront. I'd never forgive myself.'

'But I thought—I mean—there'd be just the two of us.' I couldn't keep the disappointment out of my voice.

'I know, darling,' she said, 'I'm sorry too. But...'

'I know you're fond of your family, but...'

'There'll be other times.'

'I mean you've got to break away some time. You can't always have them trailing round, following you everywhere you go.'

I hadn't proposed, or anything like that, and I didn't want to jump the gun now by letting her suspect what was on my mind.

'But they *need* the sea air. You don't really *mind*, do you?'

I sensed she was getting a bit ratty. For all I knew they were listening to the conversation.

'Oh, all right. Who's coming then, just your Mum and Dad?'

It did no harm to let her know I was reluctant. With women you've got to show you're not just a pushover. Otherwise they'll take advantage, and not just some of the time.

She seemed to hesitate for a moment before she answered 'Well, Fred and Vera asked if they could come, too, and I knew you wouldn't mind. After all, we couldn't very well leave them behind. They don't get much chance to see the sea.'

Fred and Vera were the kid brother and sister.

You can't object to kids, can you, even if they are at the age when you wish they were anywhere but with you.

But she hadn't finished yet.

'And then there's Aunt Dolly.'

'Who?'

'Aunt Dolly, Mum's sister. You'll like her. She *enjoys* everything so much, if you know what I mean.'

'But why her? I don't even know her.'

'She's a widow. She doesn't get out much, and it'll be nice for her.'

So that was it, Mum and Dad, Fred and Vera, and Aunt Dolly, all coming down by the noon train. Not much chance of a bit of fun with all that lot around, I thought, and I was fair miserable about it, I can tell you. It wasn't even as if we had a big pier like Brighton or Southend where we could leave them and meet them later, and she and I could slip back to the flat. My little amusement arcade was about the only attraction we had, apart from the beach, and a moth-eaten little cinema in the town and that only had one performance a day. They wouldn't exactly get lost in the arcade, and they wouldn't want to come all this way just to go to the cinema, even if the bloody place was open, which it wasn't.

You see my point, don't you? I mean for all the good it was going to do me I might just as well have stayed in London. I felt like rebelling; running off somewhere so that when they came there'd be no one there. But then I thought that was childish. I tried to put myself in their place. I remembered how I'd longed to get out of London.

So I met the train and there they all were and we piled as best we could into the little car my friend had lent me that went with the job, and off we went to the beach. You'd think they'd come for a week, all the stuff they'd brought. Sandwiches was right; enough to sink a battleship. Ham and corned beef and meat paste and sardine. Thermoses of tea and lemonade and mounds of currant cake. They must have spent a fortune, and you could see that they were determined to enjoy every minute of it. I hadn't the heart to mind after that. Even Aunt Dolly's face was shining. I can see her now. She was a faded and wizened little woman, old before her time, and I believe she'd been in service. I can't remember asking, but I think someone told me. She'd married this chap who worked in a radio repair shop and he'd gone off and got himself killed at Dunkirk. So she was all alone. You can see what a day by the sea with the family must have meant to her.

I can't remember the exact events of the day in proper order. I wish I could, because in view of what I found out later it might have been important—or significant, as you writers say. I remember that the kids wanted to go in the sea straight away—they felt hot and sticky after the train. Aunt Dolly wanted a sip of tea—now it comes back to me she always talked about having "sips" of everything—a sip of lemonade, a sip of port—oh, yes, we finished the day having one for the road in the Feathers while the kids sat outside drinking ginger ale. I had to go and see that the arcade was running properly; I had a young fellow in to help me over the weekends and Bank Holidays and the like—but I promised to come back and have lunch with them. I still hoped to get the girl alone in the afternoon. On the pretext of going for a walk we could slip back to the flat for a half-hour or so. That is, if she was willing. Trouble was, I couldn't get her alone to ask her.

I was later back than I expected. One of the machines had gone wrong, and you can't afford to have a machine out of order on a day when you expect to do a lot of business. It was one of the electric ones, and a contact had got bent. I won't go into the technical details, but the pennies wouldn't go in, and it took me about forty-five minutes to repair it.

When I got back to the beach Mum and Dad were having a nap, Aunt Dolly was reading a thriller, and the kids were making sandcastles. The girl wasn't readily visible.

'We thought you weren't coming back,' Mum said when I nudged her. 'We nearly ate your lunch.'

"Where's..?'

'Oh, I think she went to look for you. Corned beef or ham?'

Damn, I thought. We must have passed each other. Just the chance I want, and I muff it.

'Thanks, I'll see if I can find her first,' I said, and nipped smartly back to the arcade. There she was, standing outside it, looking at a loss what to do next.

She was so relieved to see me, that this probably made it easier for me to persuade her to come to the flat rather than return to the beach. Once indoors I looked at her more closely than I'd done before. She seemed anxious, she looked a bit pale and drawn, and I realized how much she needed this spot of sea air.

I'll skate over the next half-hour or so. After all, it doesn't really have any bearing on the story, except to confirm my previous feelings about her and to make me suspect that she felt the same way about me. I think I asked her to become engaged, but I can't really be certain. All I know is that she didn't give me a definite answer, one way or another.

'Is anything worrying you?' I had asked once.

'Why?'

I told her I thought she looked ill. All she said in answer was, 'It's nice to be here,' so I assumed that it was because she had been missing me.

When we got back to the beach Mum was beginning to look a bit put out. 'I thought you two had got lost,' she said, and I thought she looked a bit accusing.

'We decided to go for a walk,' the girl answered, quick as you like.

'Well, there's not many sandwiches left, and the tea's cold.'

It wasn't actually, because it was in the Thermos, but this was Mum's way of registering a protest.

The rest of the day passed uneventfully, as days by the sea do. The kids went in for their second swim, we all joined them, and even Aunt Dolly was persuaded to put in a tentative foot, the equivalent of a "sip". Afterwards I had to buy them all ice creams, and when it got too cold to sit out any more, as I said, we all adjourned to the Feathers for a quick one before they caught the last train home. We didn't arrange a further outing, but as soon as the season was over I would come back to town and contact them. I wish I could remember whether we had agreed to be engaged, but I honestly can't although I think in my own mind I assumed we were.

When I had seen them off and come back to the flat, I had this comfortable contented feeling, as of a good job well done, and I don't think it was only because I'd given the family a badly-needed day out, or even got the girl alone for half an hour. So thinking back on it, I think there must have been a definite understanding.

I want you to understand that the whole day was ordinary, routine, nothing queer about it at all. For the next week I went about the business of running the arcade, all the time with this contented feeling. I suppose in a way it was a bit smug. I knew I'd given all of them, including the girl, a good time. And you can't help feeling a bit noble, can you? I mean, we're all human.

Mind you, I thought it was odd that I hadn't received a "thank you" letter from them. They were the sort of people for whom things like that are important. But I didn't lose any sleep over it. At least, not then.

I had no conscience over the half-hour—after all, she'd enjoyed it as much as I had. I just felt pleased that I'd put one over on the watchdog brigade, if you know what I mean. But then after a week had gone by, and I'd heard nothing from anyone, I began to wonder if perhaps they'd questioned her about the time we'd wandered off together, and found out and given her hell. I knew she couldn't have kept up a lie or a bluff for long against concentrated attack from all sides. I began to imagine all sorts of things, and slowly but surely my satisfaction ebbed away, and I became more and more uneasy. Perhaps they'd turned her out of the house, perhaps she'd found herself with a bun in the oven and was ashamed or frightened to tell me. I mean, it would have been inconvenient and awkward, and we'd have had to hurry things along, and I hadn't enough money at the moment, but I *did* want to marry her. It wasn't as if I wanted to shirk my responsibilities.

I decided I'd have to go up to town myself to face the music. Probably I was worrying about nothing, but I had to be sure. I told you about this young fellow who came in to help me in the arcade at busy times. I decided I could safely leave the place in his hands for a day or two—midweek wasn't a busy time, even in season— while I did any sorting out that had to be done. Luckily, he was free, and could fit it in with his own work, so off I went.

I don't ask you to believe this next bit. I'm not sure I believe it myself, but I saw the evidence for it with my own eyes, and afterwards I checked at the local newspaper office.

You see, the house wasn't there anymore. It was a ruin. It looked as if a bomb had hit it. But there weren't any more bombs. I rang a neighbour's doorbell. She was a kind, motherly woman, who took me in and gave me a cup of tea. I was feeling dazed, as if none of this was really happening. A fortnight ago it was, she said. Something to do with the local gas supply. In all the papers it was, hadn't I seen it? The whole family gone, Mother, Father, three children, and a widowed sister who had come to lunch. There had been an inquiry. The mother was cooking lunch. A naked flame, a faulty gas jet, who's to say why these things happen.

I checked dates, and the dates didn't agree at all. You can guess what I mean. It had happened several days before...

You see what I mean about ghosts, don't you? I don't believe in 'em, never did! And especially not the ghosts you write about, what with your spooky old houses, your murders, your dark and stormy nights.

It still bothers me, and will to my dying day. Oh, yes, they were dead all right, there was no mistake about that. But what was the attraction? I mean, was it me or the beach? I mean Heaven is Heaven, and Angleford is no paradise by any stretch of the imagination. Perhaps when you die everything is so strange, so different, that you can't take it all at once. You need something you're used to, that you enjoy, before you leave it all for ever. One last day out, before...

She certainly didn't *feel* dead, that time in the nice soft double bed in my friend's flat. Although she *did* look anxious and worried about something.

Poor little girl! Poor little dolly! That's the thing that worries me most. Like the song says, *And Her Mother Came Too.* Even in death, she couldn't get away from her nice, ordinary, nosey family.

THE LADY BY THE STREAM

'YOU STUPID CHILD! Now you've broken it.'

She looked down helplessly. The doll lay grotesquely straddled across the stone floor of the passage, its limbs spread ea-gled, one arm reaching vainly towards the head which had rolled across the floor to the kitchen. It had stopped half-way over the threshold and now stared idiotically at the ceiling.

'Your father and I only bought it for you last week,' her mother's voice was storming on, 'really, you're quite the clumsiest child I've ever seen. Everything we give you you break—'

It wasn't her fault the wretched doll's head had come off. She had been expected by her parents to love it and she hadn't wanted to disappoint them. She had merely given it a playful squeeze and when it had squeaked in response she had turned the head round to see how far it would go. Her mother towered menacingly over her like art ogre. 'Well, you won't get another one in a hurry,' she had said finally.

And that was that. Elisabeth never did get another one. Her parents, in a vain attempt to deny that her clumsiness was an inte-gral part of her make-up, thought foolishly that by depriving her of any more new toys they could rob her of further chances of exercis-ing it. They merely drove it underground. As she grew older Elisabeth began to realize that in some strange way it manifested itself in direct proportion to her own emotional involvement. If she became fond of anything she broke it. If she found herself indifferent to it, it continued to work perfectly. This state of affairs was paralleled in her personal relationships. People whom she disliked thought her quiet and capable. Those whom she desired desperately to please, found her tactless and awkward. Her parents, not astute enough to detect her growing psychological imbalance, noticed with satisfaction that in their presence at least she was always perfectly composed.

They only noticed this, however, when she was too old for dolls. The martyred doll, last in a line of three which had all gone in more or less similar ways, became for her a symbol of her lost childhood. When she knew that she would never have another doll, she had ceased, quite simply, to be a child. In such small ways are great events brought about. At the same time she had begun, at first unconsciously but later with full realization, to dislike her parents. If asked point blank why, she could not have answered. In many ways they were all that parents should be. They fed her, they clothed her, they sent her to several good schools. It certainly wasn't the doll. After all, *she* had broken the doll, not *they*. But perhaps it was because they would not accept her for what she was. Instead they wanted her to be something she was not. Denying her clumsiness they wanted it hidden, pushed out of the way, so that by ignoring it they could pretend it didn't exist. It was something not quite nice, like sex, but breathing the foul air reserved for family skeletons it flourished and grew.

Elisabeth knew that if she concentrated on something very hard she could usually come out all right. If she had to wash up she was all right if nobody watched tier. If they did she usually dropped a cup. If she had to sew on a button she only pricked her finger if she felt her mother's eyes staring into the back of her neck. That was the first stage. When she recognized the true nature of her feelings towards her mother she didn't care whether she was watched or not. Some point of her seemed to have become dormant.

It re-awoke forty-one years after the broken doll incident. Her father had died, her mother had sold the London house and they had moved into the country. Her mother, no longer able to tower over her, had eventually sunk permanently into a wheelchair, and by so doing, had managed to tie Elisabeth firmly and irrevocably.

Elisabeth, too conscience stricken to leave her, too timid to pull down the barriers which protected her from the outside world, had collapsed into disgruntled spinsterhood.

The outside world had reached out tentative feelers towards her from time to time and she had responded in greater or lesser degree. Once she had almost broken the barrier: she had put forward a cautious toe, but had found the water too cold. She had preferred to return to her chair by the side of the pool to watch the swimmers. Now, quite suddenly, she was to jump into the deep end.

Out walking in the fields near the village where they lived she found herself reviewing these momentary disturbances. The swimmer who had approached nearest to her side of the pool was Frank. Would she, she wondered dispassionately, ever have married Frank. Not that Frank had actually asked her, but she thought that he might conceivably—

How many others had there been in her forty-six years? Had there been any others? She thought there had been, but sometimes it was difficult to say. The past seemed to retreat into a vague indefinite blur, punctuated by her mother's eternal nagging demands. Her clumsiness too had grown, especially during the last few years. She no longer tried to hide it. Perhaps it was this that frightened the boys away, although she could never tell for sure.

She found herself thinking of Frank, pinning him down in her memory, trying to remember how he had looked. She couldn't really ever have been in love with him, she supposed, because if she had, she could never have forgotten him so completely. Was she really capable of love? She had often wondered this in the past, before the pressing demands of the moment had re-engaged her attention. She was thankful to her mother for one thing: that the job of looking after her had never properly allowed her to analyze her own failure.

Why had Frank stopped seeing her so suddenly? Had she made

some tactless remark, or frightened him off in some way? Or had he just tired of her? It was irritating that in real life one never knew the answers to these questions. In films or books one was omniscient, like God. One knew more about the characters than they did themselves. If a disembodied reader were suddenly to open her life's book, what would he make of her? And the big question was, would she or would she not really care?

Frank had just stopped coming, and she was far too proud to write and ask why. Perhaps her mother had put a spoke in the wheel. Her father had just died then, and her mother was beginning to show that possessiveness towards her daughter which was to dominate her life. Perhaps Frank had only been after her money to begin with, and had become disillusioned when he found it wasn't as much as expected. There were so many reasons, but she hadn't the energy to work it out now.

Her feet were beginning to ache. She must have walked for longer than she supposed. The village was behind her, the other side of the valley. Turning round she could see its roofs sparkling in the sun. Really it was quite pretty looked at from a distance. She sat down on the grass and took out a cigarette. The cottage where she and her mother lived was the far side of the village, and she had only rarely walked in this direction before. Usually, when she took her walks, when her mother was resting after lunch, the sky was grey and she needed a thick cardigan or a coat to keep out the cold. Now though it was almost uncomfortably hot. She blew cigarette smoke defiantly into it. If only it could make me young again, if only—

Her mother had always stood in the way... Oh God, why was Frank so *negative*? That was the trouble, everyone she knew was negative. Afraid to do anything, to escape their own little net, to take any positive action. If only Frank had come to her and said— but he had gone; drifted off in his normal negative fashion, and left her alone. She was alone. Her mother didn't care tuppence for her as a person, just as an unpaid skivvy to fetch and carry, fill her hot-water bottle, stoke the boiler. If only she wasn't there, if only I were free, she thought, and for a moment pictured herself as a romantic heroine from one of the novels she read, struggling like a bird in a cage. But the difference was that the bird, like all tame birds, didn't really want to leave the cage.

She closed her eyes and felt herself drifting off into sleep. For a moment her mother's face hung before her, whining, complaining, then it was replaced by Frank's. Then that too vanished and a number of other faces, anonymous, dull, passed before her inner vision. People she'd known, or thought she'd known, or perhaps hadn't known at all.

How quiet it was. How peaceful in the country after the town. A couple of hundred yards away she could hear the splash of the stream water as it negotiated the copse through which it had to pass on its way to the main river a little below. Water had a calming effect on her nerves. She could lie beside a lake for hours, seeing nothing, hearing nothing, but the plop of an occasional fish. Now though she heard the distant cry of children playing. She looked at her watch. The school would be out, the children, released from prison for the day, on their way home. She must hurry back to *her* prison now. Mother would be wanting tea.

For some reason, all through the chores of the morning, all through lunch until her mother's rest time the next day, she found herself looking forward to returning to the same spot. It was the most beautiful place she'd found, there was no denying that. The glint of the sun on the roofs of the village behind her, the flash of the water through the trees and beyond that the widening of the river flanked by the rushes and tall grasses of the bank; while away to the west the distant hills which looked purple in the heat haze. This afternoon it seemed even hotter than the day before. She wended her way down the valley slope to the shelter of the copse. It was beautifully cool in here. The leaves were just beginning to fall. This made her sad. All good things come to an end. Only with her the good things had never started.

Again she heard the children's voices released from school. Stealing to the edge of the copse she peeped out from between the flanking elms. A little group of them were clustered round the river's edge. Two boys appeared to be fishing. Delighted squeals from three little girls watching heralded a catch.

She saw the little fair-haired boy wheel it in carefully, intently, proudly, tongue sticking out against his cheek. When she had seen the perch safely flapping on the bank, she turned slowly and went home.

At tea that afternoon her mother was more unbearable than ever. She chided her for being late, as if she had no right ever to enjoy the field and the copse and the river and the little fair-haired boy fishing for his perch.

Next day was a Sunday. Elisabeth wondered whether the boy would be there all day, as there was no school. She had a sudden desire to find out, to see whether he was really such a keen fisherman as he had looked the day before. She found herself wondering who he was, who his parents were; whether they lived in the village.

She told her mother she wanted to go to church. Strangely enough, despite so much provocation, it was the first time she had deliberately lied to her mother, and at first she didn't recognize it for what it was. She really did mean to go to church, and promised herself a little walk to the copse afterwards, before coming home to get the lunch. But once she got out of the house into the sunshine she found the thought of the stuffy church intolerable. After all, what had she got to be thankful for? Instead she went straight to the copse.

Sure enough, the boy was there. He was wearing a yellow jersey and blue jeans, and Elisabeth noticed with amusement that the colour of his jersey clashed with his hair.

He wasn't fishing though. She saw his rod and line lying beside the bank. He was paddling in the water, splashing about with a stick. His companions of the day before were nowhere about. Elisabeth wondered how he managed to whistle through his teeth so expertly.

'You'll frighten all the fish away,' she called, coming out into the open.

The boy shrugged. 'Oh, they won't go far.'

'Have you caught anything?'

'Haven't tried today.'

'What do you catch round here?'

'Perch mostly. A few roach and dace. When I'm older Dad's going to teach me to fish for trout. That's with flies. Trout can put up quite a fight.'

His enthusiasm was infectious. 'Course, there's some pike here too. You catch those best with gudgeon as bait.'

'What do you catch the gudgeon with?'

'Oh bread, if you can't get worms. It'll do as well. Dad says to mix the bread with custard powder so it won't dissolve. Or lentils is quite good. They're best for perch. Do you like to fish?'

'I haven't done much,' Elisabeth said. 'When I was a girl we always lived in London. You don't get much chance there.'

'I never been to London,' the boy said. 'Always been meaning to though.'

'D'you live in the village?'

'Yeah, Dad keeps the sweetshop. Mum helps behind the counter. I'm supposed to in the holidays and at weekends, but I like to fish best.'

'How old are you?'

'Ten next week.'

'Ten next week, eh?' Elisabeth sat down beside the rod. 'It's so hot I feel like a paddle.'

The boy called from the middle of the stream. 'Mind the stones over there. They're a bit sharp.'

A moment later Elisabeth was beside him.

'Pity you can't swim here. It's not deep enough, is it?'

'Oh we do swim further down.' He pointed to where the river broadened. 'We're not supposed to though. You're not supposed to swim in the river.'

'Where are your friends?'

'Oh they'll be along later. They don't like fishing as much as I do.'

'What's your name.'

'My parents call me Tommy, but I like Tom. Tommy sounds soppy.'

'All right,' Elisabeth said, wading back towards the bank. 'I shall call you Tom. Man to man.'

The boy laughed, poking more violently at the water so that its ripples mixed with his laughter.

'I've got some biscuits in my pocket. Would you like one?' Now Elisabeth realized why she'd taken them from the kitchen cupboard.

'Thanks.' Tom came over and took one. 'You're the lady what lives with her mother over the far side, aren't you? The one in the wheelchair?'

Elisabeth nodded.

'I'm sorry,' Tom said. 'How did it happen?'

'It's a long word called arthritis. I don't suppose you've ever heard of that.'

'Oh yes I have. Mum's sister gets it. She's not in a wheelchair though.'

'She's not as old as my mother, I don't expect, is she?'

Tom shook his head. 'Think I'll fish for a bit now. I like to catch something before the others get here.'

'They are coming then?' Surprised at her own sudden sharp

pang of disappointment, Elisabeth tried to make her voice as casual as possible.

'I 'spect so. They usually do. Pat and Doris are a bit of a nuisance really.'

'They're your girl friends?'

Tom said contemptuously. "Course not. I don't have no girl friends. They're stupid. Pat and Doris just come along to catch worms for Fred and me.'

'Oh, I see.' Elisabeth lay back in the long grass and let the sun shine directly on to her face. She felt utterly contented and at peace, for the first time for—for how long?

'Of course, you can if you like.'

'What?'

She opened her eyes, shading them with her hand. Tom was sitting on the water's edge watching her quizzically. He looked rather like a little elf.

'What did you say?'

'I said, you can if you like.'

'Can what?'

'Catch worms.'

She burst out laughing. This, this unexpectedness, was childhood. This was the charm of childhood. Why not?

'All right!' She heard herself almost shouting with glee. It was Sunday, it was hot, there was no school and she was young again. 'I'll catch you a nice fat worm!'

Tom busied himself over the rod and line. For a moment his whole world was centred on it. He was serious, dedicated. Elisabeth wandered off into the copse, looking for a worm.

When she had found one suitable to Tom's requirements, she presented it to him gingerly, as if it might bite.

'Can you thread it for me?' he asked her naughtily. Her first reaction, of course, was to say no. But when she looked into Tom's face, she realized that he could make her do anything. He was ten,

71

eagerly treading on the first rung of life's ladder. She was forty-seven and had rejected life. But he had seduced her, suddenly without warning he had come upon her, shattering her carefully built up defences, forcing his way in to her maidenly heart, making her a child again, granting her the momentary power of sharing with him childhood's all-engrossing discoveries. Without another word, she took back the worm and began to thread it on the hook. Tom watched her, with as near to cynical amusement as he was able to attain, hoping she would make a mistake so that he could correct her.

As she felt his eyes on her, the old clumsiness came back. Her fingers seemed to exert a strange will of their own. They refused to obey her brain. Several times she nearly had the hook neatly im-bedded in her hand. With the mercilessness of the ten year old Tom continued to watch her. Was he hoping for an accident, she wondered in passing.

'You must make allowances for a beginner,' she laughed, handing him the hook. 'You'll have to teach me.'

Before she realized, it was lunch time. Her mother would be waiting. 'Are you coming?' she called to Tom as she began collecting her coat and scarf.

'I've got sandwiches,' he said. 'Besides, Fred will be here soon.'

Next Sunday she determined to bring sandwiches.

'What was the sermon like?' her mother asked her over the roast lamb. 'I understand they had Mr. Sampson over from Dorchester.'

Absently, Elisabeth nodded. 'The usual thing. Not very inspiring.'

Her mother was going on, 'Of course, he's a most peculiar man, so I've heard tell. They say he—'

Shut up, a little voice in Elisabeth's brain shouted, shut up, you nagging miserable woman. Because you see only ugliness in life, why should I share your view?

In the afternoon she returned to the river. Tom's friends were there, and again Elisabeth felt that tinge of disappointment. They had stripped down to their shorts in the afternoon heat, and Elisabeth admired his bronzed body. He was beautiful, she decided, like a young faun. When he was a few years older, there'd be no girl he couldn't have, just for the asking.

She watched him from the shelter of the copse, afraid of appearing awkward and clumsy before the others.

During the week she ordered expensive fishing tackle from London. It would arrive too late for his birthday, but she would have the pleasure of giving it to him the same afternoon it did arrive. Then he'd be able to go trout fishing. She made excuses to go to the village sweet shop to buy cigarettes. Tom was always out or at school when she called. Once or twice she passed the school playground during break and was able to wave to him gaily. He returned her salutations casually, self-conscious before his class mates.

The present took a week. She waited for him at the river, and when he appeared she produced it from behind her back with a flourish. He unpacked it carefully, again with tongue half way out, that universal habit among schoolboys which denotes concentration.

'It's smashing!' he said simply. 'Thanks ever so much.' His eyes sparkled as he fondled the new rod lovingly. 'Now Dad will be able to take me trout fishing. Oh gosh!'

'What's the matter?'

'I don't know what he's going to say. It's so expensive. He'll make me give it back.'

'Now don't you worry your head about that.' Elisabeth reached out timidly and patted his shoulder. 'I'll speak to him. It'll be all right.'

But she expected squalls to follow.

The next day she was dusting in the living-room when the front doorbell rang. From the window she recognized Tom's father from the sweetshop.

He was obviously ill at ease when she opened the door. 'Can I speak to you a moment, Miss Wilson?' he said clearing his throat.

'Certainly. Come in and have some coffee.'

'No, I shan't bother with coffee, thanks.'

She showed him into the living-room. Now she had a chance to study him, now that he wasn't doling out toffees or ice cream, she saw how completely unlike Tom he was. The goose that had given birth to the swan. She remembered Tom's mother as a little pleasant dumpy woman. Tom was a miracle. She pulled herself together.

'Are you sure you won't have a coffee, Mr. Andrews? It's no trouble.'

'No really, no coffee. I—well, it's a bit difficult for me to say this.'

'Cigarette?'

He took one gratefully.

'It's about my boy Tom.'

He paused. She waited, saying nothing, gathering her forces together for whatever was coming.

'You've been seeing him.'

'Once or twice. Down by the river. He was fishing.'

'Well, to cut it short, Miss Wilson, he came home with a new expensive fly-fishing rod and tackle which he said you gave him,'

So it was out. Good. 'Yes, as a matter of fact, I did.'

The man was plainly embarrassed. He moved his feet nervously.

'It was very good of you, of course, but—but—'

'But what?'

'Well, me and his mother don't think it right he should accept it. It's too expensive. It's not even as if you was a relation—'

'Oh nonsense!' Elisabeth stood up. His obvious timidity made her impatient.

'It's good to see a boy keen on his hobby these days. He should be encouraged.'

'Yes, but—'

'Please, I don't mean to be rude. It gives me great pleasure to do it.'

'I'm sure it does, Miss Wilson. I'm not criticizing. His mother and I both realize how generous it was of you, but he's a little too young, and it's too much for—forgive me, a perfect stranger to do. It was too much to spend on my boy.'

There was an awkward pause. Elisabeth stood over him. He watched her carefully.

'Look, Mr. Andrews,' she said at last, 'I'll be perfectly frank with you. I've no one to spend my money on. My father left us reasonably well off and—I like your son. It gives me great pleasure to be able to give him something I know he will appreciate. So many people these days—well you give them something and they thank you politely, but you can tell they don't really want it. They're only waiting for you to go so they can dispose of it. But your boy—don't deprive me of that pleasure, Mr. Andrews.'

It was almost a plea.

'Yes, but—'

'I wouldn't have done it if I couldn't afford it.'

Elisabeth sensed that she had won.

'Well, if you put it like that—will you agree to one thing?'

'What's that?'

'That his mother and I keep it for him till he's older.'

'You're his father,' Elisabeth said, 'you must do as you think best.'

When she saw Tom next, she told him of this interview. 'I thought he'd do that,' Tom said. 'He said he would.'

'Well we won. You're to keep it.'

Tom smiled. 'I think you're smashing. I don't know how you

wangled it.' He squeezed her hand. This was the first time he'd actually touched her, Elisabeth realized.

'He wants to keep it till you're older. Do you mind that?'

Torn shrugged. 'All the same if I do. He's the boss.'

'Yes, but do you?'

'Not really. I told you he was going to show me how. I'd probably break it.'

'You're sensible for your age, aren't you? Other little boys would want to—'

She broke off lamely. Perhaps he wasn't as keen as she'd thought.

Tom said, 'Oh, there are lots of other fish to catch here first. Look I'll show you.'

For the next half-hour neither spoke much. He is a little boy, Elisabeth thought, he is a little boy and I am a grown woman, and I can't understand him all at once.

She had brought tea for them both, and over the currant cake she had an idea.

'Would you like me to take you to London?'

'Coo! Would you?'

She laughed at his eagerness. Perhaps he wasn't so difficult to understand, after all. Not really.

'You'd like to go to the Zoo, wouldn't you? To the aquarium, where they have all the tropical fish.'

'I sure would. Are they open on Saturdays?'

'Oh yes, and Sundays too. We'll have a day's holiday in London!'

'You *are* smashing.'

During the week she called in again at the sweetshop. Mrs. Andrews was on her own.

'You want to take Tom to London? Well, it's very nice of you, but—'

Not this again, Elisabeth thought. Always this pretence, this ritual.

'I'll take great care of him, Mrs. Andrews,' she said aloud, 'he'll be perfectly safe.'

'Oh yes, I'm sure he will,' Mrs. Andrews said hastily. 'It's not that. It's just—I don't know why you're doing all this for Tom, Miss Wilson. First the fishing rod, now—'

'But I haven't been to London for ages. It's a good excuse for me. Besides, I love the Zoo, and when you've no children of your own and—and no family, well, you've got to find an excuse for going.' She leaned forward persuasively.

'Tom will love it so much.'

And Tom did. Next Saturday they went up by the first train and Tom was immediately smitten with awe. He'd never seen a big city before, and the wonder and noise and size of London were something he had to come to terms with. They lunched at one of the big Oxford Street stores, and afterwards caught a bus to the Zoo.

All that day he never said much. He nodded at every remark Elisabeth made, and seemed much younger than his ten recently acquired years. In the darkness of the Aquarium he clutched her hand tightly as they went from tank to tank, so that she really felt herself his mother. The heat of the Zoo, the smell of the animals and the noise of the crowds almost made her regret her quixotic action, had it not been for Tom's obvious enjoyment of every minute. They had tea at a little self-service cafe near the Mappin Terraces, and afterwards he wanted to return to the Lion House, perhaps the smelliest building of all. Still, children never minded that. Actually the beauty of the great cats as they paced restlessly from side to side of their cages, the poetry of their movements, the symmetry of their bodies and the muscles rippling and rolling under their brown hides, the intelligence in their eyes, their longing to be free, called to something in herself so that she felt a sympathy with them, almost a fellow-feeling. Though, *she* was halfway out of her cage, while they would only lose *their* captivity in death. She stole a sidelong glance at Tom. He too was fascinated by their strength and grace.

'Have you never seen a lion before?' she asked softly.

'Only in books.'

'They are beautiful, aren't they? Poor things. I think I really hate animals in cages.'

She thought, if only we could all be free. All living things under the sun. Why did God allow living things to be locked up?

'Have you had enough, dear? I think we ought to wend our way to the station, or we'll miss the six o'clock train.'

As the train left Paddington, Tom moved from his corner seat next to hers.

'It's been a smashing day, Miss Wilson,' he whispered because there were other people there, 'thank you a million times. Can we come again?'

'We'll see, dear.' There was the Tower, she thought, and Madame Tussauds, and Windsor Castle. Everything a boy should see. When they got home she knew she'd have to face her mother...

'Well, I don't understand this cradle-snatching.'

'Oh don't be absurd, Mother.' She had seen Tom home, and outside the door of their shop, over which he lived with his parents, he had kissed her. Just a momentary peck, another whispered "Thanks ever so much", and he had run inside and shut the door. She had stood for a moment looking stupidly at the closed door with its sign "Donald Andrews, licensed to sell tobacco", unable to remember where she was or what she was doing there. Who was this strange little being who had kissed her? Just for a moment, then the feeling had passed. Now, with her mother's words, she was back to earth with a bump.

'Please don't make a scene, Mother. London was very hot and tiring, and I want to go straight to bed.'

'I'm not making a scene. I'm certainly not complaining because you left me alone all day—'

'You could have asked someone in—'

'—left me alone all day, and went gadding off to London. No, what I object to is all the talk there'll be.'

Elisabeth was almost too weary to listen. 'Talk? What talk will there be?'

'Your monopolizing this child, this boy from the village.'

'Oh, Mother, please. If his parents don't mind, I can't see that it is anyone else's business.'

'Well you know what people are like. And all these expensive presents.'

'One fishing rod. Must we have this tonight?'

'I've been meaning to talk to you about it before, but you're always too busy. Or else you're deliberately evasive.'

No, not this now, not tonight. Don't spoil it all. *Please...*

'Mother, if we can postpone this talk, I promise I won't be evasive tomorrow. Goodnight.'

She bent to kiss her automatically on the forehead, as usual, but stopped. 'Come on, I'll wheel you to your room.'

'I'm quite capable of putting myself to bed. And anyway, if you'll take my advice, you'll leave this boy alone. He isn't even our class.'

'Goodnight, Mother.'

She is disgusting, Elisabeth thought, as she undressed in her room. She is my mother and I must honour her, but she is disgusting. But Tom had kissed her, and somehow that thought blotted out her mother's unpleasantness, and sent her happily to sleep.

Soon after that it was the school holidays. Elisabeth took Tom several more times to London. His parents at first unwilling, realized how much he was enjoying this unexpected good fortune, and eventually gave in. After all, it was good for his education. Elisabeth began to enjoy defying her mother openly. A thing which up to a few weeks before she would not have thought possible.

Tom's attitude towards her had changed too. He began to

confide in her, to share with her the little boyish secrets which he told no one else, least of all his own parents. She was thrilled that she was able to promote in him this confidence, this ease in her company which implied affection. Until one day the bomb was dropped.

They were sitting as usual by the river when it happened. She was always to remember that they had been eating tomato and cress sandwiches which she had prepared herself.

'Dad says we're going to the sea next week.'

He was leaning back chewing a blade of grass. The August afternoon was as hot as ever. She could hear the rooks cawing over in the copse.

'Oh, that's nice,' she said mechanically. 'For the day, d'you mean?'

'Oh, no, for a fortnight. To my sister Vi in Deal. She's married there. Got a house and all. Dad's going to take me mackerel fishing.'

'For a whole fortnight. I—I shall miss you.'

'I'll send you a postcard.'

Impulsively she took his hand. 'Mind you do!'

For a moment he let it lie in hers, then jumped up and ran to the river. Fred and the girls were coming up the slope. Elisabeth sat watching them, aware once again of the barrier between age and childhood.

During the next fortnight Elisabeth went about her household tasks mechanically. She had tried joining the village Women's Institute, to give herself an outside interest, but could find none, and stopped attending their meetings. Her mother, glad of her undivided attention at last, became more unbearable than ever.

'It's a good job that boy has gone away,' she said once, 'the way you carry on, you'd think he was yours. It's not healthy.'

Elisabeth felt like saying, if it hadn't been for you—but stopped herself. It was useless and stupid to blame someone else for your own lack of courage. Perhaps her mother would have done just that if the positions had been reversed, but why bring herself down to her level? She said nothing, but bore her loss stolidly, doggedly, uncomplaining. Only once, when she felt her mother had really gone too far she said 'For God's sake shut up about Tom. You're making something big out of nothing. He's merely rather a pleasant youngster who amuses me. Please don't mention him again.'

But in bed at night, when the darkness protected her, she knew that she lied not only to her mother, but also to herself.

After an eternity of monotonous, featureless days, the fortnight was up and Tom returned. The same evening he knocked timidly on the door of their cottage. With difficulty she restrained an impulse to take him in her arms. Instead she said casually, copying the latest Americanism, 'Hi there, stranger!'

How absurd I am, she thought.

'Hi,' said Tom. 'Can I come in?'

'Did you have a good time?' She stood aside to let him pass. If possible he looked more sunburnt than ever. His fair hair stood out sharply against his bronzed skin.

'Sit over there by the window. I'll get some tea, then you can tell me all about it. Or would you rather have lemonade? I think we have some.'

'Tea would be fine, thanks.'

'How sunburnt you are!'

'I was out most of the time. Dad took me—'

'I know. Dad took you mackerel fishing. Did you catch any?'

'Not me by myself. But I helped. You see the seagulls all clustered together on the water—all in one place. Then you know there's a school of mackerel there. That's how you know.'

'Who is it?' Her mother's voice came from the bedroom.

'Does she mind me being here?' Tom whispered.

'Of course not. It's Tom, Mother.'

'Oh.' She heard her mother grunt disapprovingly.

'Is she very cross?'

'Don't worry dear. She hasn't been very well lately.'

'Is it her arthritis?'

'Yes, it's her arthritis. You never sent me a postcard.'

'Sorry.' Tom stared at the floor sheepishly.

He reminded her of his father, that day he'd come to see her... She had been hurt not to receive his promised postcard, and she didn't see why he shouldn't know it. 'You promised, and you shouldn't break promises.'

'I did mean to, honest. But the time went so quick—'

'Elisabeth.' Her mother was calling again.

Tom looked round uneasily. 'Where is she, upstairs?'

'No in her bedroom. She can't get upstairs easily with her wheelchair, so she sleeps downstairs. At the back.'

'I'd better go—'

'No, don't go—'

'I must. We haven't unpacked yet. See you.'

He was at the front door before she could stop him. 'See you. Er—'

'Yeah?'

'When are you going to the river again? Saturday?'

'I'll let you know if I can't,' Tom said.

'Promise?'

He nodded, grinning. 'I promise. See you on Saturday.'

'I'm glad you're back. Give me a kiss before you go.'

'Damn you,' Elisabeth said aloud to her mother's bedroom door, 'damn you.'

There was nothing to distinguish that Saturday morning from any other Saturday morning, except of course that Tom was back. That was the funny thing. Elisabeth thought afterward what a funny thing it was. You couldn't count on omens or hunches or "feelings", otherwise she might have been prepared.

Tom was waiting for her at the river when she got there.

She saw that he had on the same yellow sweater and jeans he had worn the first time she'd seen him. Even in that short space of time, barely a month, he had grown.

'Hi!' he called.

'Hi! I've brought some tea.'

'Good! I haven't caught anything yet.'

'D'you want to eat now, or go on fishing for a bit?'

'No, let's go for a walk.'

Elisabeth laughed. 'That's unlike you! All right. I'll leave the tea things here. Are the others coming?'

'No, I asked them not to.'

'Did you? Why?'

'Because there's something want to tell you. I thought it better if—if we could talk alone.'

Surprised, Elisabeth looked at him more carefully. His face was grave.

'What's the matter? Is something worrying you? You know I'll help if I can.'

Some tiff at home, she thought. At that age things seem so terribly important.

'Let's walk over to the copse. We can talk on the way.'

'All right. But don't look so serious. It may never happen.'

She put her arm round his shoulder. He looked up, grinning uneasily.

'Well, what is it?'

'Tell you when we get there.'

Again she heard the rooks. Through the copse she could see the sun flashing like a Morse code signaller. She was immensely flattered that he thought she could help in this juvenile crisis, whatever it was.

Inside the copse she felt its welcoming coolness. Funny how the weather stayed so obstinately hot.

'Well, out with it. What's all the mystery?'

'It's Dad. He wants to sell out. He wants to go and settle near Vi. There's this empty house in her road, near the seafront, and he wants to buy it. In fact, he did buy it while we were there.'

What is the child saying? I'm not taking it in.

'He wants to retire. Says he's had enough of shop keeping. Mum likes the idea, too. I'm not going back to school next term. They want to put me in school at Deal.'

There was a numbness creeping over her, over all her bones on this hot August afternoon.

'It means I won't be able to see you any more.'

'Won't be able to see me any more?' she repeated stupidly. 'You're joking.'

'I'm not. Honest. Mum said—'

'Go on.'

'Mum said there was another thing. I couldn't get it all, but there's talk about—about you and me, and—'

'Stop it! Stop it!'

'They don't think it a good idea for us to be together so much... And your mother—'

'My mother?'

'She wrote a letter...'

Something snapped in Elisabeth. The boy stopped, startled at what he saw.

'Wh—what's the matter, Miss Wilson?'

'Elisabeth. My name's Elisabeth.' Was that voice really hers?

'Elisabeth. What's the matter, Elisabeth?'

Timidly he put out a hand and took hers.

'That's not the main reason, honest it's not. Dad likes the sea. He always said he'd retire to the seaside. Mum does too. I'll be able to use your present—'

'No!'

'—you can come and stay with us. I'll tell them I want you to—'

'No!'

Her cry startled the birds feeding near. They flew in panic into the nearest elm. Tom, at first puzzled at what he saw in her face, began to grow alarmed. He backed away.

'It's all right, Elisabeth. Don't—'

'No! They shan't take you away. They shan't. All my life—they shan't, they shan't!'

Tears welled up in her eyes, blinding her. She grabbed at the faint blur which was Tom; before he could struggle free she pulled him towards her.

All her desire and despair came to the surface. He was hers. Her lover, her son, what did it matter.

'Let me go, you're hurting me—'

'You're mine, you're mine. They shan't take you away—'

Her fingers round his neck, drawing his head up to kiss his lips. Through her tears she saw his expression of blank, uncomprehending horror. Frank, why did you leave me when I needed you? Her mother, always her mother... Frank.

The clumsiness which was her curse, rising up to destroy her...

When it was over, she looked down at the body lying before her. It was funny, the way his hair clashed with the yellow of his sweater...

Beside the stream her tears splashed on to the pebbles, mixing with the current which ran into the river further down.

Soon, with it, they would find their way to the sea.

THE INMATE

YES, SHE IS PATHETIC, isn't she? About thirty-two, I imagine: No, I shouldn't go too near if I were you. She's quite friendly most of the time, but occasionally— That's why we have to keep her apart, of course. Can't be too careful. It's really amazing how one isolated incident of violence communicates itself to the rest of the patients. Seems to bring out all kinds of hidden tendencies. Mild old gentlemen who normally wouldn't hurt a fly, well, if they get to hear that there has been some sort of—some little spot of bother anywhere in the establishment involving a patient and a member of the Staff, or even a visitor such as yourself, you'd scarcely credit the change. Of course, it all stems from the fact that most of us, even those of us on the outside who are laughingly referred to as sane, have a streak of violence which certain stimuli can activate. Usually it is so well concealed, so well controlled that the stimuli have to be pretty powerful. But with our patients it is less under control, so that the stimuli needed are correspondingly less. I don't wish to bore you with medical jargonese, but I'm sure you realize that there is no such thing as absolute sanity. Yes, I'm sure you do, being a writer and all that. You remember that old saw about the sleeping tiger? Was it Omar Khayyam? It usually was. Well, it's true, of course. Most of us have a beast inside us just waiting to spring out, under certain circumstances...

Talking of beasts reminds me. About that poor woman. Though I don't think I ought to tell you. You might put it in a book or something. On second thoughts, even if I did you wouldn't believe me. It's not the sort of thing—

Well, come back to my office then, and I'll give you a drink to round off your tour. I keep some in case of emergencies.

Whisky? Cheers. That woman? You really want to hear? I said a beast reminded me, didn't I? Her husband, you see, was a friend of mine. That's what made it all the more distressing when she had to be brought here. Quite incurable, I'm afraid. When you hear why, you won't be surprised. Though I doubt if you'll believe me.

Her husband was an animal collector. Yes, I said was. He's dead now, poor chap. Didn't live long after the experience. Became an old man in one night. Well, he collected animals, and brought them to his own private zoo. More money than sense really. He had one of those enormous estates you still hear about occasionally in Scotland. Bought it cheap off some ancient crumbling family who found it impossible to keep up and had to sell it to pay off death duties. His family made all their money through marketing one of these detergent powders. Can't abide them myself, give me a good old fashioned packet of soap flakes any day, but there's money in it. No, I'm not going to tell you which one, and anyway, that's another story. Suffice it to say that there was a takeover bid made and accepted, and my friend found himself a very rich man. He was madly eligible, of course, and being not exactly ill-favoured, as they say in Victorian novels, he was eagerly chased after by match-making Mamas. There are still quite a few of them about as you know, as thorough and single-minded of purpose as ever, and they didn't all die off with Jane Austen.

You detect a certain flippancy in my manner? Yes, you're right. It's because I'm uneasy, because I don't know how to tell you what happened, because there's no medical explanation for it, for what I saw with my own eyes, but mostly because I don't really want to tell you. Confession won't be good for my soul. I fear it will only cause me more sleepless nights than I've had already, though God knows if that's possible.

That creature you saw in there, smiling and mumbling to herself. She was once one of the most beautiful girls in Edinburgh Society. My friend met her at some dance or other and fell hook, line, and sinker. Whether she genuinely cared for him, or was merely attracted by his money we'll never know. She had the reputation for being somewhat fast, but in this day and age most girls are, or if not, like to be thought so. At any rate, she came of a very good family as I've said, and in my friend's eyes, that made up for a lot. Braving the jealousy of her unsuccessful rivals and their equally disappointed mothers, she married him.

Everything went well at first. After the bustle of town life she found the quietness and seclusion of the Western Highlands intriguing. Still very much a young girl, she adored the romance of it all and was prepared to put up with the inconvenience of inadequate plumbing for the beauty of the mountains and lochs. Do you know that part of the world at all? The Road to the Isles that they used to sing about, from Fort William to Mallaig? Well, you should. I have a small cottage near Fort William that I sometimes escape to, so I was actually on the spot. He called me in the middle of the night, and the horror in his voice made him sound quite unrecognizable. But I'm anticipating.

Linda often used to say to me that the beauty and peace of it all actually inspired her. She was like that, you see. She said that it led her thoughts on to a higher plane, made her aware of a higher level of consciousness. In this frame of mind she turned to mysticism, and began studying the occult. I suspect that she had already begun to feel a little bored, and turned to fantasy, as many bored women will. I once taxed her with it, practically accused her of not having enough to occupy her time, but she replied that for a doctor I was surprisingly insensitive.

Her husband at that time had just embarked on this zoo idea. It all started, I believe, from a herd of white deer which had bred on the estate. White deer are extremely rare, practically extinct, in fact, and I believe there is only one other estate in Scotland which boasts a herd. He was very excited about them, and determined to cash in, though God knows he didn't need the money. He told me what he intended to do. He would start this zoo, charge people to go round it, and eventually open the house and the rest of the grounds too. Linda was dead against it at first, particularly when he started throwing money away financing expeditions to the Belgian Congo and the Indian jungles. You see, apart from the initial expense of hiring guides and equipment, there were all the costs of shipping the animals, obtaining the necessary foods and the hundred and one incidentals. It's amazing how it mounts up when you stop to think.

But none of this deterred him. He never actually went on any of the expeditions. Even if he'd wanted to, there was too much to do at home administering the estate. At least that was the excuse he gave. You see, he wasn't that adventurous. He preferred the somewhat doubtful comforts of a draughty Highland baronial hall to no comfort at all on safari in some malaria-ridden swamp, and I can't say I blamed him.

It was from the second trip to the Congo that they brought the animal in question. Oh, hadn't I mentioned him before? I find it difficult not to keep thinking of him, so I presumed I must have brought him to your attention. I see him now. He was enormous, even for a gorilla with a great brown shaggy hide, and arms so powerful that they looked as if they could crush a man with the slightest pressure. He was hideous, and yet at the same time he was beautiful. There is something beautiful in a manifestation of primitive strength, and he was a perfect example of his species. It seemed to me when I saw him that he had an uncommonly high brow, and if there are degrees of intellectual ability among the anthropoids in the same way that Man varies between idiocy and genius, he would have been nearer the latter than the former category.

Linda had previously taken no interest in her husband's "foolishness"—her description. I think she was frightened that one dark night all the animals would break out and wreak havoc on the estate. She had tried to dissuade him from carrying on with it: after all, she had pointed out, there were enough zoos in the country already. It was a needless expense, she had said. She had even tried to get me to speak to him to use my influence, but I would not be drawn into any controversy between husband and wife. After all, it was his money to spend as he wished.

However, all that changed when the gorilla arrived. To this day I cannot explain it. I wish I could, but medical science has no name for it. The very day he arrived she began to take an all-absorbing interest in him. They had to keep him under sedatives during transportation, you see, because he could have fought his way out. No, there's no law against keeping one privately that I know of. He was to be the star turn of the zoo. People were to come from miles around to see him. They had a specially strengthened cage all ready to receive him, and there was quite a welcoming committee, of whom Linda was one. You see, straight away that was out of character. She had taken absolutely no interest in the animals up to now, and all of a sudden— Yes, you can put it down to the whims of a bored woman, if you like. You can put it down to natural curiosity, you can put it down to anything you like. But what you can't put down to natural curiosity was Linda's behaviour. Even now I shouldn't be telling you, with that poor creature not fifty yards away from us, in the state in which you have just seen her. You must promise that it shall go no farther— You see, there was nothing natural about Linda's curiosity concerning the gorilla. She would spend hours beside the cage just staring at him. She seemed to be completely fascinated by him. Her husband was quite worried, well, concerned would be a better word. At first he didn't take it seriously; just another of her odd little pastimes. But when it started getting out of hand he came over to see me at Fort William. I go there for weekends when I can get away, which isn't often now since I took over this place. But when I was there, one weekend he came over, purely on a social visit you understand, and told me all about it.

I could see straight away that there was something he didn't understand. Don't get me wrong, there was no horror about it, he was just puzzled. She kept on talking about the gorilla, you know, where he came from, his natural habitat, was he lonely, shouldn't they get a mate for him, all that kind of thing. She was suddenly terribly interested in his history, the evolution of the anthropoid and mammalian species; nothing, of course, that you couldn't find in a book on natural history or biology, but for one who had previously shown no interest, even a positive antipathy for the subject, this volte-face seemed somehow unhealthy. That, at any rate, was how Bob felt. He asked me to drop in for dinner and casually talk to her: nothing doctor-patient, just a friendly chat.

When I arrived they showed me over the zoo. It was larger than I expected. I've described the gorilla to you, so I won't bore you again. But I watched Linda watching him—she insisted on accompanying us—and there was something in her expression that I didn't understand and didn't particularly like. I suddenly realized for the first time why Bob was worried. There was nothing you could put your finger on, it was just something you sensed. And the gorilla, too, sensed it. It was unbelievable, but he actually responded. How? You have asked me a difficult question, because I can't—or couldn't—give a definite answer. All I can say is that he was conscious, of her presence in some way in which he was not conscious of ours. It is too subtle to convey easily. He was less of a beast when she was there. When she left I stayed behind for a tiny minute and I could almost see the physical change. He seemed to sink in the evolutionary scale as I watched. It was not a little frightening. What possible point of contact could these two beings share, which was denied to Bob and myself? And what deep core of his being could Linda touch and we couldn't?

Linda still studied her books, in the intervals when she could tear herself away from the zoo. During the course of the evening I noticed one lying face downward on one of the occasional tables. She had evidently thrown it down when we arrived. It was concerned with reincarnation. 'Do you believe in reincarnation?' I asked, more as a conversational gambit than anything else. Linda smiled, though there was a tenseness in her eyes. 'Do you really want to know, or are you merely being polite?' 'You must tell me all about it sometime,' I said, trying to keep the conversation as casual as I could. 'I'm frightfully unversed in things of that sort.' She seemed to think I was making fun of her, because she shut up like a clam after that. Nothing I said would make her discuss it.

But it wasn't only me with whom she was irritated. Her husband seemed to vex her in various trivial ways. I saw her once or twice look at him with what actually appeared to be distaste, although he was blissfully unaware of the fact. When it was time for me to go I was relieved. There was a steadily growing atmosphere which made me uneasy, and even then I didn't put everything together—I didn't connect all the parts I'd seen or discovered to make one convincing whole, if you follow me.

I didn't see them after that for some considerable time. My duties here took up virtually all my energy, and in the intervals all I felt able to do was eat and sleep. The marital troubles of Bob and Linda went completely out of my head. I occasionally heard from Bob, of course. We had kept a desultory correspondence for many years since we had first met on holiday in Spain before the war. Only in one letter did he mention Linda's preoccupation. He had convinced himself it wasn't important and because of his casual tone, he almost convinced me. Almost, but not quite. In the letter in which he did mention it, though, he was somewhat agitated. It seems she had stayed out all night. He didn't realize it at the time. He himself had come in late and had gone straight to bed. He hadn't switched the light on so as not to disturb her. Only in the morning did he realize her bed hadn't been slept in.

They searched the grounds first, because even then he didn't imagine— Well, they found her in the gorilla's cage. Yes, actually *in* the cage, *with* the gorilla. Sound asleep. She hadn't been harmed in any way. She had somehow managed to get the key, or a duplicate of it, and her story was that she had gone outside to see him last thing and had fallen asleep. When it was suggested that she might have been killed, she had laughed and said, 'Oh, *he* wouldn't hurt me,' or words to that effect. At any rate, so Bob said, she seemed none the worse for her adventure.

I wasn't really sure that I believed what Bob had said. I put it down to the fact that he was disproportionately worried about Linda, and had, albeit unconsciously, distorted the facts. Although I couldn't quite see how facts like that could have been distorted. Apart from forbidding her to repeat the experience, I understand, he took no further action.

You see, even then I wasn't really worried. Not worried enough to take any positive action. I was having certain changes made, certain structural alterations done to this place, and I can only plead this in excuse for my remissness. I was busy to the exclusion of all else, as they say. You won't judge me too harshly I feel, when I tell you that Bob's next letter drove what little unease I felt clean away. Linda was pregnant. This was the best thing that could have happened. It was just what she needed to drive all this morbid nonsense out of her head. I determined to drive up to Fort William at the first opportunity I could get away, to congratulate them.

As luck would have it, I had just taken on Doctor Cannon. You met him earlier this afternoon. Young fellow, but very capable. I have every confidence in leaving the place in his charge, so I had no qualms in taking another long weekend off. I went over to the house on the Sunday. When I saw Linda, I realized at once how right my opinion was. She looked happier and prettier than she had since before. she was married. I offered my heartfelt congratulations, and I must say that she accepted them without any of the apparent coolness which had seemed to grow up between us. It had probably been because she was nervous and upset on the pre-vious occasion, and not meant for me personally at all. I was even quite willing to put it down to my highly developed imagination that her relations with Bob still seemed a trifle strained. It takes a certain effort of adjustment on the part of the Mother-to-be when she first hears the news, and the husband is the obvious person to suffer. I still thought it would pass. Linda was happy about it, that was the main thing.

In the evening, over our coffee in the drawing-room, I determined to make quite sure the breach between us had closed. The best way to do this, so I fondly imagined, would be to re-examine the original cause. 'You promised to tell me about reincarnation,' I said, deliberately ignoring Bob's startled look.

'I believe in it implicitly,' Linda said, quite calmly, broaching no argument. 'I'm quite certain I have lived before.'

'But how *can* you be so certain? You don't remember—' It seemed to me that they both jumped up simultaneously, though I now realize that Linda was the first one to get to her feet.

'But that's just it, Tim. I do remember! Oh, nothing connected, of course. I'm no Bridey Murphy, or anything like that. But suddenly, for no reason at all things came into my head. Little pictures of places I couldn't possibly have seen.'

'You've seen them in books.'

Linda laughed. 'I won't try to convince you. I know I couldn't do that, so I won't try.' And she didn't. I was sorry because I would have liked to discuss it further, but I could see that nothing I could have said would have shaken her faith in what to her was an incon-trovertible fact. What she did tell me though was about her dream. It seems that for some time past, long before she was pregnant, she had been having this recurrent dream. At first it had frightened her by its very intensity, then she had come to accept it and eventually to welcome it. I asked her to describe it, but she was cagey. I think she felt that in some way it was encroaching upon her privacy.

Outside the night was cold. Smoking Bob's cigars and drinking his very excellent brandy, I was loath to move, although my car was heated and the drive back to Fort William would have taken fifteen minutes at the most. When Bob suggested I stay the night, I didn't put up any very strong resistance.

It seemed I had hardly put my head down on the pillow, when I was awakened by sounds of shouts and cries corning from outside the window. I could see waving lights coming from the bushes at the end of the lawn, and as I was about to throw on some clothes to discover what had happened, I heard the sharp report of a rifle. A moment later Bob burst in, eyes wild with excitement, and collapsed into the armchair. 'What on earth—' I began, but he held up his hand to stop me. He was so breathless that it was some time before he could speak. At last he managed to get out, 'The gorilla. He escaped from his cage!'

'My God—' I was almost out of the door and down the stairs before he shouted, 'It's all right, Tom got him. He's dead.'

'Was anyone hurt?'

'He went for Tom, but Tom got out of the way and he lumbered off in the direction of the wood. One of Tom's assistants always carried a rifle, and I told him to shoot to kill.'

'It was a pity you had to do that.'

'There was no other way. He was a dangerous brute, and I couldn't take any chances.'

I saw the body. Tom, the head keeper, still white and shaken from his narrow escape, had covered it with a tarpaulin. As I folded it back to take one last look at the magnificent specimen, I heard a woman's voice, shaking with anger, cry out, 'You damned fools.'

A moment later Linda burst upon us. I say that, because there was no other way to describe her entrance. She threw herself down on top of the tarpaulin, sobbing as if her heart would break.

'Oh God,' I heard her moaning, 'why did they have to do it. All that beauty, all that strength. Oh God.'

I put my arm on hers to try and restrain her.

'They had to, Linda,' I said, as calmly as I could. 'He was dangerous.'

She drew away from me sharply, as if my very contact repelled her. 'What do you know about it,' she shouted out, beside herself. 'You can't possibly understand. Nobody can. Nobody can appreciate beauty as I saw it.'

She turned round. Bob was standing behind her looking helpless and unhappy. 'It was wanton cruelty,' she said, throwing him a look of bitter hatred and contempt. 'I'll never forgive you.'

And she never did. I left early the next morning, and Linda did not put in an appearance. When I came back to Town, I had an anguished letter from Bob saying that Linda positively refused to speak to him. Her behaviour seemed out of all proportion. Bob was really very much in love with her, you know, and her silence hurt him more than he could put into words. He still couldn't properly understand why she was so furious at the gorilla's death. I still blame myself for not writing to her personally asking her to make it up with Bob, if only for the child's sake, but then she might have written me an abusive letter telling me to mind my own business, and after that, well, I could hardly have visited the house again could I? But then, I blame myself for so much, for not seeing what I should have seen. The trouble was that whether or not I suspected the truth subconsciously I would have rejected it.

I made excuses even to myself after that night for not revisiting Scotland. I was busy here. That was certainly true, but I capitalized on it if you follow me. Although deep down I knew that Linda needed help, I preferred not to become involved, and perhaps with my well meaning but clumsy attempts to help only widen the rift between the two of them.

When the final event occurred it was only sheer coincidence that I was on the spot. At least that is how I argued it to myself, though I was having a spot of conscience trouble by that time. Idle curiosity played its part, too, I think, on looking back. The nine months were approximately up and I wanted to see if Linda's baby would have the desired effect.

In the middle of the night after I got to Fort William the telephone rang. I hardly recognized Bob's voice. I told you this before, didn't I? He sounded as if as if he'd caught a glimpse of Hell. And he had, of course. You think I sound melodramatic? He could hardly speak, but he managed to gasp out a plea for me to come at once. When I arrived, he met me at the front door. He had been waiting for me. His face was ashen, his eyes were dazed with horror. Without a word he grabbed me by the arm and led me into a little room. What I saw nearly made me vomit.

Even now I can hardly bear—it had Linda's features you see. Linda lay in bed, eyes staring up at the ceiling, smiling happily. She was more or less as you saw her today. They'd engaged a nurse, a midwife she was, and when she saw— Well, they'd wanted to destroy it, but Linda moaned and moaned for it. When I'd seen, Bob pushed me into the corridor. He told me what Linda had been like for the past few weeks, pushing him away with disgust every time he'd tried to go near her, telling him he wasn't the father... He'd put it all down to the whims of pregnancy, as anyone would. She'd told him about her dream too, *all* about it; about the jungle, how she'd lived as mate to— Her reincarnation belief was all mixed up with it. He was sobbing, holding his head in his hands, still stupid with unbelief. But suddenly he stopped, became calm, ominously calm as I knew. He told me what he intended to do, first to—it, then to himself. I told him not to be a fool, even then I should have stayed with him, never left him for a minute. Even now I can't forget the last thing he said to me, and the way he said it.

With eyes clouded with horror, he told me what would stay with him forever, both this side of the grave and beyond it—how Linda had gazed upon it, and her expression of thankful relief when the thing had first been placed into her arms...

A NICE CUT OFF THE JOINT

'ARE YOU *SURE* you won't stay for dinner, Julia? I've got a nice shoulder in.'

'No, my dear. It's sweet of you, but Fred will be in soon, panting for food. You know what a glutton he is. I must go and cook for him.'

Julia Simpson got to her feet heavily. Helen noticed how fat she was. Positively obese. 'Husbands,' she was saying, 'what bores they can be at times. I would have loved to stay and have a real old hen session.'

At the door Helen pressed her hand. 'Do come again soon. I get so lonely when Tom's away. I'm really not used to it, you know, and I notice it so dreadfully.'

'Well, it won't be long, dear. He'll be back before you know it. Meanwhile you ought to seize your opportunity.'

'Seize my opportunity?'

'Yes. Make a little hay while the sun's shining. Get out a bit, see people, go to theatres—'

'Oh, it's no fun alone, Julia.'

'You've been out of England so long, you ought to catch up on things. There's a marvellous new musical at the—'

Helen smiled what she hoped was a brave smile.

'We'll see, dear.'

'And you must put on some weight. You're looking alarmingly thin, you know.'

Helen stared at herself in the long mirror in the bedroom. Was she really too thin? She thought she had rather a nice figure, especially for a woman of her age. Remarkably well preserved, that was the phrase, wasn't it?

Behind her she could see the other end of the room reflected in the mirror. She'd put a thick white dust-sheet over the large double bed in the corner, as a temporary measure. Now she noticed what an eyesore it looked against the pink and blue furnishings of the rest of the room. She'd chosen the colour scheme herself. She went out quickly, and closed and double-locked the door. Time enough to deal with that, she thought. After all, there was no Tom to come poking and prying and disturbing her.

It was amazing; it never ceased to astonish her, how suddenly the feeling always came upon her. Thank God there was that shoulder in the kitchen, that sweet, fresh, juicy shoulder, that could be popped straight into the oven and cooked until it was ready to satisfy her enormous hunger. Hunger that drove out every other consideration, that dominated her whole being.

Of course, when she and Tom had first returned to England she had noticed the difference in quality of the food at once. Everything seemed tasteless, insipid. It was all this frozen stuff. All the meat shipped over to England had been lying in some hold for weeks, frozen solid; all the vegetables were either tinned or pre-packed—the plastic bag civilization. Nothing came straight from the ground anymore; everything was sifted and strained through a hundred and one aggressively hygienic hands. Before the war Helen had never noticed this insistent craving for fresh meat that now attacked her with increasing regularity: in vain she searched the butchers' shops for the kind of food she remembered with nostalgia. For weeks her problem had remained unsolved.

Presently the kitchen was filled with the delicious smell of cooking. Helen licked her lips in eager anticipation. If only Julia had stayed, how she would have enjoyed herself. Her girth testified to her fondness for her stomach. Even Tom, poor Tom, how he would have revelled in the unaccustomed taste of fresh meat unsullied by the various synthetic processes through which everything passed nowadays.

It was nearly ten years now since Helen Bentley had married Tom Simpson, the young construction engineer. Tom was five years older than Helen, good-looking, so her contemporaries agreed, but undeniably dull. It was a wicked waste, as more than one young man murmured into his cups, confidentially but wistfully. The more so because she was considered to be one of the most brilliant medical students of her year. A woman surgeon was still a rarity, and for a promising career, which besides bringing honour to the name of womanhood, would stand on its own merit anywhere where the medical fraternity gathered, to be nipped in the bud in quite such a cavalier fashion, was a crime of the darkest nature. Helen's fellow students blamed Tom in the most unambiguous terms. He had swept her off her feet. Overnight, as it were, she lost all interest in a medical career, to be ready at a moment's notice to follow the young engineer to whatever part of the world the demands of some new hydro-electric scheme, or the orders of some new untried Government, might lead him.

The social life of the College suffered to no less a degree. As well as being clever, Helen was also pretty, and was well able to hold her own against the claims of various assorted nurses and probationers who were readily available as dancing partners.

In vain on the eve of her wedding her teachers, as well as her contemporaries, urged her not to give up her career. In that respect, though, Tom was adamant. A wife could either have a home or a career, not both. She must choose. And he didn't want a wife whose home and family came second. Because she was madly in love with him she agreed, but not without an inward struggle which was both hard and bitter. Her parents, who were sweet old-fashioned things, were in favour of her giving up because they had never been able to rid themselves of the notion that a lady doctor was not quite nice, and this went a long way towards deciding her finally. After all, as she told herself, her medical knowledge would always prove useful, and her surgical skill might come in handy if she and Tom should find themselves forced to live in a primitive community, while he was engaged in building a dam in some under -developed country or other. To this effect she found herself, with due pomp and ritual, presented with a complete kit of surgical instruments by her fellow students as a sort of secondary wedding present. And as many a true word was spoken in jest, she took it away with her on her numerous trips abroad, as an adjunct to her hand-luggage

She did indeed find herself in under-developed communities, and had all the travel she wanted. But with it all she remained inactive. As soon as she'd made one home temporarily comfortable, Tom's job would be over and they'd be on the move again. She found this at first frustrating, and later merely boring. Boredom became her greatest adversary. Tom was good at his job, and his services were soon in great demand. She longed to return to England and settle down for good, but he loved being forever on the move. Consequently, she made vast sets of acquaintances, but few friends. She felt herself to be merely a piece of Tom's luggage, to be carried round with his suitcases, but because she loved him she had to fall in with his plans. He would not compromise.

While he was actually engaged on a construction job, there was little for her to do. She would go for endless long walks, and badly in need of a friend as she was, she felt afraid to advance along more than the first few tentative steps towards intimacy with anyone because she knew she'd have to leave them before long.

It was when they went to Brazil that she ran into danger. The Brazilian Government had launched out on a vast new programme of development, and Tom's name was put forward as a top man in the dam construction field. The dam itself was to serve various small new townships springing up along the edge of the Amazon Basin, and he was lent by the British Government as being particularly informed about specific problems to be met with in exploiting jungle terrain.

The village where they were to stay looked to Helen's dismayed glance exactly as if it had been got together hastily overnight. These hideous collections of tents, adobe huts and sheds thatched with matted grass, spring up inevitably on the site of every large construction job, and although the quarters to which she was assigned were a cut above the rest, Tom gave her a sympathetic shrug when he saw them. He asked her if she would care to return to England and wait for him, but the thought even of England without him was intolerable. She had laughed when she thought of what her parents would have said if they could see her now. Better a career in surgery!

She always kept her case of surgical instruments by her, together with various other assorted items of first aid, and although she had never had to go so far as to perform an operation, the first aid stuff had come in useful. In a sense the presentation case was a symbol of her past: she could look back with satisfaction on her comparative success; she could remember her friends with affection, if not with regret; but the logical result was dissatisfaction with her present. She longed to be doing something useful; of course she knew nothing about engineering, but she urged Tom to find her some kind of subsidiary work—perhaps vaguely secretarial, or even domestic. Unfortunately, there were numerous cooks, and she couldn't fancy the kitchens anyway.

It was in this spirit of rebellion that she heard one day by bush telegraph that the chief of one of the neighbouring tribes was dangerously ill and not expected to live. Apparently one of the warriors out on a hunt had strayed on to the building site, attracted by curiosity, and primed with drink, had talked. She grabbed at the chance at last to be of some use, and determined to visit the chief. As soon as Tom heard what she intended, he hit the roof.

'Are you insane?' he shouted at her. 'Thousands of miles of unexplored jungle, snakes, crocodiles, God knows what. You, the plucky little woman, going in alone. Florence Nightingale of the Amazon!'

His ridicule only made her more determined. 'Of course I can't actually tie you up,' he told her. 'But it'll be your own funeral. I'm not interfering.'

She shrugged. 'I'm perfectly prepared to take all the risks,' she announced.

'Oh, for God's sake!' He stamped out. A moment later he was back. 'D'you know anything about native customs? You've heard about the head-hunters, I suppose? If you go, you'd better be prepared to have your head shrunk and put on a stick outside the Witch Doctor's hut!'

'Oh, don't be so stupid!'

'If you go, you go alone. I can't spare any men.'

'Thanks!' This time she stamped out.

She wondered how Tom would feel, seeing her head on the end of a stick. He wouldn't mind too much, she thought, he'd get over it.

She found the native sleeping it off in the back of one of the trucks. She got into the front seat and started the engine. As the vehicle sprang into life, he came to himself with a grunt, and began to rattle the door. She turned round, and in a mixture of Pidgin English and sign language, intimated to him what she wanted. To her surprise he understood more English than she expected. She held up her case, and imitated sickness. He nodded, beaming.

'Truck no good,' he told her. 'We walk.'

Half an hour later they reached the tribe's village. After the formal preliminaries, she was ushered into the presence of the chief. She saw at once that he was very ill indeed. Although they still tolerated the appointment of a witch doctor, they knew enough about white man's medicine to realize his position was only a cypher—a concession to tradition. They were more sophisticated than she gave them credit for.

The chief had cancer of the stomach. An immediate operation was the only hope. Even then it was touch and go. Afterwards she remembered the operation fairly clearly, but what came next was still vague and hazy. For what came next was infinitely the most terrible and appalling thing that could ever have happened to her. The operation was a success, there was no doubt about that. The old man would recover. The cancer hadn't had time to spread too far. Presumably out of gratitude he had issued instructions that she was to be suitably rewarded and feted.

Then the drums had begun. Softly at first, insistently, subtly, they had lulled her into a feeling of security, until all her nervousness had gone. Then they had grown in volume, gradually, without her registering the difference consciously, until suddenly it seemed they took over completely, blotting everything else out. For the first time she realized the significance of drums in stories she had read about Voodoo. Here, of course, they called it Macumba. These natives, indeed all primitive peoples, had realized the existence and potency of hypnotism long before Mesmer had come on the scene.

But then the nightmare had begun. They had instigated her into certain ancient and abominable rites, customs probably peculiar to this tribe alone in this part of the world, some freak survival. The shock had numbed first her feelings, then her mind, and through it all burst the realization that with some indescribably old part of herself she was enjoying it. She lost all sense of time, and Tom later told her that after an agonized two-day search, they found her on the edge of the jungle in an advanced state of shock. Whether she had walked there, or been transported in some way, she never discovered. They took her to a hospital, but there were no facilities for treating illnesses of the mind, and the doctor who was sent for urged Tom to get her back to England as soon as possible, where she would be able to undergo the correct psychiatric treatment. She had passed through some severe traumatic experience, and while there was no physical evidence of sexual assault, the assault to her sensibilities was no less severe in its result.

She lay in the white little bed in the scrubbed hygienic little room, gazing up at the sky through the window for several weeks. She learnt to identify numerous species of brightly coloured jungle bird by its cry alone. And it was during those weeks that the craving for fresh meat first came upon her. As soon as they judged it safe for her to get up she would seize the opportunity to slip out, back through the jungle, hardly realizing where she was going. Tom took to guarding her himself, and she came to look on him as her jailer.

Eventually, of course, as soon as a replacement could be sent over, he was released from his assignment, and they returned to England. On the way over, she seemed to him so much better and so urgent in her pleas for him to take no further medical steps, that he judged her to know what she was talking about.

Arriving in London they went to their usual hotel. Their first night back they had a long and serious talk. Tom pledged to her solemnly that in future he would only accept jobs which would not take him too far afield. They would find a flat, which she could furnish to her exact requirements, and use as a permanent home. She was content for the first time in her married life.

They had enough money put by to furnish a very attractive little place, and for the first time Helen found herself able to make friends without the fear of imminent separation. The one cloud on her horizon was the incessant craving which soon developed into a chronic condition. Tom, at first inclined to dismiss the whole thing as a symptom of restlessness with a belatedly ordered life after their nomadic existence, tried to ridicule her out of it. But continual dissatisfaction with all the food available in the shops, and the daily half-left meals, soon took its toll. She lost weight and grew thin, although to Tom's surprise, she didn't appear to notice it herself. Worse than this, her hospitality towards her husband, which had begun after her ghastly experience in Brazil, instead of lessening with her contentment, grew more intense. Everything he said or did seemed to annoy her. With her thinness, grew her irritability. Occasionally he saw her giving him strange, almost terrifying looks, when she thought she was unobserved. Now that he too was forced into comparative inactivity, this didn't help his own mood. It was almost a relief when he was called urgently up to Scotland to supervise the building of a new dam in the West Highlands.

Helen had been alone now for two days. She had enjoyed her tea party with Julia the day before, and she had enjoyed even more the evening meal she had cooked after Julia had left. For the first time since leaving Brazil she had felt replete and satisfied. She enjoyed too being alone in her own home, complete mistress of her environment. Of course Tom was a dear, but he could be nerve-wracking. For a moment she forgot where Tom was, almost expecting him to walk in at the front door. It was true what she had told Julia. She did get fits of loneliness when she was glad to see people, Julia particularly. But they soon passed. She laughed.

She was roused by the ringing of the telephone. An urgent voice demanded where Tom was. For a moment she was at a loss. 'Tom—Tom—?' Of course, her husband Tom. It seemed that Tom hadn't reported for duty. Where was he? If he'd been delayed, why hadn't he let them know? Everyone was ready to start. Carefully she replaced the receiver.

It made her nervous when people shouted at her. It wasn't fair. She felt her heart pounding uncomfortably. When she was nervous, it always made her hungry. Nothing for it, she'd better have something more to eat.

Carefully she took down her case of surgical instruments and went into the bedroom. There was the bed covered with the dust sheet, just as she'd left it. Stripping back the sheet, she revealed what was left of the body. Carefully, methodically, she made a further incision...

GUY FAWKES NIGHT

'PENNY FOR THE GUY, MISTER?'
The old gentleman at the bus stop thought, 'Really, they get earlier and earlier every year. They'll be starting up in the summer holidays next. Their parents really ought to—'

'Penny for the guy, Mister?'

He looked down at the grimy hand tugging his sleeve. 'Where is it?'

'Over there.' The thumb jerked over in the direction of a small wall which divided the pavement from the sodden lawn behind it. Sitting propped up against it was a glum apology for a guy.

'They're not like the guys *we* used to make,' he thought wistfully. 'We really took some trouble. Now it's just a six-penny mask from Woolworth's and a pair of Dad's old reach-me-downs. Why, if you pick them up they all fall to pieces!'

The guy certainly looked somewhat precariously strung together.

'Well, Mister?' The hand tugged more impatiently. 'What about it?'

'There's my bus! But the penny appeared nonetheless. He found it more or less impossible to refuse, so pressing was the request.

'Somebody,' he thought, as the crowd pushed and pulled past him, 'Somebody will *have* to do something about this wholesale begging...'

'Mind yer backs, please. Hurry along there!'

In the bus as he was jostled and jammed, the old gentleman thought sadly of his long lost youth. He had not been just an old gentleman in a bus then; an anonymous old gentleman hurrying home from an anonymous job to an equally anonymous semi-detached. No, he had been Jerry Williams of Tedham, of whom great things were predicted. Strange how he could remember things that had happened then with far greater clarity than what had happened only yesterday. Silly, childish, irrelevant things, most of them, too. But a scene or a person came creeping into his mind, and before he knew what was happening, had taken over completely.

'Fares, please. Have your correct money ready, please.'

Like that wonderful bonfire. He still remembered that bonfire in every detail. It glared at him from the recesses of his memory, with all the shining clarity of those leaping, dancing flames. They said that folks had come from miles around to see it, even the neighbouring gentry had come. Of course, a lot of the gentry were friends of the Thomases so it was natural that they should have had invitations.

Jerry had heard that there had been supper and dancing up at the Hall before the great fire was lit. So that the open-air festivities had only been a culmination of what had gone before. But to Jerry and the other villagers, the bonfire was everything. They had looked forward to it for what had seemed months. And when the great day came, they were not disappointed. There was no feeling of anti-climax as so often happens when one has looked forward to something too hard.

And the guy! Jerry still remembered the guy. It was, he felt sure now, a work of art. Life-size, it had seemed a fitting crown for the best bonfire he had ever seen. Again be reflected how poor these modern guys were. Like everything else in the modern world, there was no craftsmanship.

A voice was speaking into his ear.

'Have I your fare, sir?'

A woman a few seats ahead was getting up to leave. Eagerly he grabbed the seat, and for a time stared dismally out at the

November fog which was beginning slowly to envelop the City.
    'Every night at the same time,' he thought...

He wondered what had become of the Hall, in this National Trust
age. They were an odd family, the Thomases. His mother used to go
up to do sewing and various other odd jobs for Mrs. Thomas. That,
of course, was before the poor lady had her attack. The first time
he, Jerry, had ever been taken to the Hall was on one of his mother's visits, when he was too young to be left alone. He had been giv-
en an immense tea, and Mrs. Thomas had brought young David in
to play with him.
    He and David were almost the same age, but David had been far
shyer than Jerry, and had at first refused positively to play with
this strange boy. Both mothers had coaxed and cajoled, and
eventually David had been prevailed upon to show Jerry the new
train set he had been given for Christmas. Jerry had never even
seen a train set, let alone played with one, and he was vastly
impressed. His eager interest softened David's heart towards him,
and on subsequent visits the two boys had played happily for
hours while Mrs. Williams sewed and pinned and altered. Sometimes Mrs. Thomas would stay with them, but more often she was
off on one of her numerous visits to the village.
    This had been the beginning of an intermittent friendship
between the two boys. Occasionally David would come to tea at
Jerry's cottage, and then out would come the best cloth and teaset.
David's manners were perfect and as he grew older, he charmed
Mrs. Williams more and more; he was continually held up as an
example to the less inhibited Jerry. But it was this inhibition in
David that had been the cause of the gradual cooling of their
friendship. Not that they had ever fallen out—far from it. In fact,
they hardly ever quarreled. David invariably gave in to Jerry if there
was a disagreement; he seemed to lack the spirit for a really good
set-to.

No, it was just that David seemed to prefer his own company, or the company of animals, to that of other boys. When he did want other boys, it was usually to Jerry that he turned. But he was quite content to go off for long walks by himself, or perhaps with a dog. He had always been fond of dogs. Jerry remembered how his eyes shone when he first showed him his new puppy.

The bus came to a violent stop, jerking him out of his reverie. The driver swore at an Austin van which had swung out of a turning just in front. Various passengers grabbed the opportunity to get off. When eventually the bus did begin to move again, Jerry tried to collect his scattered thoughts.

Where was he? Oh yes, David and his dog. Jerry tried to remember that dog. It had gone everywhere with David, refusing to be parted from him for even a minute. And David had returned the affection. It was a little wire-haired terrier: Jerry couldn't remember whether it had been a stray, or whether David had been given it. In any event, it was very much a one-man dog. Jerry himself had tried periodically to make tentative advances to it, but it had run back to David at the first opportunity, much, he felt, to David's secret satisfaction. Sometimes when David thought himself unobserved he had kissed and fondled the dog in a demonstration of affection Jerry had never seen him show towards his parents.

In fact, Jerry thought that he had never got on particularly well with his parents. His father was a bluff genial typical county Squire, who had very little sympathy with his son's strange aloof ways. In fact, he seemed to be attracted more by Jerry himself, as indeed did Mrs. Thomas, who also found it difficult to meet her son on common ground. Perhaps because he and David were so different, Jerry and Mrs. Thomas became firm friends, and even after her mental collapse, Jerry was the only person in whose company she remained reasonably calm. When his father, who had worked on the estate, was killed on the Somme, she used to bring over enormous food parcels and in a hundred ways helped to tide them over a difficult time. Her husband had tried to dissuade her from bestowing too much bounty on the tenants, but in many ways he was known to be surprisingly hard.

It was also known that the Thomases disagreed on practically everything. It was said that their marriage had begun to go wrong even before David was born. There were no other surviving children, and for a long time before David had reached what is popularly but sometimes erroneously called the age of discretion, wild rumours had been circulating in the village concerning the Squire's roving affections. To most people who knew the Thomases these were considered not only wildly untrue but also grossly libellous; but nevertheless doubt remained. Indeed, it was true that nobody had actually seen the Squire out with any other woman: it was just the look in his eye perhaps that made wise women nod their heads and say they wouldn't put it past him, and fond mothers turn anxious looks towards their daughters. That, and a certain haggard look which was sometimes noticeable in Mrs. Thomas. Jerry, who of course was really too young to take any interest in such things, had heard his mother relate in muted tones to his father at the end of one of her days up at the Hall, that *things* had been said and done, and that all was not as it should be between them. But nevertheless it was true that any dirty linen was safely and securely washed in private. Only the haggard look remained as testimony.

Jerry had read enough whodunits to know that one of the basic rules of the game from the author's point of view was that a person should have knowledge of a certain vital piece of information concerning the crime without actually being aware that he knows it. And this certainly applied to himself. It was only after the Squire's sudden disappearance that the rumours crystallized into proven fact, and he remembered his mother's discreet utterances. He could not recollect that he'd ever heard any rumours till afterwards, when he suddenly became aware that actually he'd heard a great many. It was strange the way that after the police had searched and searched without finding any trace of the missing gentleman, it seemed the most natural thing in the world that he should have run away with one of his lady-loves. And he certainly covered his traces well: no hint of his whereabouts ever had been discovered.

Jerry tried to remember, after an interval of forty years, what Mr. Thomas had really been like. The only thing he *could* remember, at first, without consciously trying, was that he had never got on well with his son, David. But Jerry had always seen things from David's viewpoint, never from his father's. Now he realized how trying it must have been to have had a son so different from oneself, both in temperament and every kind of taste. Jerry had never had a son himself, but he could imagine how frustrated a father might feel. Perhaps in some obscure way he had blamed his wife, and that was why they had had scenes that had given rise to his wife's haggard looks.

Now other incidents began to return. He remembered the Squire's violent temper, and that when he lost it a little vein used to appear in his forehead and throb and throb. Like the time when poachers had been caught on the property. They had had a lot of trouble for some time, and certain village louts were suspected. One evening the gamekeeper had burst into his study in a state of intense excitement to say that they had been chased into a coppice and were surrounded. Squire had ordered them to be smoked out. David had later told Jerry how disgusted and degraded he had felt at the whole sordid spectacle. Torches had been lit and soon the whole copse was a circle of flame. Nothing happened. David had been present, but in the background, crying with fear and pain for the wretches inside. They had stuck it out till the last possible moment, and then three sorry-looking specimens, blackened and scorched, their clothes half off their bodies, and wriggling with pain, had emerged. One of them had later died in the cottage hospital, so David had said. His father had shrugged at this, imply-ing that he had brought it on himself, but David had remembered his smile of triumph on that memorable night.

Perhaps after that the idol had toppled, David took to avoiding his father's company altogether, and went off with his little dog for whole days at a time. Even Jerry was banned from the secret fraternity, though reading Huck Finn at the time he had begged to be allowed to accompany them. Mrs. Thomas was in an almost continual state of anxiety, and soon after this had arranged for the child to be sent away to boarding school. David had at first seemed pleased at the idea, but later had agreed to go only on condition that he could take his dog with him. Mrs. Thomas had appealed to her husband, who as might be expected, scoffed at the idea, and told the boy not to be such a damn sissy. He had all but implied, so David later said, that there was something almost unhealthy in the boy's preference for canine company.

Jerry remembered the climax to this situation. After the catching of the poachers Mr. Thomas had taken to putting down traps. Hideous lethal-looking things they were too, that could break a man's leg. Word got round the village, and no poacher was seen again in that region. But one day David had burst into Jerry's bedroom in a state of near hysteria. It seemed that Rusty had disappeared. He had hunted high and low but the dog was nowhere to be found, and David was brokenhearted. Jerry promised to come and help him search.

For hours the two boys whistled and called, until it was quite dark and the search had to be temporarily postponed. Early the next morning before Jerry was up, David was round at the cottage. There were dark lines under his eyes, which were red and swollen. Mrs. Williams was quite alarmed. His distress seemed to be quite disproportionate; when at the most Rusty had probably wandered off after a rabbit or something and would return when he was hungry. She tried to reassure the boy, who at length assented somewhat doubtfully, and agreed to eat breakfast with the family. She promised herself that at the first opportunity she would have a talk with Mrs. Thomas. How best, she wondered, to broach the subject, and suggest tactfully that the boy be given a nerve tonic...

But Rusty did not return. Some workers on the estate found him later that day and tried to keep the sight from David. Mrs. Williams' guess must have been right, and he must indeed have chased a rabbit. At any rate, he had been caught in one of the traps, and it was evident from the state of the body that the poor little animal bad been struggling for hours. His hind paw had been crushed completely. David saw the men returning with the forlorn little bundle wrapped in a sheet, and had somehow wormed the truth out of one of the party.

He didn't say much, Jerry remembered. In fact, he'd never said much about it. He just went deathly quiet, and his face was so white it reminded Jerry of one of the clowns in a travelling fair he'd seen the week before. For a week after that he was very ill and Jerry wasn't allowed to see him. When he was free of chores for his mother, Jerry would sometimes wander up to the house and hang about outside David's bedroom window, idly kicking the gravel and hoping for a glimpse of him. He saw a number of important looking men with top hats and preoccupied faces drive up in carriages, and learnt from the between-maid that they were medical men, and one, so it was said, an eminent Harley Street specialist. When he asked what was the matter with him, she said it was brain fever, and when he asked what that was, he was told not to ask so many questions and sent about his business. Once he collared Mrs. Thomas, slipping out on one of her errands of mercy to the village, but she only smiled sadly and distantly and said he would be all right in time. Even his own mother was scarcely more forthcoming.

When at last he did appear he seemed to have grown much older. Something warned Jerry not to mention Rusty, and Rusty was never mentioned between them. David was even reconciled to the idea of going away to school, and looked forward to it. After all, as he said, there was nothing to keep him at Tedham.

Jerry was anxious to hear all about his illness, and on this subject, surprisingly, he was less reticent. In fact he rather delighted in recounting the symptoms. Jerry told him that he had seen the doctors, and how important they'd looked, and David said that he'd decided to be a doctor when he grew up...

'Excuse me.'

A large businessman was nudging Jerry to move over as he wanted to sit dawn. Jerry's raincoat was overflowing on to his neighbour's part of the seat, and with a muttered apology, he gathered himself together. The businessman sat down and opened his evening paper.

...Yes, that must have been when David had first decided he wanted to become a doctor. And now he was one of the most eminent neurologists in the country, with his own rooms in Harley Street. For a moment Jerry felt himself the possessor of an intimate and coveted secret. Probably, and because David did not confide in his parents, he, Jerry, had been the first one to know what was in David's mind.

Shame, really, that he hadn't kept up with him. Though he doubted whether David Thomas would want to be bothered with a small fry like himself. He had had very little of what the world terms success, though he had to admit he had married quite a nice wife. He had had no children so, he reflected wistfully, his line would die out. Funny David had never married. Jerry had collected various news items through the years, and he knew that Sir David lived alone, with only a housekeeper to look after him. The last time he had seen him was at poor Mrs. Thomas's funeral. Then they had barely said two words to each other. It seemed that all they had ever had to unite them was gone, and they had nothing left in common. In fact, when David left for the large Public School in the North, they had gone their separate ways. That was soon after Mr. Thomas's disappearance, and his wife's mental collapse. In fact, the year of the Bonfire.

Funny how important the night of the bonfire had become in his mind. Everything had changed that night. It was almost like the end of an era. Jerry tried to remember the exact year. It must have been after the War, because his own father had been dead then—probably about 1919 or 1920.

If he closed his eyes he could still see it as vividly as the little boy he had once been. About ten then, he had been, and David going on for twelve. David was the taller, but still with that queer strained look which betrayed his recent illness. Although he had looked forward to the great day with as much eagerness as anyone.

Jerry had read many books since the Tedham days. He had branched out on strange uninhabited byways of literature. The occult interested him, and witchcraft. He even fancied himself in some way psychic. He often had uncomfortable hints of foreknowledge of events; rather like the common experience we have all had of thinking about someone for no apparent reason, and then suddenly seeing them. Except in his case it was heightened. Now something seemed to warn him to go no farther. If the affairs of the Thomas family had come into his mind, they had come there unbidden, and he would do best to let sleeping dogs lie.

But this was nonsense and he knew it. What possible harm could there be in thinking about a Guy Fawkes Night celebration of forty years ago? He pushed the warning voice away, and rejoined the young Jerry Williams of *circa* 1919.

But something sinister had crept into the proceedings. It must have been planted there by time itself, for he had found nothing then to frighten him. It had just been a glorious holocaust, throwing out its arms to brighten the whole countryside. But now, though...

The scene was assuming unfamiliar proportions. It reminded

him now of some ancient witches' Sabbat or Walpurgis Night dance: the naked bodies thrown into sharp relief by the leaping flames against a gigantic, primeval backcloth of forest or mountain. And then it wasn't the Sabbat anymore, but the burning of the witches themselves, found guilty and condemned by the solemn pronouncements of the Church; and their screams of agony were mixed with the shouting of the onlookers in one diabolic opera of death in which the orchestrated accompaniment was the crackling of the flames as they ate into the wood of the funeral pyre...

All this he saw in one brief second, and then it was gone, the screams of mortal agony were after all only the delighted squeals of ecstatic children, and of course this picture was not the Fire, *his* Fire, but some uninvited intruder from the world of nightmare.

With a conscious effort he tried to recapture his own experience, uncluttered by alien impressions.

Plans had first been laid for Guy Fawkes Night weeks before. Everyone in the village had co-operated by searching their attics and cellars for all the old furniture and lumber they could throw out. All the children had united together, ranging far and wide in their search for combustible material. Odd jobs were requested and carried out with inflammable articles as payment. Surrounding trees were practically denuded of their branches: vast stacks of twigs and dead leaves were swept into position. Even the adults agreed that they had never seen preparations for a bonfire on such a grand scale, and as the great day dawned, even the older population of Tedham and surrounding districts looked forward, with something like excitement to the evening. Anxious parents crossed their fingers that there would be no accidents, but the delighted faces of their offspring were sufficient compensation for any momentary misgiving.

Even Mr. Thomas entered into the spirit of the thing, allowing the party to be held in the grounds of the Hall. In those days fireworks did not constitute the menace they do now, and consequently the bonfire was everything. From the first David took the greatest interest in the preparations and volunteered to make the guy. It wasn't till afterwards when the events of the night were discussed over and over again, that someone remembered that the whole thing had originally been his suggestion.

Instantly his consuming interest became the fashioning of the guy, making it as lifelike as possible. His mother noted with satisfaction his gradual return to health, and as he never mentioned Rusty's death, she convinced herself at length that he had forgotten it. His reawakening energy was now concentrated almost entirely on the guy, and he was tireless in his efforts in constructing something as above the normal run of guys as he could make it.

Mrs. Thomas confided to Mrs. Williams that she suspected the dawning of latent artistic talent in David, though she was unsure how her husband would react, should he choose an artistic career. Well, he didn't. He became a doctor, and then a neurologist: but, Jerry reflected from his height of forty years, it was probably a certain basic knowledge of anatomy, gleaned in his first tentative steps down the road of medicine, that had enabled him to construct such an uncannily life-like figure. Perhaps he had scrounged an anatomical book from the local doctor's surgery.

When. Jerry had first seen the guy he had had a shock. He had almost fancied the thing alive and breathing. He looked at David with admiration. It was almost too good to put on the fire.

He had gone with the other village children up to the Hall to fetch it. David had placed it in the large wing chair in his fathers' study, in as lifelike an attitude as possible. Now they trundled the old wheelbarrow they had taken from the gardener's shed up to the French window, and David with four other boys lifted it through. He had fastened its head back to a wooden plank so that the head wouldn't loll forward and the straw fall out, as he explained. The height of the fire was so great that they needed a ladder to get the thing into position, but eventually it was done with the plank firmly wedged. David himself saw to that, and it was David who lit the fire, with due pomp and ceremony.

Immediately the night was transformed into a fairyland of splendour. The fog, which had been threatening, was held severely at bay. There were hot roast potatoes, and paper bags full of hot chestnuts for the children, and hot spiced and mulled wine for the grownups. Now came the next surprise of the evening. A pig had been roasted whole, and now delicious plates of steaming meat were handed out through the kitchen windows. Only Jerry was checked at the last minute from accepting any, by a slightly pungent odour which seemed to be hanging on the atmosphere, and which he connected in some vague indefinite way with the meat. He noticed, however, that David was eating with relish, so he guessed it was probably the smoke-laden fog.

He did accept the chestnuts, however, and was just eating one when he was tapped on the shoulder by Mrs. Thomas.

'Hello, Jerry,' she said, 'enjoying yourself?'

'Yes, thanks, Mrs. Thomas.'

He had been too young then to note the tone of forced casualness in her voice.

'Have you seen Mr. Thomas anywhere?'

'No, I haven't.'

'That's funny. He promised to join us in time to see the lighting of the fire. Now I can't find him anywhere,'

She wandered off. The world of adult affairs did not impinge very heavily on Jerry's consciousness, and he soon forgot the incident. He caught sight of David watching the blaze intently. David's face was ecstatic.

'Terrific, isn't it?' be called when he became aware of Jerry's eye upon him.

'I'll say! Did you make the guy all by yourself?'

'Yes, but it's a state secret how I made it Effective though, isn't it?'

They both watched the guy, now surrounded by a wall of flame. It seemed to Jerry to be dancing with joy as the branches on which it was supported shifted this way and that. As the flame finally touched its feet, delighted cries went up on all sides from the children who flew round and round shouting and singing. Leading the singing was David, eyes shining with excitement.

And then Jerry saw it. He saw it without for one moment taking in all the implications of what he saw. That funny huddled figure on the outside of the crowd, pressing in behind them as far up to the fire as the heat would allow, was Mrs. Thomas. Jerry never saw the expression on her face, except for one brief moment when the light from the flames threw her eyes into sharp relief, and then a shadow blotted it out She was gesticulating and pointing up at the guy, and then her arms were flailing about in a queer way. Then he lost sight of her completely, until he noticed that the people round her were clearing a hurried space. There was something on the ground, which looked like a heap of clothes: a party of servants had trooped out of the house and were coming towards them. They picked up the bundle, and then Jerry saw that it was Mrs. Thomas and that she had fainted. They carried her back to the house; some children nearby had begun to cry and were taken home. The older ones stayed, but the best of the night was over, and the fire burnt itself out. Jerry looked round for David, but he was nowhere to be seen. He guessed that he'd gone to his mother. Soon after that he too went home.

He never saw Mrs. Thomas again until he was twenty.

A few weeks later David went away to boarding school. Jerry saw him only a couple of times before he left, and each time he seemed ill at ease in Jerry's company. When Jerry asked after his mother he was reticent and evasive. Jerry gathered only that she had had to go away for a time. It was from Mrs. Williams that various snippets of information filtered through. It appeared that

Mr. Thomas's brother and his wife had come to the Hall, ostensibly to look after David, but also to help in the search for David's Father, They had been summoned by a frantic housekeeper, at the same time as the doctor was sent for, and had arrived in the small hours.

Much later Jerry heard all the details, pieced together from various sources. Mrs. Thomas had had a complete mental break-down, and it was doubted whether she would ever recover fully. David's father was missing—in fact, he hadn't been seen since the night of the party. A complete search was instigated, and only after every possibility had been explored thoroughly was it concluded that he had run off with, or to, someone he had kept successfully concealed in the background of his life. Mrs. Thomas was not capable of answering questions: she was kept under sedatives, and the doctors in whose care she was placed by her brother-in-law forbade her to be worried unduly whether by police or any other interested parties. It was assumed that the shock of her husband's defection had been too much for her, and that in all probability he had left her a note which in her distraction she must have screwed up and thrown into the bonfire.

The nine days' wonder in the village died down, as nine days' wonders do, and eventually the Hall was sold...

Jerry saw David only rarely after that. In the school holidays David was shunted about among numerous aunts, uncles, cousins, and grandmothers, and when he went up to Oxford Jerry supposed that his friendship with the Thomases belonged to a past chapter in his life.

It was not till ten years later that he was to learn anything further. He was working in an Insurance Office in the City, and living in furnished lodgings at the time, when, on arriving home one evening his landlady informed him that a gentleman had called to see him, and that she had shown him up to his room.

'David Thomas! Good heavens, after all this time! How on earth

125

did you know where to find me?'

'I went to see your mother at Tedham.'

David had just come down from medical school, he explained, and was looking up old friends before settling down to work.

'I've decided to specialize in neurology. You know, nerves and the mind. There's an opening on the staff of St Andrew's as a house surgeon, and I can study while I'm there.'

'I wish you luck.' Jerry poured a sherry. 'Tell me, about yourself.'

He was looking well, Jerry thought, except that he had never lost that strained look about the eyes.

He shrugged, 'Not much to tell. I read medicine, and got through the finals last week.'

"Congratulations.'

'Thanks. What are you doing for dinner?'

'Mrs. Richards usually cooks me a chop. Stay and have one with me.'

'No, you come out with me. You look as if you could eat a decent meal.'

Over their food Jerry steered the conversation towards David's father.

'Father? He's dead as far as I'm concerned,'

The vehemence in David's tone startled him.

'You've heard something then?' Jerry leaned forward eagerly.

David shook his head. 'No, nothing. And I've never bothered to inquire.'

'Haven't you? I'm sure I would have done in your place.'

'I loathe and detest the ground he walked on. He was a brute when he was here and I hope to God he's dead now.'

Jerry stared in amazement. David's face was a living mask of hate, and he noticed the little vein in his forehead, throbbing until it looked as if it would burst, a legacy from the man he hated.

Jerry felt as if he hazarded the next remark at the risk of his life.

'Surely you're being unreasonable. I know you and him didn't always see eye to eye, but—'

'Jerry, I know you don't mean to annoy me, but if you value my friendship you'll drop the topic.'

There was an awkward pause after Jerry's fumbled apology, and it was only over the mellowing effect of the brandy that David calmed down sufficiently to re-open the subject of his own free will.

'I'm sorry about that outburst. Actually, I do owe you an explanation—'

'No, of course you don't. It's your affair after all.'

'Well, I'll give you one anyway.'

'I must admit I am curious. What exactly *did* happen that night?'

'Which night?'

Jerry found himself becoming a trifle impatient at David's equanimity, which he felt sure was assumed.

'Why the night of the bonfire, of course. The night of your father's disappearance.'

David shrugged. 'I don't really know. As far as I remember, we had some people up for dinner, and my parents had arranged a small dance afterwards, Then the guests were all to go out on to the terrace to watch the fireworks and all the quaint village goings -on. Sorry, that was stupid.'

'Go on.'

'I sat next to father at dinner. He always got rather drowsy after a big meal, especially when he had to engage in a lot of small talk with people who bored him. He complained of feeling tired and announced that subject to the permission of rest of the party, he would go into his study for a short nap so as to feel fresh for the later festivities. Apparently the dance was to continue into the small hours. You may remember that rather enormous wing chair he had in his study?'

'Vaguely.'

'Well, he frequently fell asleep in it. He hated being disturbed, and there was a tacit understanding with Mother that whenever he announced that he wanted ten minutes' sleep she would wait until she was summoned at the end of it.'

His lip curled slightly, and Jerry fancied that there must have been scenes over the disobeying of this rule.

'He retired into his study, the dance began, and—that was it! He was never seen again, as they say in books.'

Jerry remembered Mrs. Thomas's inquiry.

'She asked me if I'd seen him, I remember.'

'Oh, when?'

'I think it was just after you'd lit the bonfire. It never dawned on me that there was anything seriously wrong.'

'No, of course not. Why should it?'

'Did they have to force the door of the study?'

'No, he never locked the door. Anyway, the study was quite accessible by the French window. He quite simply wasn't sitting in the wing chair.'

Something about the French window struck a chord in Jerry's memory. 'Were the servants questioned?'

'Oh, of course. Everyone was questioned.'

'Was foul play suspected?'

David laughed. 'Foul play! You've been reading too many whodunits.'

Jerry acknowledged that he enjoyed whodunits.

'Who would want to murder Father?'

'Had he no enemies?'

'All right, Sherlock Holmes! Not that I know of.'

Jerry remembered some incident involving poachers.

'Poachers? Oh yes, I remember.'

Not the smallest change of expression, Jerry noted. Nothing but that strained look, the constant factor.

'Didn't one of them die?'

'Yes, I believe so. First degree burns. No, it couldn't have been anything to do with that... Revenge you mean? He had a wife I believe, but I heard she died fairly soon afterwards. There were no children. Besides—'

'Still, it could have been someone else who remembered the incident.'

'Well the police were fairly satisfied on that score. As I say, all the servants were closely questioned, and no one remembered seeing any suspicious strangers hanging around. After father put down those bloody traps we never had anyone near the place. They were all too scared. Word got round, you know.'

Jerry thought it wiser not to pursue this aspect of the question. He didn't know whether Rusty's death would still affect him to any great degree, but he hadn't forgotten that this had been responsible for a nervous breakdown once, and he didn't want to take chances.

'Was any suitcase missing at all?' he asked instead.

'You mean did he take anything with him? No, just what he stood up in'

'That in itself was suspicious, surely?'

'Not if he intended to cut himself off completely. Make a fresh start. It's been done before, you know. And you must remember, they hadn't been happy together for some considerable time.'

'Yes I had heard.'

'No, he had some little piece set up and waiting for him. The villainous country squire. All he lacked was twirling moustaches and a title.'

He began to sing softly.

'Oh, Sir Jasper do not touch me—

'Anyway, let's forget it. Another brandy.'

David ordered two more, and Jerry leaned back contentedly. 'Marvellous meal, David.'

'Yes, this place was quite a find. Actually...'

'Yes?

'Well, I might as well be frank.'

For one ghastly moment Jerry thought he was going to be asked to pay the bill. The next, however, he was reassured.

'The fact is' David went on, 'it wasn't only disinterested friend-ship that made me come and see you tonight. The reason I let you go on about Father was because I thought it would form a natural lead-in to—to what I really wanted to see you about.'

He paused.

'Spit it out,' said Jerry, trying to keep his voice casual. But he half knew what was coming.

'It's about— about Mother. You must know what—what happened to her? It's that more than anything else I cannot forgive Father for. Though God knows—it was such a great shock. The police thought he must have left her a note saying he'd run off and—'

'I understand.' Jerry patted his arm. David's face was working.

'Well, you see she's no better. She lives in this place in Sussex, on the Downs it is. The doctors and nurses are very kind to her, but,' he shrugged, 'it seems her mind is gone.'

'Oh, David, I'm so sorry. Is it hopeless, quite hopeless?'

David nodded. His voice began to shake. 'But the most awful part, Jerry, is that she can't stand me.'

'Can't stand you?' Jerry repeated incredulously.

'Not at any price. Can't bear to have me in the same room with her. And I don't know why. Can you understand that? Now the doctors say it's better if I don't go to see her at all.'

'David, I don't know what to say.'

'There's nothing you can say. Oh God, it's so awful. The three of us, bound together in some silken bond of hate—'

He buried his face in his hands. The other diners began to look round uneasily. Jerry half rose. David's voice came from between his fingers.

'It's all right, sit down. I'll be all right in a minute. You see, that's what decided me to become a nerve specialist. Mother's illness I mean. But now it's all so hopeless, I feel I've done it all for nothing. There's no cure.'

'David, you don't know yet. Your work hasn't begun. You may find some new wonder drug.'

But David's interest in medicine had begun before that night, he thought.

'No. You see the doctors have just told me that Mother hasn't long to live. She's going to die, and she's going to die hating me.'

'Die hating you?' Jerry repeated the last words as if they held no meaning. All this was so foreign to anything in his own experience.

Now, thirty years later, he remembered this conversation in almost every detail. He saw the young man David had been then, sitting opposite him at that cosy table for two, surrounded by all the opulence of the twenties in that fashionable restaurant; hand-some, clever, rich, seemingly with all the world before him and yet with that cloud of darkness and grief pressing down on him. Yes, there had been tales of insanity in the Sadler family, tales to explain the plight of poor Mrs. Thomas, tales of hopelessness and terror and dark unnameable and blasphemous doings: handed down from villager to villager, there were skeletons that rattled as they do in most long-established county families, though these perhaps rattled rather more loudly than some. But never, until that moment in the restaurant, confronted as he was by that specimen of human misery before him, had these tales come home so forcibly to Jerry as now. For a mother to die hating her son was as intolerable as it was unnatural. In fact it was monstrous.

David was speaking again. 'Sorry if I've shocked you. I didn't mean to spoil your dinner. Look here, I'll get to the point. I want you to go and see her.'

'Go and see her?' Jerry repeated stupidly.

'Yes. See if you can talk to her. She always liked you. More than

131

me, in some ways I think. She'll be pleased to see you, I'm sure of it. She has rational spells you know. But the sight of me only distresses her. Find out if you can why she hates me so.'

'But—'

'Will you do it?'

Jerry gazed at David intently.

'Yes, of course I'll go and see her.'

It was arranged that on the following Saturday when Jerry was free from his office David would call for him at his "digs" and drive him in his new motor to the Nursing Home. During the interview be would wait outside, and then they would go somewhere to discuss it.

All David's anxious preparation did not prevent Jerry's shock when he first saw Mrs. Thomas. She was sitting on the bed at the far end of the severe room, huddled and emaciated, her hair grey and lank. Jerry remembered her former copper tresses, and a great surge of pity for this unfortunate creature welled up inside him.

He advanced tentatively into the centre of the room. 'Mrs. Thomas?' he murmured, then stopped, at a loss. She looked up without much interest.

'I'm Jerry—Jerry Williams. Do you remember me?'

She repeated the name to herself several times, and he was just about to explain further, when to his relief and joy he saw the dawning recognition in her eyes.

'Jerry Williams. Little Jerry! But it's big Jerry now, isn't it? Come closer and let me look at you. How old are you?'

'Nineteen.'

She nodded. 'Nineteen. And how is your dear mother? She used to do sewing for me, and help me with all my pretty dresses.'

It was Jerry's turn to nod. He felt tongue-tied, like a little boy again 'She's very well, thank you.'

'Give her my love, dear. Now be sure to do as I say.'

'I will indeed.'

'Little Jerry Williams.' She sighed. 'How nice of you to come and see me. But you were always a nice boy. Yes, you were. A kind, dear, thoughtful boy.' Jerry shifted uneasily. He had always hated being praised. It made him feel somehow a fraud.

Mrs. Thomas sighed again, then she shivered violently.

'Are you cold, Mrs. Thomas?'

'A little. Hand me that coat will you? That's better. Just someone passing over my grave, I expect. My—grave.' Her voice tailed off.

'Are you tired? Shall I go, Mrs. Thomas?'

'Nonsense, you've only just come. Sit down. There, that's right. Now talk to me. About yourself. Tell me all the news.'

Jerry began to talk to her, retailing little pieces of gossip which he thought would amuse her. He knew he wasn't a very good talker, but she seemed entertained. Several times, in passing as it were, he mentioned David, but a shadow crossed her face at the name, and a warning voice bade him beware.

This was the first of several visits. Each time David took him there, and each time he waited for him outside, but at the end of the fifth visit Jerry was no nearer to solving the mystery of the violent antagonism he sensed in her towards her son. They would play draughts together, and Mrs. Thomas's delight when she won gave new encouragement to her doctors. She began to look forward to Jerry's visits, and Jerry too in some strange way began to welcome them. He wrote to his mother, telling her of the latest development, but when she wrote back offering herself to come up, the doctors warned Jerry that Mrs. Thomas was not quite so amenable with other visitors.

It was after the fifth visit that David came round to beg Jerry to come at once as she was not expected to last the night. Although Jerry had known she was dying, latterly she had seemed so much better that this new shock struck him all the more forcibly.

When she saw him her words were so feeble that he had to bend right over her to catch them. David hovered at the door, but Jerry screened him from her sight.

Now or never, he thought. He whispered, so that only she could hear.

'Mrs. Thomas, your son—'

But he got no farther. She pushed him back violently away from her and sat up, saying in clear, ringing tones: 'I have no son.'

The doctor eased her gently back, frowning at Jerry and telling him on no account to excite her. David shrank back out of sight.

But it seemed she had asked for Jerry specifically, and now she gestured for him again. He bent forward. 'Jerry,' she whispered.

'I'm here, Mrs. Thomas.'

'Jerry, the smell, the smell—'

This bemused him completely.

'What smell? What smell, Mrs. Thomas? Is it stuffy in here? Shall I open a window?'

He saw that she was trying to shake her head, and there was a look of impatience in her eyes.

'The p-pills. The sleeping pills. He took the sleeping pills—'

But the effort was too much for her. Jerry was guided gently but firmly from the room.

Half an hour later he heard that she was dead.

'What did she mean about sleeping pills? Have you any idea?'

Jerry was talking to David in the matron's office where they had been taken after they had heard it was all over.

David shook his head. 'Not the remotest. Did you ask the doctor?'

But the doctor hadn't known either. It seemed that she had mentioned sleeping pills before, but as she had never had access to any, no one had taken her ramblings very seriously. David now remembered that in the old days at Tedham after a quarrel with his

134

father she had sometimes had to take one to compose herself, but when her illness had necessitated her removal from the Hall, the box had been thrown away. No, he didn't know what they were; only that they were quite strong.

However, the thought of sleeping pills had led invariably to one of her periodic outbursts of violence, during which she had shouted various unconnected words and phrases, often coupling her son's name to that of her husband. When one of the doctors had suggested that they try to trace the missing husband, she had given way to peals of hysterical laughter, often losing all control so that they had had to subdue her by force. After that it was considered unwise to mention the husband in her presence at all.

Had she ever mentioned this mysterious smell before? The doctor was not sure, but had thought that she had.

Jerry wished now, not for the first time, that psychiatry had been as advanced and as widely practised in 1929 as it was in 1959.

He had remained with David for the rest of that night, and spent as much time as he could with him until after the funeral. But David had told him then that he would be taking up his new post at St Andrew's in a few days, and as Jerry himself was more than half concerned in a certain affair of the heart, they had again drifted apart.

That was the last Jerry saw of David Thomas. At first they had written desultory letters, but as they had always moved in different worlds they continued to do so now. David went up and up the ladder of medical eminence while Jerry more or less remained stationary in his own field. He was bothered too by a slight conscience as far as David was concerned. David had come to him in distress asking him to perform a desperately important service. The fact remained that he had failed. Had he tried hard enough? Although David never reproached him, he wondered whether David felt he had let him down.

He still kept himself informed of David's affairs through the

medium of the Press, however. He was thin skinned enough to imagine that in the rarefied atmosphere that David now breathed his
continued friendship would seem an encumbrance to him. So that
was that. He must remain at a distance, but—

He now realized just how many questions remained
unanswered. How different life was from books where every "i"
was dotted, and every "t" so very tidily crossed. Now he would
never know the truth: not one truth alone but many. He
determined, though, to take every fact he knew and, see where, if
anywhere, it led. He remembered the golden rule of every
whodunit worth the name, and determined to see whether he was
the possessor of any such vital piece of information.

Right, here goes:

Mrs. Thomas's last words, for instance. Had they any
significance? The sleeping pills. Had sleeping pills figured at any
time in the story? Could she have meant her husband, when she
referred to the mysterious "he" who took the sleeping pills? An
overdose of sleeping pills perhaps? But if so, they would have found
the body. And in the middle of a party? Impossible. But if not her
husband, who had taken sleeping pills, and why?

He remembered how very rational she had seemed during those
last visits, and found it very hard to believe that the words she had
uttered had been the mere ramblings of a madwoman.

And the smell. What did she mean by that? If anything. There
was some kind of association in his mind with a disagreeable
unexplained odour, but for the life of him he couldn't remember
what it was.

'Hyde Park Corner!' He came to himself with a start. Good Lord,
he was nearly home. He noticed that the businessman next to him
had gone, leaving his evening paper on the seat. He picked it up
absently.

Again he was unpleasantly conscious of that warning voice.
What did it say? Leave well alone, it was saying, don't trespass.

Some things it is better not to know. Yes, but what?

That smell now. Yes, of course, he'd got it. The night of the bonfire. He'd noticed a vague smell in the air that he'd connected with the November fog. Or had he? No, he'd connected it with the meat. But why *had* he connected that smell with the meat? It was perfectly ordinary Pork, wasn't it?

The French window. Odd, that he should think of the French window. What French window? Of the study, of course!

Stop, said the voice. Stop!

He had gone through the French window to fetch the guy. It had been in the study. The wing chair. David's father had been sitting in the wing chair.

You fool, said the voice, proceed at your peril!

David had hated his father. Poor Mrs. Thomas, insanity in the family. Rusty's death. Traps. Guy Fawkes, The burning of the poachers. *David's father had been sitting in the wing chair!*

Impressions poured one after the other into Jerry's mind, and now he realized he was powerless to stop them, He had ignored the warning, and now he had to follow, wherever it should lead. It had taken forty years, but now he had to remember.

And David's father had been sitting in the wing chair!

This phrase repeated itself over and over again like a refrain.

And now he had gripped the rail of the seat in front of him, and was pressing and pressing so hard that his knuckles showed white; because he knew what that smell was.

'Are you all right, dear?'

The conductress was standing over him anxiously.

'You've gone a very funny colour.'

Jerry felt as if he answered through thick layers of cotton wool.

'Y-es. I'm all right, thank you.'

'Bit travel sick, are you?'

'Yes, a bit—travel sick.' Oh, go away, go away! I don't want to think about this, but I must, I must.

No trace. The fire would have consumed everything. Who would have noticed a piece of charred and blackened bone among the litter of paper bags and nutshells and rubbish when the bonfire had burnt itself out? And if they had, hadn't roast pork been served that evening?

And Mrs. Thomas must have seen it—in the fire, twisting and turning. Screams drowned by the noise of the flames and the cries of the children and the grotesque mask of the guy. But Mrs. Thomas had known. And she had known who had done it. And knowing it, her mind couldn't bear the monstrous burden of this knowledge.

A vision was forming itself into Jerry's consciousness. A vision at first cloudy and indistinct as if seen through water, but forcing upwards through the water with the insistence of compulsion. A little boy making a. guy; a little boy with that strained look about the eyes, making the guy as lifelike as possible, showing it to his mother, and getting an old suit of clothes for it. And then a mask for the guy, a grotesque, staring mask.

And then the picture dissolved like a cinema film. But the little boy reappeared. He was opening a cupboard and taking out a little white bottle. He was taking four little pills out of the bottle, and putting them in his pocket.

Then he was sitting at the dinner table, and there was a large party and music and laughter. He was sitting next to a man who had disappeared forty years ago, and when the man was talking to someone on his other side the little boy had his hand poised over the wine-glass.

Jerry tried to force his mind away from what he knew was coming next, but the picture demanded his attention. For a second everything was dark, vague and indeterminate, then he saw a corridor. A small figure stood outside the door, listened for a minute, then opened it slowly and soundlessly. Another figure lay sleeping in a wing chair, in a room surrounded by book-lined shelves, a room Jerry recognized only too well. The small figure carried a jacket and trousers over his arm, patched and ragged and bulging with what Jerry knew was straw. In his hand was something else, and when he put the suit down, Jerry saw that it was the mask of the guy.

'No.' Jerry felt that he was shouting, but no word came from his lips. 'It is impossible. It is monstrous.'

But he knew that it was true.

He saw another picture now, and perhaps to Jerry this was the most terrible picture of all, because he recognized himself. A group of children stood outside the French window, with a wheelbarrow, and the same little boy handed out to them a guy. The head of the guy was fastened to a plank, arid he saw now that the hands were tied...

I will not see any more. I will not. It is a nightmare. I am ill. I must get off the bus. Who will believe me? I *didn't* know this all the time. Why now? Why now?'

Many thoughts bombarded Jerry's mind in the split second before his eye focused on the crumpled newspaper he found himself clutching. But then he saw it. On the front page:

DEATH OF FAMOUS NEUROLOGIST

Sir David Thomas, the well-known nerve specialist, was found dead in his fiat in Harley Street early this morning. When his housekeeper failed to get any answer to her repeated knockings she became alarmed and called for assistance to force the door. Sir David had apparently died from a heart attack brought on by overwork, according to the diagnosis of his consultant physician.

When questioned by our reporter, Doctor Fielding confirmed that Sir David had lately been suffering from severe nervous debility, and that he had advised him to go away for a long rest. He was 52. Sir David lived over his consulting rooms, and was unmarried. He was looked after by a housekeeper.

Note: One slightly odd aspect of the affair was that near the body police found traces of some burnt substance including what was later identified as human bone. Sir David's housekeeper denied that he had been in the habit of burning anything in. his room, but the police are of the opinion that she was mistaken. They are satisfied with cause of death as given by Doctor Fielding.

Jerry had only the faintest recollection of getting off the bus, superintended anxiously by the conductress, who advised him to take a strong, dose of salts and go straight to bed, She confided to one of the other passengers, as the bus drew off, that she didn't like his colour one bit. Greenish, it was.

But Jerry knew none of this. One question and one question only, still occupied his mind. He felt he would positively never rest until he knew the answer.

What on earth had David done with the original guy?

THE TIME OF WAITING

THE WOMAN WAS MY WIFE; and she was having a baby. This much I remembered, as I sat in the cheerless waiting room. Up till the time I had entered the hospital everything had been normally clear, normally pat. And now suddenly it was as if I were no longer sure of my own identity. I began to feel giddy. I clutched at the sides of the chair to prevent myself from falling. The walls of the room seemed to shake and shimmer and begin to dissolve; through them I saw a frightening abyss. The chaos beyond the order. Frantically I grabbed at a magazine and tried to concentrate on it. The usual parade of trivia, I thought, the art of the ephemeral. If I could occupy my mind with that, I told myself, if I could push out these insane fancies which had come so suddenly, so much without warning, I should be safe. I made a conscious effort to confine the boundaries of my mind, but it was useless. I could feel the thing getting out of control, I could feel my own identity *slipping* away, and I knew that if I did not do something positive, make some active attempt at self-assertion, in five minutes I should be mad.

I got up to ring the bell. Physical movement seemed to help. I felt a sense of returning. The waiting-room resumed its normal aspect. But, chillingly, I knew it was only temporary. If no-one came, if I continued to be left alone, I knew—I felt instinctively— that the attack, or whatever it was, would return, but this time with doubled strength.

The nurse, the same nurse I had seen before, appeared. Our eyes met, and we looked at each other for a moment in silence, before she spoke. I knew she must be thinking what a nuisance I was.

'Did you ring the bell?' she said at last, 'is anything wrong?'

My voice came out thick and woolly. My throat was absurdly dry.

'I—I'm sorry to trouble you, but—'

'It's no trouble—'

'—could I possibly have a cup of tea?'

'Certainly,' she laughed. 'We're used to nervous fathers.'

'My—my wife. How is she?'

'As well as can be expected. It'll take some time yet of course. Why don't you go home, and we'll ring you when the baby's here.'

She was trying to put me at my ease, to be aggressively but professionally encouraging, and it wasn't her fault that if I went home now I would be lost.

'No!' I couldn't keep the sharpness, the fear, out of my voice. 'I—I'm sorry,' I shouted. 'I'm a little on edge. But I'd really rather stay.'

She smiled. 'Very well. I'll get the tea.'

'Stay and drink it with me.' I needed company. If she were there, if we could talk, I might be able to keep this thing, whatever it was, from happening again.

'I shouldn't really,' she said, 'I'm on duty. But—we'll see.'

I was alone again. I sat down in the high-backed chair and tried to focus my attention again on the magazine: Royal Ascot. And then, the fear began to creep back...

I'm not really a fanciful man. My natural inclination has always been to steer clear of any thoughts which weren't concerned with my immediate environment, and I fought desperately shy of any idea remotely bordering on the abstract. My critics I suppose would call it a lack of imagination. This was partly because I didn't believe in any world other than the concrete physical one. I wasn't an atheist so much as an agnostic. God was the unknown factor, the number one cause which had produced the effect which was the physical universe, but obviously subject to very definite physical laws even if we hadn't learnt them yet, and any discussion or argument or system of philosophy which advocated the existence of a spiritual universe, of whatever kind, was misguided and pointless. This, for me, made life very simple, and according to those tenets I had lived it.

I was twenty-two when I married Betty. I had thought myself seriously and indisputably in love, without of course being able to analyze what love was. I suppose, if asked, which I never was, I would have said it was a sexual urge, in the same way that animals have sexual urges, except that we are rather more sophisticated and choosy about the objects we pick for its gratification. Betty and I, then, being modern, wasted no time on sweet nothings. We lived together for three weeks before we agreed to become engaged, and finding that we suited each other in bed as well as out of it, fixed a date. I was a reporter on the local paper and she was the Editor's secretary, and we both agreed that she should continue working after we were married, at least for the first year or two. The night before the wedding the office gave us a party, and I don't remember the end of it. I'd always read that journalists drink to excess; but this must be in Fleet Street. On local papers they can't afford to. So none of us was really prepared for the vast quantities of Scotch which Jennings produced from under the "Out" tray like a rabbit from a hat. He was a good boss to work for, and this was a kind gesture I never forgot. The next day Betty and I both had slight hangovers, but I want to stress that at no time did I have any regrets, or second thoughts about going through with it. Now eighteen months had gone by, and we both wanted the baby. My main feeling, as I rushed Betty at breakneck speed down the busy High Street in the middle of the rush hour, was one of elation and excitement that the great day had finally arrived. I still wanted the baby when Betty had been received at the hospital desk and safely packed off to Maternity. When the little nurse at the desk asked me to wait in the hospital waiting-room, I had wanted to stay because I still wanted the baby. But when I got into the waiting room and sat down with the magazine, I didn't want the baby.

It was the last rational thought I had experienced before my irrational attack had first started. If you can call it rational. Suddenly the mere thought of that poor innocent life so soon to begin filled me with horror, with such nausea that I wanted to vomit on the floor as I sat.

The magazine with the vacuous Royal Ascot faces lay discarded on the floor. Again the fear advanced towards me. 'I won't let it—I won't let it,' I said aloud, as I gripped the arm of the chair. I knew the whole scene in front of me and around me was about to dissolve like a cinema film, and I fought desperately to try and stop it. I seemed about to float out of my body, almost as if were I to look back I would see myself still sitting in the chair. You must remember that I had always fought shy of anything to do with spiritualism or astral levitation or anything of that sort; the whole thing I regarded as a waste of time. I had never even read a book about them. So I had no yardstick by which to judge this experience. I only knew that I had to fight as hard as I could, weak and unprepared as I was, to retain not only my sanity but my very identity, And that if this could happen to me now it could happen to me at any time in the future; that a fit like this would go on happening, if I didn't do something about it. And like so many uninformed people I had an unreasoning horror of insanity.

All this I thought—I was still able to think comparatively clearly—while at the same time my identity was slipping away from me. It was a conscious, definite process. I felt, as I hovered somewhere between my body and infinity, that the very self I had fought so hard to maintain and develop over most of the last twenty-four years, was being pitifully and fatally assailed. I was no longer sure who the woman having the baby was, only that she bore some close emotional kinship with myself. A moment more, and this, too, seemed an illusion.

I wonder if you can imagine the utter desolation—the appalling hopelessness of feeling—of *knowing* that you yourself are no longer real. My very individuality was ebbing away, was being attracted and absorbed into something infinitely greater, was being sucked—that was the word my disembodied reporter's mind chose as being most apt—into annihilation. Yet I could still soundlessly yell out: "Oh, God, come quickly. Come and save me before it's too late!" For I knew that somewhere, aeons away, a nurse was preparing tea for an entity called John Daniels.

For I was no longer in the hospital waiting-room. I was in— nothingness. I was drowning, and as time stood still for me my whole life passed swiftly, almost subliminally before my eyes. And it added up to nothing. I would be remembered for nothing, I had accomplished nothing—this I saw more clearly than I'd seen anything in my whole life, and like a blinding light it blotted out everything, so that the last remembrance of Betty and who she was, left me. And perhaps the worst thing of all was that I no long-er minded.

I welcomed the annihilation of myself, and as I made this conscious but involuntary decision to fight no longer, the mists of obscurity round me cleared, and I found myself in a definite place again.

For a moment I could take in no more information than that. I was too thankful to be out of that mind-stopping chaos, and while I had lost knowledge of my own identity, I knew that I was in some physical place bounded by finite laws.

My sense of time was gone, so that I had no remote idea how long my period of recovery lasted: that is, before I could begin to take any notice at all of *where* I was, even though *who* I was no long-er concerned me. But miraculously I was able ultimately to investi-gate; and, like a dream, when the information and realization fil-tered through to my shattered senses it seemed the only logical, the only appropriate place to be.

I seemed to be in some vast arena, and it was right and fitting that I should be here. This much I knew for a certainty. The entity I now was seemed, just lately, to have passed through some very tense emotional conflict; I felt the aftermath of this, but I knew that the decision I had finally arrived at had been the only possible one I *could* have made. That I was happy I did not doubt for a moment, although the situation I was now in was desperate and would prove inevitably fatal. But I had accepted this and now felt no fear. All this was fed to me as if my mind had been programmed like a computer.

Then I became aware that my hands were tied behind my back. I was practically naked—I felt this rather than saw it, because my head too was tied back. I could feel the rope cutting into my neck, and then I became aware of the heat. I realized that I was in the direct line of the sun, and that it was beating down upon me pitilessly. One by one my senses were returning, were starting again to perform their normal functions. What they revealed wasn't pleasant. I heard an immense roaring, as from a vast crowd. And then another kind of roaring, and there was a pungent smell of human and animal sweat mixed.

I tried desperately to move my head. I could feel that the rope had been contracting for some time, and I knew that my throat was bleeding as the strands pressed into it. There was a voice somehow above the roaring. How could I hear it when it was only whispering? But I knew beyond a shadow of doubt that this voice was indisputably the most important thing, the *only* important thing about this whole scene.

'I can't hear what you're saying,' I shouted aloud. 'Please, oh please, speak louder.'

I knew that it meant so desperately much to hear what it was saying. On my left, out of the corner of my eye I could see a glint as of copper in the sun. It was the hair of a girl, and it was the girl who was speaking to me. She too was tied, and soon she too would die.

'My darling,' she was saying, 'oh my heart, my only love.'

Tears blinded my eyes. Pain, so searingly intense that for a moment it blotted out the whole scene, overwhelmed me. I knew that this pain had nothing to do with the ropes around my neck and my hands, or the savage beasts that would presently tear me to pieces. For deep within the pain, and irrevocably intermixed, was a fierce and white-hot pleasure. Her words bore into my brain, so that I felt rather than heard them now.

'Soon we'll be together. For always and for always. And when that happens nothing, ever, will separate us.'

Again the scene dissolved. Again the mindless, hideous chaos annihilating self. But this time the voice seemed to be carried over. The voice that now I would never forget. Her first words seemed to drift with me, through ageless lands and numberless centuries, back to that shabby little hospital waiting-room where I was to find myself—how many millions of aeons later. "I will wait for you, even if it takes all eternity" —

The little nurse was standing over me. 'Wake up, Mr. Daniels,' she was chirping brightly. 'You were dead to the world! And your wife's just had a bouncing baby boy. Congratulations! And here's your tea.'

I stared at her uncomprehending. Even when the sense of what she was saying had forced itself into my consciousness, and I knew that I was happy and thrilled at the news, the full significance of something else that had happened was still lost.

'Now you must be very quiet,' she whispered to me, hands on lips as if she were addressing a naughty child, as we tiptoed down the passage.

And it was not until she whispered that I was sure why her voice was familiar.

THE SICK ROOM

'THIS IS THE ONE,' Mrs. Hayter said proudly as she stood aside to let the young couple pass through. She judged the girl to be about sixteen, the boy not more than eighteen.

'It's very nice,' the boy said timidly. Mrs. Hayter noted his nervousness. Terrified of making a mistake he is, she said to herself. Obviously his first time at the game. Still, money was money and you couldn't be too fussy these days. Not with a husband unable to work, you couldn't.

'Yes, it is nice, isn't it? All newly decorated too. Matter of fact we only just moved in ourselves. Spent a fortune on this place we did. Hope you'll be comfy.'

'I'm sure we will.' The girl spoke for the first time. She smiled at Mrs. Hayter, as if anxious to make her an ally. Mrs. Hayter remained aloof but amused. 'Twenty-five shillings, bed and breakfast, and dinner at seven if you want it. That's extra, of course.'

'Thanks, we'll have dinner.'

Mrs. Hayter smiled, knowingly, and went out.

'Might as well be hung for a sheep as a lamb,' the boy said, trying not to sound gauche, but suddenly feeling very young.

'Would you like to unpack first, or shall we go for a walk?'

The girl shrugged. 'Don't mind.' She sat down abruptly on the bed. The boy came over quickly.

'What's the matter? Anything wrong?'

'My legs started to shake a bit. I'll be all right in a minute.'

'Can I get you something?'

She shook her head. 'No, I told you I'll be all right in a minute.'

The boy sat down beside her and took her hand. 'You haven't

got cold feet, have you? I mean—'

'Course not, silly,' the girl answered scornfully. 'Wouldn't be here if I had, would I?'

'Yes, but if your Mum knew—'

'If my Mum knew she'd tan the living daylights out of you.'

'Out of me? What about you?'

'I'd tell her I was young and innocent, that I'd been swept off my feet by all your promises, and that—'

'Would she believe you, then?'

The girl laughed, throwing back her head so that her copper hair caught the last rays of the sun from the open window. 'No, but it would've been a good try!'

The boy put his arm round her waist. 'Gosh, you're beautiful, you know that?'

'Oh, don't be soppy.'

'No, I mean it. You are, you really are.'

He bent forward to kiss her, but she evaded him.

'Let's go for a walk before it gets dark. Then we'll have dinner.'

'How you can think of your stomach at a time like this!' The boy laughed, though he was disappointed. She was a good catch, he decided. It was obviously her first time, but it was his too, and he was anxious not to make a fool of himself. He looked at her for a moment as she stood by the door waiting for him.

'Come on, slow-coach!'

'All right, all right. We've got the whole weekend.' He straightened his tie in the mirror, purposely keeping her waiting. After all, he must show her he was boss at all times. Begin as you mean to go on.

Mrs. Hayter saw them go out. She stood in the front room behind the curtain, watching them. The boy was less intimidated, now that he was out of the house. Young for his age, she decided. Probably never had a girl before in his life. Well, let him find out the hard way. Once he'd been to bed—that was it. An over-rated pastime. She watched them cross the road. The boy was going to buy cigarettes. The girl waited for him outside the shop, tapping her stiletto heel on the kerb. Flighty bit of goods, though probably still a virgin. She saw the boy come out, stop to light a cigarette, then take the girl's arm.

They were going to the sea front. How long ago it seemed since she, Elsie Hayter, had been for a walk on the arm of a beau. She wondered if they still talked the same rubbish nowadays that she and Albert had talked all those years ago. Before she had grown up and learnt what a let-down life really was. Behind her in the armchair Albert had begun to snore. With a sigh she left her place at the window, and went to the kitchen to prepare supper.

'Doesn't the sea look lovely with the sun on it like that?' Mary Carter said delightedly.

They were down on the beach, and Johnny was throwing pebbles. 'Oh, Johnny, I do think you were clever to find this place.'

Johnny shrugged. 'Trust yours truly,' he said. 'Let's sit down for a bit. It's sandy just here.'

'We mustn't be late for dinner.'

'Oh, blow dinner! I want to kiss you. I haven't kissed you for at least an hour.'

There was no doubt about it, Mary decided, Johnny's kisses excited her far more than she had thought possible.

He whispered, 'Let's go back.'

'It's nearly supper time.'

'I know, but let's go upstairs first.'

Was love all impatience, Mary wondered. Impatience to be over with something which should be savoured at leisure, like old wine?

On their way back Johnny said, 'Suppose your Mum checks up that you haven't gone to your aunt's. Had you thought of that?'

'She won't. She trusts me.'

'Suppose you do the same thing to me when we're married. Can

I trust you?'

'Don't be stupid.' Mary squeezed his arm.

As they went up to their room they could hear Mrs. Hayter bustling about in the kitchen.

'I think we're the only guests,' Mary said on the stairs.

'It's early in the season. What is it?'

They had reached the door of their room. Mary hung back. Johnny turned round. 'Come on. What are you waiting for?'

'I—don't know. You go in first.'

He opened the door. She fancied the room was waiting for them. It was really rather a hideous room, freshly done up as Mrs. Hayter had said, in Mrs. Hayter's execrable taste. The Victorian flowered wallpaper particularly made her blanch. She couldn't imagine why she hadn't noticed its ugliness before, when they had first been shown it. Perhaps because she had been too nervous.

She looked again at the cheap ring Johnny had given her to wear for appearance sake. Had Mrs. Hayter been fooled? True, Mrs. Hayter had asked no questions, but perhaps she was the sort of woman who'd go with the room.

'Johnny, I—don't think I could sleep in this room. See if you can get her to change it.'

'Oh come on! There's nothing wrong with the room. If we made ourselves a nuisance she might start being funny—you know what I mean?'

'Johnny, I don't like the room.'

'You'll feel better after a bit of food. Come over here.'

He was on the bed. Half unwilling she went over. He pulled her down beside him. The springs creaked protestingly.

'A whole weekend,' he was saying, 'a whole weekend with you. A whole weekend with you. A whole weekend away from that ruddy garage.' He began exploring her body, exploring its curves. His fingers were soft and delicate, more a boy's than a man's.

'Do you love me, Johnny?'

'Course I do. We're going to get married, aren't we?'

'Yes, but—'

'Don't talk.'

She put her arms round him. It was the first time she'd ever properly held a boy in her arms, and the sensation made her tingle. Was it the nearness of his body, or was it something else that made her shiver?

The gong sounded for dinner. Ashamed, they drew away. Johnny grinned. 'Saved by the bell.'

'We haven't even unpacked yet. We really ought to change. It's expected.'

'What, in a dump like this? They'll be lucky!'

Over dinner Mary saw that she was right. They were the only guests. Mrs. Hayter saw to them personally. Her constant scrutiny made Mary nervous. She realized that quite literally she did not dare to ask for another room. Several times she caught Johnny's eye while they were being served, and they winked at each other. They were both uneasy and embarrassed. They couldn't talk much, because she was always in the room. If she wasn't attending to them she was polishing one of the other tables, picking up articles and dusting them. Several times she moved things to new positions, then she came back and returned them to where they were before. She's spying on us, Mary thought. She began to long for Johnny's arms, they were strong, they were safe, they could protect her from Mrs. Hayter. Suddenly, she realized Mrs. Hayter was speaking.

'Pardon?'

'I said, would you like some cheese?'

'No, thank you.'

'Only coffee thanks,' Johnny cut in.

Silly young fools, Mrs. Hayter was thinking. The great adventure. So what? She wondered what the boy would be like as a lover. Fumbling and inexperienced, of course. Not that Albert was much cop.

'Have you finished?' Mary whispered across to Johnny. He nodded, kicked back his chair so that it scraped on the linoleum floor. 'I'm ready.'

'Let's unpack. Then we can go out again.'

Johnny nodded. 'Anything you say.'

She was determined to face the room, to challenge and conquer her dislike of it, before they actually had to go to bed in it. After all, it's really because I'm het up, she thought, and anyway it's only for two more nights.

She unpacked slowly, carefully averting her eyes from the wall-paper. The bed was one of those fearfully solid Victorian brass bedsteads. She could see it out of the corner of her eye, drawing the rest of the room round it, taunting her. Her nightdress lay exposed. Johnny was sitting in the armchair. He too was watching her. He too seemed part of the room, part of something which she was beginning to feel in some undefined way hostile to her. In her ears she heard a distant pounding. Was it her heart, or her blood racing, or what? Was she really as nervous as that?

'That's nice,' Johnny said, looking at the night-dress. He loved her, didn't he, he was her protector, she was safe with him. Then what on earth was she getting so steamed up about?

'Hurry up. When you're finished we'll go and have a drink before we—turn in.'

Johnny was thinking, she's the first one I've ever truly wanted to sleep with. I mustn't muff this. I mustn't let her see I'm inexperienced. I must keep this bird, even if I have to marry her. He couldn't see what she had against the room, it wasn't *that* bad. Besides, what did it matter in the dark?

He leaned back in the armchair. Yes, it was really rather a nice room, in a period sort of way. He'd seen pictures of the house where his mother had been born. That was a bit like this. Odd that anyone would want to decorate a modern room like it, but as he always said, there was no accounting for tastes. He looked at her nightdress lying neatly across the bed where she'd left it. It was a frilly sort of thing, transparent, hardly worth wearing at all. Wait till he told his mates he'd made this bird. When he'd first met her at the dance, what was it, two weeks ago, he'd thought her stuck-up. Pretty, but stuck-up. Well, she wasn't stuck-up now, although she was nervous.

The room watched them both, the boy and the girl, and the room waited.

It was over his second beer that Johnny suddenly went quiet.

'Is anything wrong? D'you want to go?' Mary asked.

'It's hot in here. Let's get some air.'

They left the crowded pub, and wandered down to the sea-front. The lights were out along the promenade. Far out to sea they could see a liner. They leant over the rail that separated the promenade from the beach, and Mary felt for Johnny's hand. She found it clenched tight.

'What is it, Johnny? Why are you so tense?'

'Nothing. Don't be silly.'

'Are you sorry?'

'Sorry? What for?'

'For bringing me. We can go back to London if you like.'

Johnny turned round, forcing a smile. She could see that his face was white against tile light from the fairy lamps.

'Course I'm not sorry. What d'you take me for?'

'Oh Johnny, you sound it. You sound sorry. And it could all have been so lovely.' She found to her shame that she was going to cry.

She started back towards Mrs. Hayter's. Something had gone wrong. You can't force an idyll.

'Hi, wait. Wait.' Johnny caught her up, pulled her round to kiss her.

'Course I'm not sorry. I told you. I don't know what's got into you. First the room, now these tantrums. Come on, snap out of it.'

Arm in arm they returned to the room. But Mary saw that his face was still white.

It must have been about three o'clock. She couldn't sleep. She'd heard the clock downstairs strike a short time before. It was a big grandfather clock that stood in the hall. She thought it had struck three though she hadn't consciously counted the chimes. Her wrist watch was on the bedside table. Gingerly, so as not to wake Johnny, she leant sideways to examine it. Yes, it was a few minutes after three.

She felt Johnny beside her. He hardly moved in his sleep. I needn't worry, she thought, nothing will disturb him.

It had all gone wrong. She felt very old, very experienced, very miserable. She had really loved Johnny, she thought he loved her. What had happened to spoil it? Oh God, she thought, almost starting to cry again. It had all been so wonderful, all the prepara- tion, all the anticipation, all the fixing, the squaring, the arranging. Both sets of parents thought they were somewhere else, their suspicions safely lulled. Johnny had even bought her that ridiculous ring. Had he bought it, or had he got it out of a cracker? In any event, it didn't matter. He'd thought of it, that was the main thing. Everything they'd done, all the lies they'd told, all for nothing. All crushed and useless in this tremendous anticlimax.

She felt her own body. She felt the curve of her own breasts under the nightdress. She'd always thought of herself as attractive to men. But Johnny had rejected her. He'd drawn away, aloof and remote, 'Johnny,' she'd moaned, 'Johnny.' But his white face in the darkness had shown her something alien to herself, something that had made her shudder. She lay alone, agonized. What had she done? Had she said something to make him hate her?

She stole a glance at him as he lay beside her. He was so white he might have been a marble statue. For a moment she thought he was dead. His eyes were open, staring in front of him. Alarmed she touched his face. He sat up abruptly.

'What's the matter?'

'I—I'm sorry. I couldn't sleep. You looked so quiet, I thought you were ill.'

Again she heard the pounding in her ears.

'I'm all right. Go back to sleep,' Johnny said.

He remained sitting bolt upright.

Mary murmured miserably. 'Oh Johnny, what have I done?'

'Nothing.' The word startled her with its vehemence. 'You ain't done nothing. Go to sleep.'

The voice was Johnny's, but somehow it seemed to be coming from miles away. It seemed to be all mixed up with the pounding in her head. Outside it was beginning to get light. She could see the hideous wallpaper, the china jug and washing bowl, gradually taking on their daytime shapes. She was frightened of the room, she was frightened of Johnny sitting up beside her so white and still. He was naked, but she had no desire for him now. Only a fear that was coming up from the pit of her stomach like nausea.

'I'm thirsty. I'm going to get a drink of water,' he said. Then he turned to her. 'Go to sleep.' But the tone of his voice was hostile. She heard him shuffling down the passage in his dressing-gown and slippers. When he had gone the room seemed to close in on her, stifling her, so that she could hardly breathe. It seemed to shout soundlessly at her from all its four corners, nudging her out of bed, beckoning to her. It smelt of a world long dead, of Victoriana mildewing in some long-forgotten attic, fighting against the twentieth century, the generation of whom she was a member, this shabby squalid hole-and-corner affair with Johnny which had failed so miserably. She felt very small, alone in this enormous bed, which seemed to be growing to fill the whole room.

'Johnny, come back. Don't leave me.' Had she spoken aloud, or were these merely her thoughts? She now knew that her fear was not of Johnny, but solely of the room. When Johnny came back they could pack up and move somewhere else. Things would be all right then.

She shut her eyes, and when she opened them Johnny was back. She smiled up at him. Things were sorted out now. She was going to get up, get dressed and packed, and leave Mrs. Hayter's. She didn't have to put up with rooms that hated her, that whispered in corners. Johnny bent over her, smiling. He understood too. She put up her arms to draw his head down to her breast. It was all right now. He understood.

The knife glinted in the dawn light from the open window. Desperately she struggled to avoid it as it plunged into her neck again and again. Then it tore a jagged line down her flesh till it found her heart. She thrashed at the bedclothes, as the blood splashed out over the sheets and blankets, and over Johnny's naked body as he stabbed again and again and again.

When he had killed her, he put the bread knife carefully on the bedside table next to Mary's wristwatch. It was just before half past three. As he got back into bed he heard the grandfather clock chime the half-hour. He lay down beside her. The sheets were wet and sticky, but he was very tired.

That was how they found them the next morning. Johnny said one more thing. He said 'Goodbye, Mary,' and those were the last consecutive words he ever uttered.

The room had claimed two more victims.

'I don't care what you say about it, I think it's more than coincidence.' Elsie Hayter was sitting in the kitchen drinking tea. Albert, she noted with distaste, was picking his teeth.

'I said at the time we'd have trouble, but you pooh-poohed me as usual.'

'You're talking rubbish,' said Albert. 'Just because some painter broke his back, you take it as the gipsy's warning.'

'But he died in hospital, they told me.'

'Oh, let me read the paper in peace.'

'I never liked that room, never. I always felt there was something wrong with it. But you wouldn't listen. You never listen to me, that's the trouble.'

Some months had passed, but Mrs. Hayter still couldn't bring herself to stay in the room upstairs for any length of time. Whenever she was dusting, and she caught sight of the reflection of the bed in the mirror, she fancied she could still see the blood. All over the bed, it had been. And that boy... When they had first had the room decorated, one of the painters had fallen off the ladder and broken his back. He said later that something had made him turn round and he had lost his balance. Complications had set in and he had died in hospital. Elsie had wanted to leave the house straight away, but Albert wouldn't let her. Riddled with superstition, he had called her. And then the first time they had let the room, this ghastly tragedy had happened. She had been proved right, but still Albert wouldn't listen.

All over the house the police had tramped. Questions, questions, until Elsie thought she should go mad. Then the Press had come. For days and nights they had camped outside the house until Elsie screamed from an upstairs window for them to go away. They were like vultures, growing fat on people's misfortunes. Albert assured her that the fuss would die down in a week or so, but what did Albert know about it? He was so insensitive. She looked at him now over her teacup. Albert sat opposite, his thick coarse features immersed in the newspaper. What madness had possessed her to marry him?

'Course, you know what's going to happen now, don't you?' she said at last.

'No. You surprise me.'

'And you needn't be so clever, Albert Hayter. There's nothing to be clever about, nothing at all. I'll tell you what'll happen. We won't let any more rooms, that's what'll happen. How d'you think we'll be able to let rooms after this?'

'It'll die down. Just you see. Things like this always do .'We'll let more rooms than ever once this house gets known.'

That was so like Albert. Always look on the bright side, Elsie thought with irritation. Every cloud has a silver lining, that should have been written for Albert.

'And I'll tell you *what* we'll get,' she snorted. 'Morbid sensation-seekers, nasty perverts. "Show us where it happened", they'll say, "Where were they lying? Was there much blood?" Disgusting!'

But Elsie wondered whether Albert was right.

And Albert was right. They got more enquiries than they could cope with. True, the sensation seekers came, eyes popping, but they were careful to be on their best behaviour in front of Mrs. Hayter. She was thus enabled to accept their rent money, while at the same time preserving the air of formidable respectability with which she had come to be associated, and which in the eyes of both her guests and her neighbours, nothing, not even a murder, could shatter. She was able to convey in subtle ways which a casual observer would have thought beyond her, that the goings-on of her lodgers were no concern of hers, that she was aloof and remote from those who needed to ask the favour of her hospitality, and that she fully intended to preserve intact the *status quo.*

But not all her guests were of the kind which made it necessary for Elsie to assume a defensive attitude, albeit an unconscious one. Mrs. Walsingham certainly was not.

'I am divorced from my husband,' she wrote in her letter, 'and I need to get away from my home and my friends. I thought of going abroad, but I feel too exhausted to cope alone. I need somewhere quiet and restful. I wonder whether you—'

'But we have nowhere to put her,' Elsie moaned, 'and you could hardly call this house quiet and restful.'

'We could put her in the Victorian room,' Albert said.

Elsie sprang to her feet. She was as usual drinking tea, and the cup slopped over on to the floor. 'You're joking! The Victorian room! After what happened!'

'She won't know which room it was, will she? If she remembers the case at all.'

'There were pictures taken, weren't there? And I couldn't put anyone in that room. I simply couldn't!'

Elsie repeated those words to herself later that evening, when she was alone. Mrs. Walsingham's letter lay on the table before her. She wrote from Cadogan Square, on expensive notepaper, and Elsie knew enough to know that Cadogan Square was worth anybody's money. Despite the fact that the house was otherwise full, she had never put anyone in the Victorian room. It was as much as she could do even to enter it herself, to air the bed, or dust, or sweep the floor. But Cadogan Square... And after all, perhaps Mrs. Walsingham didn't know.

But .Mrs. Walsingham most emphatically did know.

'No, I don't mind at all,' she told Elsie, 'of course I'm not super-stitious. I'm only sorry for people who commit these senseless crimes. I think they should have far more understanding than they get. Of course, I don't mind sleeping in your Victorian room. Oh, by the way, I hope you don't mind dogs.'

The dog in question was a Pekinese. Mrs. Hayter, aware in some vague way that she was doing the other woman an ill turn by allowing her to set foot in the room at all, was glad of the opportunity of being able to offer compensation

'Isn't she sweet?' she cried with feeling, although she detested dogs.

'She's quite housetrained, perfectly quiet and absolutely no trouble.'

The room welcomed Mrs. Walsingham and her dog.

'We don't usually accept dogs,' Elsie said from the door, 'but in *her* case—'

She nodded to herself. The balance was restored.

'Alone at last,' Dorothy Walsingham said as she relaxed luxuriously on the bed, kicking her shoes off across the carpet. Yvette, after exploring every corner carefully, lay down under the dressing-table, head on paws, and went to sleep.

Dorothy, from her earliest years, had had a fascination for crime. She was thrilled in a way she couldn't describe by the thought of the murder that had been committed in this room. She patted the bed beside her. Here the girl had lain, splattered in her own blood. What made people do such things? What drove them to it?

Would Fred ever have killed her, she wondered? Would Fred, like that poor boy who had been found guilty but insane, stung by her own bitter cruel words, would Fred suddenly have risen up and struck her down? Who knew what any human being was capable of? She remembered some quotation about the sleeping tiger.

Yvette growled in her sleep. Dorothy could hear the sea. Strange how distinct it was, because the room itself was at the back of the house, and the house was really quite far away from the sea front.

Still, she doubted whether Fred really had much of a sleeping tiger in him. He had been the perfect gentleman, stepping out of the way graciously, allowing her to divorce him although she was the guilty party, hardly even scolding her for her infidelities. Quaintly he was anxious for her to preserve what was left of her somewhat tarnished reputation. He was naive enough to believe that she was still respected among her friends. Old-fashioned of him, and rather sweet, but definitely stupid to imagine that women, or at any rate, women in her particular circle, were anything other than cats. She knew he hadn't cared for her for years, that he was just waiting for the excuse to get rid of her, but he still believed that some women weren't cats, and for that he was willing to spare her.

Thinking of cats brought her back to dogs. Yvette was grunting heavily, as if she were having bad dreams, and moving about uneasily under the dressing-table. She went over and patted the dog absently. Then she looked out of the window.

You can't see a damn thing, she thought. Whatever possessed me to come here? I can hear the sea, but I can't see a bloody thing except those hot-water pipes from the lavatory. She wondered whether the boy who had killed his girl in that bed had had a glimpse of the future: had seen how the first passionate love of youth grows stale and sour, and because of what he had seen, because of what must always happen, he had gone mad and killed the object of his passion. Even the landlady looked as if she despised her husband. She had said he was disabled or something, and couldn't work. That was why she had to let rooms.

The room watched Dorothy Walsingham with amusement.

Yvette suddenly woke up and began walking round and round under the dressing-table as if investigating something that Dorothy couldn't see.

'Stop it, you silly dog,' she said aloud, 'you'll make yourself giddy.'

'Would you like a cup of tea?' Elsie Hayter called from the door. 'We're just making some.'

'Thanks, I would. Could you bring it to me here? I'm just going to unpack. Oh, and could you bring some milk for Yvettte ? I think she's thirsty.'

Yvette's tongue was certainly hanging out rather a long way, as she investigated whatever it was she saw.

That was the joy of having a Peke, Dorothy decided. They were so adaptable.

She took out a cigarette, and went back to her place on the bed. It really wasn't such a bad room when you got used to it. The wallpaper was hideous, of course. Probably something Mrs. Hayter had bought in a job lot. But the rest of the room was really rather quaint. Not her taste, of course, but it definitely had personality, and there was something to be said for that these days.

The dog had stopped its prowling and was sitting down looking intently at its mistress. Dorothy beckoned to her. 'Here then, Yvette, here then, darling.'

Animals were so much less complicated than people. Particularly husbands. Or even lovers. Such a comfort.

'Come, Yvette. Come here. Come and sit on the bed beside me.'

Yvette came, at first it seemed unwillingly.

Then her tail began to wag, and then she jumped up to the bed, snorting happily as is the way with Pekes.

'Oh, Yvette,' Dorothy caressed the silken ears. 'What am I going to do?'

Yvette began to growl again. She jumped on to Dorothy's lap. Foam flecked the corners of her mouth. Dorothy, startled, cried out sharply 'What's the matter? Yvette! Yve—'

She heard the sea pounding in her ears, as her mouth filled with the warm taste of her own blood. She felt the dog's teeth meet in her throat.

Elsie Hayter, coming up with a cup of tea, dropped it and ran screaming down the stairs.

They had put a round table in the room and three People sat round it, fingers touching, palms downwards in front of them.

Albert Hayter looked embarrassed and uncomfortable, glad that his friends from the Crown couldn't see him in this ridiculous posture. He had only been prevailed upon to take part in this absurd mumbo-jumbo much against his will because it was the only thing that would keep Elsie quiet. She sat opposite to him now, shivering slightly although the room was far from cold.

'D'you want a scarf?' The words came out so suddenly that both women started and Albert, surprised at the impression his words had created, looked more sheepish than ever. Elsie shook her head sharply, and frowned.

'I must ask for complete silence,' the other woman rebuked him sternly. 'Empty your mind of all mundane thoughts. If I don't have your total cooperation we shall get nowhere.'

Elsie sat as motionless as she could. If she tried very hard she could control the fear that threatened to rise up and destroy her. She felt it like nausea, a dull ache in the pit of her stomach. If she closed her eyes, she thought, she could shut out the forces, the presences she felt all round her, the evil vibrating in the very air itself. This sense of evil had grown during the past few weeks, ever since that poor woman had been killed by her dog. Every detail of that terrible evening stood out clearly in her memory. For twenty minutes the ghastly little dog had played and yapped round its mistress's body; even the police had had to approach it with caution. They had called the local vet to come in and destroy it, and when he arrived the dog was as playful and happy as ever. Only when the police doctor had come to take a closer look at the body did they discover that both the eyes had gone...

With the courage borne of desperation Elsie knew that it was the room itself that was responsible, and knowing this, knew also that it was vital for her own sanity that whatever was troubling the room had it be exposed and exorcised. A Medium seemed to only logical answer.

When Albert heard this he had first of all laughed, then exploded. 'You must be mad. A Medium! I'd rather leave this house than give money to support that—that—it's all fake, don't you know that?'

Elsie found herself, uncharacteristically, almost pleading with him.

'Oh, Albert, you must. You must try it. For my peace of mind.'

Why she suddenly didn't want to leave any more, she couldn't understand. The house repelled her, yet fascinated her at the same time. It was as if she had detected a sickness, and there was only one way to deal with sicknesses. You had to try and cure them.

'You see, it's the room,' she tried to explain to the Medium when that formidable lady arrived. 'There's something wrong with it.'

'I read about the murder, of course,' Mrs. Forrester said doubtfully. 'But it seemed to me straightforward. I mean they got the young man who was responsible, didn't they? In what way were psychical forces—did psychical forces manifest themselves?' Elsie Hayter, out of her depth, began to stammer.

'I—we—well, it's... hard to say. I can't explain. There's something about the room that seems to—make people do things.'

To her surprise Mrs. Forrester nodded, as if she understood the symptoms perfectly.

'Ah—possession, you mean. A form of demoniac possession. Well that is interesting. I haven't come across a case like this myself, though I've often read about them, of course.'

Albert grunted.

'You see,' went on Elsie, flashing her husband a look of reproof, 'that wasn't the only incident connected with the room. There was a decorator who fell off his ladder, and died in hospital, then this awful—I can't bear to talk about it, can I, Albert? This woman and her dog.

But she had to tell Mrs. Forrester about the woman and her dag. At the end of the recital Mrs. Forrester nodded harder than ever.

'Yes, it definitely sounds like demoniac possession,' she said, and Elsie could almost swear there was pleasure in her voice. 'And what is more, highly dangerous to yourselves. If I were you, I would leave this house. Sell up, and move somewhere else.'

'But the guests,' said Elsie, 'we've just got together a flourishing little guest-house. It's so hard to have to give it all up. Especially when Albert—'

Mrs. Forrester interrupted her, 'Your husband is unable to work, is he, Mrs. Hayter?'

'Yes, that is so. At least it's what the doctors say.'

Despite herself, a hard note had crept into Elsie's voice as she answered. 'In the war he was shell-shocked. Mental, his trouble is.' She looked at Albert, sitting smug in his chair. Why add an account of her own grievances? Why tell this nosy, probing woman that she couldn't see it herself, couldn't see why Albert couldn't earn *some* sort of money, however small, instead of loafing round the house all day; why she had to be the sole breadwinner as well as looking after all the guests. She couldn't tell this woman how sometimes Albert's very presence so got on her nerves that she could cheerfully have throttled him as he sat; that if Albert had gone halfway towards satisfying her in other ways life would have been more tolerable. No, she couldn't tell Mrs. Forrester all this, and the less so because Albert was sitting in his chair between them.

Mrs. Forrester was speaking again. 'Of course there is another explanation,' she was saying.

'Pardon?'

'About the room. I mean I quite understand that you don't want to leave if it can possibly be avoided.'

'I did once,' Elsie said. 'After the first murder. It was as much as I could do even to go into the room. Now, it doesn't seem so bad. I can't explain why. One just gets past things.'

'Yes, that is a common occurrence. A lot of people feel like that. The greater the challenge the more keyed up you become to meet it. And the challenge of that room is very great... But I must tell you what I mean. What you may have up there is a poltergeist.'

Albert grunted again, and picked up the evening paper.

'I fear your husband is not interested.'

'Albert, put the paper down and don't be rude. Please go on, Mrs. Forrester.'

'Do you know what a poltergeist is, Mrs. Hayter?'

'I thought they threw things.'

167

'Some of them do, it's true. But some of them can be more dangerous. They can attract to themselves energy from some frustrated, adolescent person and use that energy for their own purposes. That is why in recorded cases of poltergeist phenomena some young teenage girl usually becomes the centre of activity. Energy is extracted in the same way as ectoplasm is extracted from a physical Medium, and used by the poltergeist for its own ends.'

Elsie was not sure she understood, still less believed what the woman was saying.

'But there's no young girl living here,' she said, and into her voice the hard note had crept again. 'Apart from the guests who come and go, no young person lives here permanently.'

And now they were sitting upstairs in the room itself, she and Mrs. Forrester and, under protest, Albert. Now after Mrs. Forrester's admonition to Albert there was silence: silence so profound that Elsie could hear it. She could hear in her ears the roaring and pounding of the silence, so that it sounded like the sea.

'Oh, there is a presence here,' Mrs. Forrester said suddenly, and then after a moment she went on slowly, almost unwillingly, as if the words were being forced out of her: 'Oh, there is a great presence here. It is pressing all round me. I can hardly breathe. It is stifling me. It is tremendous, so tremendous that I am helpless before it. It is lifting me up, drawing me to itself...'

Her voice tailed off. Elsie could see in the darkness the woman's body go limp as if she were asleep. She could hear no breathing because the noise in her car shut out everything else.

There they sat, the three of them, for what seemed hours, she and that great oafish Albert, and Mrs. Forrester, and no one spoke. All round her she could hear the humming, and still it sounded like the sea.

She dared not speak, or break the spell in any way, because the woman opposite seemed to be fighting her own private battle.

She wondered whether the Forrester woman was in any

difficulties. Should Albert offer to help her? After all, it was a man's place... But then Albert never did anything for anybody. He was useless, a lump. All her hard work and he just sat around all day criticizing. Shell-shock indeed! There were places where they give the disabled work, weren't there? He wouldn't leave her alone, that was the trouble: wouldn't even go to the pub until she practically forced him out of the house. If she had her time over again... What was it the woman had said? Frustrated energy, channelled by some alien force. What she was getting at, of course, was sex. That was the only thing anybody ever talked about nowadays. Frustrated sex. Well, she, Elsie Hayter, was very far from being an adolescent girl...

Her thoughts rambled on. She found it impossible to keep her mind blank, despite what Mrs. Forrester had said. She thought of Albert when he had been young and comparatively sane. Even then he had been hideously clumsy with her so that she had found herself shrinking from him in disgust. That young boy and girl, now, had they had time to find out that sex was a ludicrous and grotesque let-down? Perhaps they had, perhaps that was why the boy in his shame and contempt had killed her.

She was disturbed by an odd trickling sound, like water dripping from a tap. Even before she roused herself to put the lights on she knew what she would find. As expected the woman was dead, head back across the chair, and blood dripping from her mouth to form a little pool on the floor. The doctors pronounced it a stroke, but Elsie Hayter knew that in some way she herself was responsible...

The room was empty. In fact, the whole house was empty, and had remained so for just under a year. At long last it had acquired a reputation, so that no one who lived locally would set foot in it after dark. In the room itself a thick pall of silence had settled, encroached upon but never really broken by the noise of the traffic outside. Elsie Hayter had taken away her Victorian knick-knacks, but somehow traces of her still remained, clinging to the walls and the floor and the ceiling. Already the house had assumed that un-lived-in, neglected look, but this room had lagged behind, enclosing within itself traces of the human element. If one were standing within it one would hardly have been surprised at the sound of the voice that now wafted up the stairs, the thin precise voice that could only belong to a house agent.

'...upstairs,' it was saying, 'a very charming, room although unfortunately there is no view. It is certainly the best bedroom.'

The room held itself in readiness for a new invasion, gathering its forces together for the defensive, preparatory to renewed attack, as the footsteps ascended the stairs outside. A moment lat-er the door opened, as the new young husband who had just bought the house held it open politely for his wife to enter.

THE CLUMP

'YOU KNOW, THERE'S ONE THING about magic that is important to remember. It's really a question of balance, like all natural forces. Good and evil. You tap the forces of one at the expense of the other. And vice versa. The scales start off by being evenly weighted. If you upset the balance—there has to be compensation.'

These words, spoken by the absurd Mr. Durnley as if for dramatic effect, now came back vividly to Danny for no apparent reason as he drooped over the ship's rail, craning his eyes for the first sight of land. He so very badly wanted to be first in the queue for disembarkation that he'd barely had time to gulp lunch. He had escaped as soon as he decently could, right off to "B" deck, camera dangling precariously round his neck, relieved to find when he arrived that there was no one before him, and that the indigestion he risked was, after all, justified.

Only a few were going ashore. The island jetty was so tiny that the cruise liner had to remain at anchor out in the bay, disgorging the boats that could carry only a small group of passengers. "Going to St Arthur" was a badge of status amongst those on board to whom symbols of exclusivity were essential. Others, however, to whom the cruise was merely an indulgence for rest, recuperation, or for the recharging of internal batteries, were indifferent to, and really rather looked down upon, mere *sightseeing*. Barbados, Trinidad, Martinique, St Thomas—names and islands approached and receded, and were remembered, if at all, primarily as interruptions to the routine of shipboard life: hectic rounds of cabin bridge, cocktail parties, jealous acquisition of a deeper suntan than that sported by one's neighbour; or perhaps only the continuance of a middle-class community life of gossip and petty malevolence transferred from home environment to that of the cruise-boat.

Few passengers wealthy enough to be able to afford a Caribbean cruise could have brought themselves to admit readily the prime attraction of sightseeing as an occupation. If indulged in at all, one did it accompanied by a faintly apologetic air: shamefacedly, because others *expected* it. Therefore the more conventional tourist Meccas were disclaimed. Perhaps that was why St Arthur still held value: alone, of all the boat's ports of-call, it remained comparatively rare and unspoilt. Gamblers could still speculate on its accessibility—the element of uncertainty added, for many, to its piquancy. A name placed on a cruise's scheduled itinerary in no way ensured that it would actually be reached—only a combination of favourable outside circumstances could decide that. 'Perhaps', Mr. Durnley had remarked to Danny's parents over his third glass of burgundy at lunch in the first class dining saloon, 'it's like Mary Rose's island, and doesn't really *like* to be visited.'

But today it seemed that these desperate elements had united favourably. A truce, Mr. Durnley might have said. The weather, currents, and the vagaries of island politics—in roughly that order—each stretched forth hesitant hands, albeit defensively and guardedly, to the American dollar.

And the American dollar responded.

Worthy representatives of that dollar were the Tuckers. Partner in a firm of real estate brokers on the West coast, Keith Tucker believed firmly that he was on the way up. The value of real estate was appreciating; Keith could at last afford a really expensive holiday. A trip to the West Indies would confirm his potential to those he wished to impress.

If asked, he would of course have been unwilling to admit that this was the prime motivation. He would have asserted, and believed, that it was done largely for Danny's sake. It was true that, according to Keith's lights, Danny would benefit. In a society where status was worshipped with religious intensity, Danny's place, even in the school where Keith had fought to send him, would be usefully consolidated, because of the enhancement of his prestige value.

The only fly in the ointment was Liz.

Keith realized that he couldn't very easily have left Liz at home. He had thought about it often enough. Up to the very morning they were due to leave, with Liz fussing eternally about passports, visas, and travellers' cheques, he had debated the possibility in his mind, casting about for some pretext, some straw at which to clutch. But there had been none. The presence of Liz loomed inevitably ahead—unadulterated Liz, because there was no office to intervene, his curse and his cross, a blight to turn to grey the blue of the Caribbean.

The wedding cake had been scarcely eaten, the champagne barely drunk, when Keith had first become aware of the magnitude of his miscalculation. And so had started that endless procession of petty annoyances, grievances at first unacknowledged and allowed to fester quietly, to add to the self-perpetuating morass of irritation and remorse for a mistake—now irrevocable because Liz was pregnant. Was it soft-heartedness that had made him decide to put up with the best of a bad job, because he hadn't wanted to hurt Liz and risk her losing the child, or was it merely weakness? There was more to it than that, of course. A fairly hefty proportion of self interest had soon forced Keith to admit that any sort of scandal would have jeopardized his position in the community; and the directorship that was about to be offered to him. But Danny was now twelve, and still Keith regretted the momentary rashness of his marriage to Liz.

It would have been trite to suggest that a Caribbean cruise could ever have served as the occasion for a second honeymoon. Even if the first one had proved satisfactory, Keith would have remained dubious, lacking the necessary faith, though he would have made a determined effort to patch up whatever breaches were repairable. But that was before Anthea. Ridiculously, Anthea had happened to him on the very day that he had made his reservations. She had come into the office to discuss with him some property that she was interested in buying, but it was soon obvious to both of them that the range of her requirements was to prove wider than either had anticipated...

At first it seemed to Danny that a heat haze concealed almost completely the tops of the trees. As the island approached the mists cleared, or perhaps it was that the ship had penetrated inside the enchanted area.

Later he could see that the trees were confined to a smallish clump which formed the summit of a tiny hill which ran down to the beach. Even from this distance the clump looked dark and forbidding, as if no ray of the tropic sun ever penetrated.

'St Arthur,' said a voice behind him. 'I take it you're going ashore?'

Danny nodded. All islands fascinated him, but this one more than most. Although he'd never before left the States, he knew instinctively that for him islands symbolized escape, quietness, refuge—if only from his parents' continued bickering. He wasn't yet familiar with the word sanctuary.

He hadn't heard Mr. Durnley come up behind him. Mr. Durnley had a habit of approaching noiselessly and disconcertingly.

Like the time he had first collared Keith and Liz during a pre-dinner cocktail in the Bamboo Bar. Danny had later joined the party for an orange juice, when the conversation on folklore and superstition was well under way. Mr. Durnley, travelling alone, was apparently engaged preparing a book on this very subject.

'I've really done most of the research,' he had assured them, 'though it's amazing what unsuspected sources you can tap just by being on the spot. St Arthur, for instance. I expect you've gathered that it's not easy to get to St Arthur. Under your own steam, that is. They don't welcome casual visitors—least of all people like me who would want to ask a lot of questions. Since the De Santos regime began, there's been almost a total shutdown. They just about tolerate cruise liners, because they'll be in and out in a few hours, and even De Santos can't afford to ignore the revenue they bring in. But God help you if you hang about too long in any one place. And take my advice and steer clear of asking questions.'

'You mean questions about politics,' said Liz.

Mr. Durnley didn't answer at once. 'Yes, mainly about politics,' he said, apparently choosing his answer carefully. 'But I wasn't thinking entirely about politics. You know how rife superstition still is in the Islands. Well St Arthur is a veritable hotbed. Perhaps because it *has* been comparatively unexposed to commercialization up to now. And there are a great many people who want to keep it that way.'

'You mean De Santos' bully-boys?' said Keith. Liz looked round uneasily, as if one or two might have strayed into the bar, to hide behind the curtains.

'Not entirely. I mean the Obeah men.'

'Obeah men?'

'*Obi.* The West Indian name for witchcraft. The Islands are riddled with it. Especially in the smaller ones. It's not of course immediately accessible to visitors.'

Liz shivered. 'And St Arthur is one of the smaller islands. I don't think I shall land after all.'

'What nonsense, Liz,' Keith exploded. 'The witch-doctors have got better things to do with their time than have a go at you!'

'You're right of course,' said Mr. Durnley, 'though it's amazing how much power these Obeah men exert. I believe that De Santos keeps several on his payroll. He uses *Obi* to enforce his power over the people.'

'Like Papa Doc,' said Keith.

'Like Papa Doc. And it's extraordinarily effective.'

'You talk as if you really believe in it,' said Liz.

'I don't think it really matters whether I believe in it or not, Mrs. Tucker. Logically, the argument supporting its existence can be demolished in five minutes. But its victims don't know that, so the curse, or spell, or hex, or whatever it is—*works*.'

'Thank God neither my wife nor I are gullible enough to believe that our own destiny isn't totally manageable by us,' said Keith. He saw Danny threading his way through the tables towards them. 'All man-made religion is hypocrisy.'

'And your son?'

Keith glanced at Mr. Durnley sharply. The question was unexpected, almost as if a hint of urgency had crept into the man's normally rather pontifical voice.

'We've brought Danny up to be totally independent and self-reliant, and not to place the blame for his mistakes and misdeeds on some impersonal deity. If, when he reaches the age of so-called discretion he wishes to choose to follow some conventional religion, that's up to him. Personally, I hope he has better sense.'

'Don't you think,' remarked Mr. Durnley as Danny dragged a stool over to join them, 'that that might make him rather—er—vulnerable?'

Only two boatloads of passengers were landing. The rest had decided that they were far too comfortable where they were. There was a proportion indeed, care for whose stomachs outweighed all other holiday consideration, who wished to preserve them intact and unsullied for the challenge of the gastronomic delights of the French restaurants on Martinique, the next port-of-call. Still others had scarcely left their cabins for days, bewailing the apparent inoperability of the ship's stabilisers over Biscay. But the

Tuckers and Mr. Durnley wished to lose no opportunity to see as much as possible, despite Liz's momentary foreboding.

She had later argued to herself that it had been solely the effect of the slightly baneful conversation that had acted on her nerves: indeed the evening had later taken an even darker turn, though despite herself she had found what Mr. Durnley had to say about the Occult and Occultists fascinating, as most people do. It was during their subsequent talk that he had made his remark about the balance of magic and magical forces, and much in the same vein. She had learnt about Adepts of the Right and Left Hand Paths, how one used White and one Black Magic, and much else besides. She learnt too about certain dark and ancient West Indian gods, and Mr. Durnley discussed some really spectacularly ugly survivals that lurked in lonely places... but of the dark forces that stirred about them at their own table as they talked, she still had no inkling, nor the slightest hint or suspicion that her husband was planning to kill her.

As the boat landed them on the tiny jetty, Liz said that she wanted a drink. The nearest cafe, attached to a small *adobe* bungalow which served as a hotel, was five minutes along the cobbled track, and the Tuckers set off together, having said their adieux to Mr. Durnley who would join them later. The stop on St Arthur was only to be approximately four hours: there really wasn't much to see on St Arthur, and at the eleventh hour Liz's misgivings about coming had returned. Keith had rather hoped that she wouldn't. He wanted to get away from her, if only for four hours, and to think about Anthea, and what he was to do. He had momentarily been far-fetched enough to imagine that being on an island only influenced minimally by tourists might clear his mind of the clutter which prevented him from seeing clearly. But then she had insisted on coming, suddenly, as if she had sensed that he didn't want her.

They ordered drinks, and while they waited, she began to talk.

She went on talking when the drinks arrived, scarcely stopping for breath as she sipped her planter's punch, on and on, gossip and small-talk, unimportant and trivial, some of it about their life at home, most of it about their fellow passengers. Inside, Keith was screaming for her to stop. Even Mr. Durnley, who had now wandered off by himself, didn't escape. He was a fool, Liz said. He was pretentious. All that stuff about magic. As if it mattered— Perhaps he'd miss the boat back, and they'd be spared his presence for the rest of the voyage.

Keith put his hand in his pocket, and his fingers closed round the comforting shape of the bottle of sleeping tablets. If only he dared, it would solve so many problems. Poor Liz, no one had guessed that alcohol, taken on top of the tablets, could have had such a lethal effect. She was always taking them, Keith would say at the inquest, though I begged her to be careful. Yes she *had* taken one or two sometimes after lunch. She had begun to complain of headaches, and the tablets eased them. No, only a couple of rum punches Nothing to excess. She must have forgotten that the boat was docking at St Arthur immediately after lunch, and there wouldn't be time for a nap. Yes, she had looked tired. Yes, a cruise can take it out of you if you're not used to it, particularly the West Indian sun...

All he had to do was wait until she went to the john, and then slip a dose into her last drink.

So easy. Oddly, it was a last-minute decision to grab the pills from the bedside table when they were both leaving the cabin...

'Can I go for a swim, Dad?' Danny, bored, was finishing the last of his pineapple juice.

'Can't you use the pool when we get back? We've only got four hours.' That was Liz.

'It's not the same as the sea.'

Let the boy go, Keith's inner voice said. He might see something, and remember later. There'd be a bottle to dispose of.

Aloud he said, 'Wouldn't you rather explore? God knows when you'll get another chance.'

'I could do both,' said Danny.

The clump, the same clump of cabbage palms that he'd seen from the boat, now seemed darker than ever, sharply contrasted with the gleaming sands—so white that they hurt the eyes—which ran from directly beneath it as if trying to escape to the sea. One or two palms fringed the beach's boundary, but the trees that bounded the wood were casuarinas, tall, thick and majestic, giving nothing away that went on beyond them.

'I want to see that wood,' said Danny.

'You'll probably be shot for trespassing on private property. They do that here. Ask Mr. Durnley.'

'Mr. Durnley!' snorted Liz.

'Dad, you told me to explore. Now when I say I want to—'

'Okay, okay. Explore. But don't say I didn't warn you.'

'I'll be careful, I promise.' Danny got up, knowing that if he didn't go at once he'd be over-ruled.

'What about snakes? I know there'll be snakes,' Liz piped up.

'There'll probably be mongooses to take care of the snakes,' said Keith. 'If you get into difficulties, just yell.'

The waiter approached with a further round. 'You talk about that clump?' he demanded abruptly. 'I saw the boy point to it. Don't let him go there. Bad place.'

Keith and Liz both looked up. The man appeared to be in earnest.

'You mean that the wood is private property?'

The boy *should* stand on his own two feet. We all like adventure, Keith argued to himself, but Liz saw only visions of a firing-squad personally supervised by De Santos himself, a picture that speedily assumed a disconcerting tangibility.

'No. That place taboo. Don't let the boy go there.'

But Danny had already left, striding purposefully, and chose to be considered out of earshot, as he tackled the path which, skirting the edge of the island's largest sugar plantation, led towards the clump of palms.

As he passed between the rough trunks of the palms the first aspect that struck Danny was the silence. Always over the Islands there was a constant background of sounds—birds screeched, insects hummed sleepily... now, suddenly, there was nothing, as if a tape recorder had been switched off, or as if the giant casuarinas, the tamarinds, the pines, formed some sort of a soundproof curtain. It was like stepping onto a stage.

He picked his way at first gingerly, then with more confidence, over the densely-weeded ground, until he discovered by trial and error that there was indeed a path of sorts. So he wasn't the only person ever to have set foot in this wood since the dawn of history...

Back home, Danny had always loved forests, and the times he'd spent in Summer Camp had been the happiest of his life. And islands too had always held for him the attraction of the Romantic Unknown. To be able to combine the two, must constitute a fair proportion of Total Bliss. He felt a momentary regret that he hadn't brought his pocket torch with him, but this soon passed, or was absorbed into the delicious awareness that he was a pioneer exploring virgin territory.

He craned his eyes ahead for a glimpse of the sandy beach running down into the Bay which he knew must lie beyond the bordering palms ahead. He was convinced that the actual wood must in reality cover a fairly small area, albeit one densely packed, though in here, above and around him, it felt immense enough to carry on into infinity. Overhead, the sun flashed its way through the foliage like a Morse code signaller, but not really helping to light the scene. He knew that once his eyes grew more accustomed to the sudden unbelievable contrast they'd be of more use, and the slightly claustrophobic feeling that the vegetation was actually pressing down upon him, would go. Danny was really very sensible for his age.

He picked himself a cane-like twig, and still keeping to the path, began to slash his way through. His sense of direction was good, he assured himself. At school he had come near the top of his grade in woodmanship, though it was true that he had a compass then and the woods at home hadn't been too thick to enable an embryo tracker to read one.

Not that that mattered. He knew that as he had stuck to the path the whole time he'd been in the wood, all he had to do to get out of it was to turn around and retrace his steps. He determined to press on as far as possible while he had the time. There must be *something* to see.

And there was. He began to notice that he wasn't alone after all. And even the silence wasn't as deep as he'd at first supposed. His ears, as well as his eyes, must have got accustomed to the conditions of the wood, because now he realized that what at first he'd mistaken for silence was actually composed of myriad rustlings all round him, as perhaps countless tiny creatures, and other creatures not so tiny, fought and jostled their way out of the path of this interloper.

Oddly it never crossed his mind that any of the denizens of the wood might be poisonous. He hadn't taken seriously his mother's casually thrown-out warning about snakes: in Danny's life there had always been a mongoose around to fight whatever snake had slithered out of the bushes to threaten him, and he didn't see why a benevolent and watchful Providence should cease its function now.

And it was then that he noticed the figure just ahead.

At first he wasn't clear that he could actually see anything. The rustlings and creakings around him had increased in volume, and now that both his eyes and ears were sensitised to receive impressions, he fancied that he detected movements in the air and on the ground and even above him in the trees. The normal every-day life of the tropical wood fascinated and intrigued him, and while he was aware that the movements were happening at the corners of his eyes, and that when he looked directly at the spot all was as still as before, he made up his mind to stand motionless for a moment or two so that whatever the creatures were that hid at his approach, they could be induced to come out as soon as they realized that the explorer meant them no harm.

Crouching at the bole of a tree, a path of greater darkness against the surrounding murk, the shape ahead of him began, if he was not mistaken, to whimper.

'Hello,' he called out, 'who's there?'

The whimpering stopped, and for a moment there was silence. Then a small voice said, 'I'm lost. I want my tea, and I'm lost.'

The words sounded disconcertingly like something out of a nursery book, and definitely not what Danny expected. But it *was* apparently a small girl, though impossible to make out her actual size. Danny was still chauvinistic enough to feel that girls had to be protected, and suddenly all his instinctive male domination rushed to the fore.

'Gee, that's okay.' He made the tone as reassuring as he knew how. It was good to realize how comforting the correct assumption of sexual roles was, in territory as unknown as a wood. 'I've just come in myself, and I've stuck to the path all the way. Just follow me.' A moment later he added, 'Come over here so that I can see you.'

The shape slowly raised itself from where it had been squatting. Now Danny could see that it was indeed a small girl, not more than eight or nine, so Danny judged. Her back was towards him, though a patch of white indicated that she was wearing what appeared to be a Panama hat. Probably she belonged to one of the workers on the plantation, he told himself. He was aware that his judgment as an adult was being called into play, perhaps for the first time. It was tremendously important that he should do the right thing within the next five minutes.

'Are you all right?' he said, thinking suddenly of his own parents, and the sort of questions they would have asked. 'I mean you're not hurt or anything?'

There might even be a reward, if the child were returned unhurt.

'No, I'm not hurt,' the child said. 'I did fall down a while ago. Twisted my ankle or something. But it's all right now.'

'Then you can walk over to me?'

'Yes.' The child, still with her back to him, turned round with a sort of swivelling motion, and began to approach him.

She obviously wasn't hurt. She hadn't even been bitten by one of those snakes that he didn't really believe in. There was no reason why he should be compelled to carry her out of the wood. But nonetheless he couldn't exactly order her to remain while he finished his exploration. Irritation that this kid had curtailed his plans for the afternoon took him over.

'I don't see how you could have got lost. You were hardly off the path at all. Are you a tourist or something?'

That was really *a very* good card to play.

'Oh no. I live here.'

The girl had now reached him. As the sun flashed its semaphore message through the crowding branches, and before sick and agonizing terror grabbed his mind, mercifully shutting out consciousness, he saw her fully for the first time.

Whatever else the thing might be, it certainly wasn't a child. Between the fringe of the hair which circled the hat, and the top of the neck-high cotton dress, was a blank void, innocent of features.

Mr. Durnley had joined them soon after the waiter's dramatic warning, and confirmed that the wood was not, in fact, private property. 'I gather,' he said, 'that no one on the island would actually dare to lay claim to it.'

Even at this stage, when the Dark Powers had taken in hand the destinies of the three Tuckers, Keith's mind still remained closed to the St Arthur influences. Liz had been for calling the boy back immediately the waiter had spoken his dire pronouncement, but Keith had effectively overruled her.

Danny was old enough to take care of himself. And besides, he had to be got out of the way. Keith fingered the small round bottle in his pocket, and waited for Liz's absence from the table.

Liz shivered in the afternoon St Arthur heat.

'What's the reason, do you know? Is there a story connected with the wood?'

'Some primitive childish superstition,' Keith muttered.

Mr. Durnley shrugged. A hint of the apologetic crept into his tone. 'Interesting only from a folklorist's point of view,' he said. 'Odd, though. What one may term a quaint survival.

'Hitherto I'd only come across it before on Tobago. You know that each island has its own set of myths and legends? They rarely cross from one to another unadulterated. Perhaps in this case the Obeah men instituted it here because they didn't want people trampling round in their clump. That is what the natives call a wood—a *clump.*'

Mr. Durnley drank a hot coffee slowly and thoughtfully, and Keith guessed that another footnote would be added to his tiresome book.

'On Tobago, the Donens are children who die before being baptized. They haunt the clumps and lure other children to their deaths. They wear white Panama hats, and don't have any faces!'

Keith and Liz laughed dutifully, as Mr. Durnley finished his coffee.

'And that, my dears, is the extent of the taboo on the clump. I don't think your Danny has much to worry about. Besides, on

Tobago the Donens only haunt on moonlit nights.'

'I was frightened,' Liz said, 'that De Santos' thugs had placed the wood out of bounds.'

'Oh no. If he had, there would have been barbed wire up every-where. Besides, whatever else he may be, he's astute enough to know which side his bread is buttered. He still wants to placate the tourist trade as much as possible.'

Mr. Durnley got up abruptly. 'From time to time children *have* been lost in the clump. The last time was about seven months ago. The young daughter of one of the estate workers disappeared. My informant was—unwilling to say too much about it. But she was much younger than Danny, and it later transpired that her father had fallen foul of the Party...

'And now, if you will forgive me, I'll return to the boat. My afternoon siesta calls. I find that too much of this heat debilitates me for the evening's jollity. We will meet no doubt for a pre-dinner drink.'

'I think you should get him back,' said Liz.

'Crap. Are you frightened of ghosts now?'

'Of course not. As I said before, there may be snakes. Perhaps a snake got that other child.'

'You heard what Durnley said. More likely she was murdered by—'

'Careful what you say.'

'D'you want another drink? It'll do you good.'

'I'm going to the john,' said Liz. 'Then we'll *both* go to the wood.'

'Okay, if it worries you so much, I'll go. You stay here. I'll collect Danny, and we'll go back to the boat.'

Keith, alone at the table, waited for the new drinks to arrive. It was now or never. Perhaps never again would he find the courage...

He unscrewed the lid as Liz's rum punch arrived, tipped the bottle and—

Something, he wasn't sure what, made him look up towards the wood. Okay, *Clump*. Was it a voice, far away, calling him? A voice born from remote distances on a practically non-existent wind, ineffably distant, but with an urgency of terror so intense that he froze where he sat, his hand still clutching the tilted bottle so that the tablets spilled harmlessly away to lie unheeded beside Liz's chair.

He sprang to his feet, because the terror, the horror in that voice couldn't be denied, because a child called to its father for help, and Keith was running towards the Clump slipping and sliding over the loose stones and shale that covered the approaching path.

Long before he reached the towering palms, he saw the figure of his son, arms waving frantically, trying to pull himself free from something that held him, that was trying to pull him back into the wood.

Badly out of training, Keith hadn't run since College. Now he felt as if his lungs were bursting as they snatched ineffectively at the heat-laden air, but he dared not stop because he knew that if he let up for one moment, his son would be irrevocably lost.

Pudgy American tourists weren't intended to sprint through a West Indian August afternoon, and it was surprising that despite the pain which burst all over his left side as he reached that figure standing on the edge of the wood, he still had breath enough left to scream.

For as Danny turned round, Keith could see that he had no face.

Afterwards, Liz could never tell how long she had been alone at the cafe before realizing that something had happened. She never saw the pills lying beside her chair, so that when she finally was made aware of her double bereavement, and through long years of loneliness that lay ahead for her, she never suspected the powers of those dark and native gods, jealously guarded on the island against intruders that had momentarily allied with her and saved her life.

THE NONDESCRIPT

'DAD, WHAT'S A NONDESCRIPT?'
Bob's father looked up from the sports page. 'Not a Nondescript, it's an adjective. It means indescribable, no particular kind.'

Bob's sister had already dived for the dictionary.

'You're wrong, Daddy, it's a noun too... see?'

'"Something not easily described or classed",' read her father resignedly. 'There's a clever girl.'

'It's rude to correct your father like that, Carol,' said Mum.

'But Mummy...'

'All right, Carol,' said Dad. 'Anyway, Bob, why did you ask?'

'Because there's one in the attic!'

'Eh?'

'There's a—a Nondescript in the attic. At least, that's what it says on the case. I think it's stuffed.'

'We'd better have a look,' said Dad. 'Fetch it down.'

'It's too big for me to carry, Dad.'

'Right-ho,' sighed Dad, putting his paper aside, 'I'll get it.'

'You're not bringing dusty old cases into my clean lounge!' cried Mum.

'Carol will spread some newspaper,' said Dad, and he and Bob plodded upstairs, leaving Mum grumbling about the boy spending Sunday afternoon in that filthy attic, then treading dust into the carpet and putting his grubby paws on the walls. The family had recently moved into the old house in the country, and Bob had been delighted to find the attic full of junk, undisturbed for years.

Dad returned carrying a dusty glass-fronted case, and everyone gathered round to stare at the thing inside.

'Ugh, what *a horrid* thing!' cried Mum.

Carol backed smartly behind the sofa.

'Good grief!' said Dad.

Bob smiled proudly.

'I'm not coming any nearer,' declared Carol. 'It might bite!'

And indeed, the Nondescript looked capable of it.

It was like a mermaid, or rather a merman, but not the romantic story-book kind. It was about four feet long, with its scaly fishtail curved gracefully under it. From the waist up it was, as Mum said, *horrid.* A skinny, leathery body, with thin but strong-looking arms ending in clawed, graspy hands. Worst of all was the head. A bit like a monkey's, but uglier than any monkey you ever saw—pale glaring eyes, scanty black hair, and a wide snarling mouth filled with pointed fangs.

'Isn't it smashing?' laughed Bob. 'Straight out of *Doctor Who!*'

'If they had him on the telly, people would ring up complaining,' said Dad, 'and I wouldn't blame them. He is a splendid piece of work, though. What do you reckon he's made from?'

'You mean it's not real?' cried Carol. 'Thank goodness...'

'Of course not, silly,' said Bob. 'There are no such things as mermaids. The bottom half must be a fish, Dad, but the top... I don't know. It looks awfully like a man, a very ugly little man.'

'I should think it's a monkey, doctored up a bit—those glass eyes, for instance. Well, you've made quite a find, my son. What shall we do with him?'

'I want him in my room,' said Bob.

'You're not putting that hideous thing on show,' said Mum.

'Be fair, dear,' said Dad. 'When we moved in, we told the boy that was his room. We don't have to look at the thing, and Bob will keep it clean.'

'Well, you heard what your Dad said, you'll have to dust it. I'd have nightmares if I touch it. Now you go and have your bath, my lad. Time you were in bed!'

Bob went happily to sleep, dreaming strange and rather scary dreams.

Next evening his father arrived home triumphant.

'I spent my lunchtime in the library, finding out about Nondescripts. I couldn't bring the book—it was in the reference section—but I copied it out...'

Nondescripts, it appeared, were not uncommon in the eighteenth and nineteenth centuries, being manufactured for gullible travellers, particularly in the East. They were made from shaven monkey torsos, sewn to fish tails. Bob's was a fine specimen, with additional touches in the splendid glass eyes and the teeth filed to sharp points. The best Nondescripts were so well made that the join between fish and monkey could scarcely be detected without surgery or X-ray.

'You can have fun with your friends,' said Dad, as he applied varnish to the newly scrubbed case. 'Tell them it's a real monster your grandfather caught!'

Over the next couple of weeks Bob did just that, and the Nondescript in its gleaming case was his proudest possession. Gradually, however, it lost its novelty, and although he wouldn't have parted with it for worlds, he didn't think about it much except when some new friend was invited to admire it.

And that might have been all there was to tell, but for that fateful weekend...

This time it was Mum who made the discovery. Clearing out a cupboard, she found a box of papers belonging to a previous owner of the house. Among the fading legal documents and yellowed letters was a book with cracked leather covers—a journal.

Mr. Thurston Bayliss owned the house in the early nineteenth century—the journal covered the years 1838 to 1843. Dad read out pieces of it, and everyone was fascinated, but the real surprise came at the end...

'May 14th, 1843—Acquired a curiosity today, from Dr. Creighton, a naturalist and a great traveller, who lives at Fosset House. In conversation yesterday after church where he seldom comes! —we happened to discuss curios, which I collect, and he said he had something I might like.

'Today he sent over to me a splendid Nondescript in a case, with a polite letter saying he had no further use for it, and besides he'd a guest who disliked it strongly. I know of no guest at Fosset House, but then, neither I nor anyone here has seen inside the place, for Creighton is pretty much a recluse.'

'I'll have to ask Mr. Keith if he knows anything about Bayliss and Creighton,' said Dad. Mr. Keith was a retired solicitor whose hobby was local history.

Bob went straight to the map, and although Fosset House was not marked, to his excitement there was a Fosset Pool a few miles away. The next day—Saturday—Bob set off to find it. It turned out to be a neglected pond about thirty yards across, hidden behind a tall unkempt hedge. Nearby was some overgrown rubble that might once have been a house. Fosset House!

This hot summer, the water had sunk far below its usual level, and the shrunken pool was ringed with a slope of hard-baked mud. Bob amused himself tossing stones into the water. But he couldn't move *this* one—a fine stone, big as a football. It would make a grand splash if he could get it out of the rock-hard mud. He dug with his pocket knife and at last levered the stone from its socket.

It had been stuck in the opening of a hole and... there was something inside! Bob was sure he could see a dark shape. He knelt, peering into the muddy depths—there *was* something. Plucking up his courage he reached in and felt a leathery mass, eased it out of the hole and—no, surely, it couldn't be...

A Nondescript!

Another Nondescript, just like the one at home, only curled into a ball and very muddy. Scarcely able to believe it, Bob took the thing to the water, washed the dirt off, then carried it back and laid it on the grass. Cleaned, it was an even handsomer specimen than his own: there was a sheen on the tail, and a more natural look to the skin.

Had the mysterious Dr. Creighton run a Nondescript factory?

Two—in a few weeks! It was almost spooky. Still, if all these Nondescripts wanted to queue up at Bob's door, he wouldn't turn them away. He picked up the creature, wrapped it in his jacket, and set off for home. He didn't want the neighbours to see him carrying the weird beast.

'Hello, Bob,' said his father, who was cutting the front hedge. 'What have you got there?'

'You'll never guess, Dad.'

'Oh, I don't know... another Nondescript?'

'Right first time!' laughed Bob, unwrapping his find. Dad's jaw dropped. 'Good Lord! Where on earth did you find that one? Here, bring it indoors.'

Going in, Bob collided with Carol, who jumped back with a squeal of alarm.

'Mum! For goodness sake, look what Bob's got—another of those dreadful whatsits!'

Everyone was as amazed as Bob had been himself. His mother and sister, of course, were disgusted, and complained about the house filling up with monsters, so Bob and Dad retreated upstairs to examine the new Nondescript.

'There's no doubt about it,' said Dad. 'It's even better made than the other one—you can't see the stitches. No wonder Dr. Creighton didn't mind giving away the other one if he had this beauty! I tell you what, Bob, let's take the old one out of the case and put this one in. Tell me again how you found it...'

The new merman looked most impressive, sitting in state in his case; Bob went proudly down to tea. That evening he went to bed earlier than usual, without being told, and lay for some time surveying his new treasure. The old Nondescript looked rather sad and drab now, lying on its back on the chest of drawers. Sooner than he'd expected, Bob yawned and settled down to sleep. He'd had an exciting day and he was tired.

It must have been about three in the morning when he woke up, though he didn't look at the clock. Something had wakened him, a sound, a faint scratching. A mouse would be rather fun, though Mum wouldn't see it that way! He reached out and switched on the bedside lamp.

There was no sign of a mouse or anything else moving. The new Nondescript looked sinister in its case, the slanted light of the lamp throwing dark shadows across the ferocious face.

Bob gasped. He thought he saw... it was impossible...

The Nondescript had moved.

Very, very slightly—there!—the tail switched its tip like a sleeping cat's. There was no mistaking it, the thing really was moving. Bob sat frozen with amazement.

Slowly, ever so slowly, the curled tail straightened, the head lifted. The stringy arms quivered and stretched, and the fanged mouth opened in a ghastly yawn and snapped shut like a trap. Pale eyes opened, closing at once as if dazzled by the lamp. After a moment they opened again and focused on Bob, and they seemed to light up. Bob flinched at the hatred that filled the hideous face, curling the black lips back from the pointed fangs. The taloned hands clutched convulsively as if they felt themselves already at Bob's throat. He wanted to shout for help, but... but...

The Nondescript's gleaming eyes fastened on his own, and he felt all the strength ebbing from his limbs. His hands could barely grasp the bedclothes. The beast was moving... he must do something... he must warn...

The shining, glaring eyes seemed to grow bigger, until they were all he could see, while his own eyes drooped shut and a deadly, chilling sleep crept over him. He could not move, he could no longer see the eyes except as twin glowing discs...

'Bob! Wake up. Bob!'

What was it? From miles away someone was calling, someone was shaking him. But he didn't want to wake or move, he just wanted to sleep.

Abruptly Bob was awake, to see his mother bending over him, concern on her face.

'Hello, Mum. What's up?'

'Bob, thank goodness you're awake! What's been going on, what have you been up to? Look at the state of this room.'

Bob struggled to a sitting position and looked round. The case! The glass case lay shattered, and the Nondescript was gone! Wait a minute, where was the other one, the old one? It wasn't on the chest of drawers... There! It lay on the floor, scattered in pieces across the carpet—torn to bits.

Bob's mother could see at once from his baffled expression that he was not responsible. She walked to the window, which was left open these hot summer nights, and leaned out.

'Well,' she said after a moment, 'there's no sign of it in the garden.'

She ducked back into the room and said with decision: 'You go and get washed, Bob. I'm going to get to the bottom of this.'

While Bob washed, he could hear her re-enter his room with Dad, and both looked very serious when he arrived at the breakfast table.

'You're quite sure, Bob, that you didn't do it? I mean, you haven't started sleepwalking?' said Dad with a poor attempt at a grin.

'No, no,' said Bob firmly, 'I didn't do it. Why would I? But wait a minute, I'm beginning to remember something...'

And he told briefly what he had seen—or thought he had seen—during the night. As he talked, another memory came: he seemed dimly to remember waking, or half waking, and seeing the Nondescript rocking the case back and forth as if trying to tip it over. But perhaps he was imagining that after what he had seen this morning.

The whole family trooped up to Bob's room and inspected the remains of the old Nondescript, then searched the garden for signs of the other one, but without success. A burglar seemed unlikely—and why would he destroy one? Dad eventually said a cat must have done it all, though why, nobody could guess. Anyhow, it wasn't a job for the police.

Sunday passed without any more clues to the mystery, and Bob, though he was sad at losing his treasures, was not at all sure he wanted to see a Nondescript ever again. That night he fastened his window firmly shut, and left his door open, but nothing disturbed him and he passed an unexpectedly restful night. He didn't even dream. It was as though a weight was off his mind.

When Bob came home from school the following evening, he found his mother talking to one of the neighbours. They stopped talking abruptly when he arrived, but it must have been decided there was no harm in his hearing, because over tea Mum told Dad how the neighbourhood was buzzing with the strange tragedy of Mr. Maybrick, an elderly gentleman living half a mile away, alone except for a housekeeper.

The housekeeper, visiting relations for the weekend, had returned early this morning—Monday—to find the old man drowned in the goldfish pond at the bottom of his garden. She'd fled in hysterics and the matter was now in police hands, but it looked like a simple heart attack. Mr. Maybrick must have visited the pond the evening before, had an attack, and fallen into the water. There was one funny thing. It was only a rumour, and not yet confirmed, but Mum had heard that the housekeeper had said that all the goldfish in the pond had gone...

Neither Bob nor any of his family said anything about the affair of the Nondescripts, but Bob had an uncomfortable feeling that there was a connection somewhere. Water, or pools, had to do with both events, and for some reason he couldn't pin down, he was glad he'd seen the last of his Nondescripts.

Despite the succession of macabre happenings, Bob slept well again that night, and felt cheerful enough next day. That is, until lunchtime, when he was talking in the school yard to some of his friends. Steve Hopkins, a boy who lived the other end of the little town, had a story to tell.

'Here, Bob, you know that business of poor old Mr. Maybrick?'

'Yes,' said Bob, feeling an unaccountable shiver down his spine.

'Well, the lady next door to us—Miss Ingles, you know?—she's got a goldfish pond, and she's had exactly the same thing happen! She was telling my Mum. Apparently she looked at the pond this morning first thing, and—not a fish to be seen.'

'What do you suppose it is?' asked Bob, though he had his own ideas.

'I think it's a cat gone wild,' said Steve. 'Cats can learn to catch fish. Old Maybrick caught it in the act, but he had a heart attack.'

Bob didn't pursue the discussion, but the rest of the afternoon he was very quiet, and when he got home he made straight for the bookcase and took out a map of the town. 'What are you looking for?' asked Carol.

'Penrick Lane—where Steve lives—it's on the way to Fosset pool, I think... Yes, it is,' muttered Bob, more to himself than to his sister. 'And Mr. Maybrick's house is in the same direction.'

'Why?'

'Oh, nothing,' said Bob, and went in to tea. As soon as he'd finished he went out, scarcely speaking to anyone, and Carol made a face at her mother as if to say, 'What's up with *him*?'

When Dad arrived, he too looked preoccupied and a bit puzzled. 'Sorry I'm late, dear, I was waylaid by old Keith. You remember I asked him about that journal?'

'Yes, dear,' said Mum, not really listening.

'Well, he's come up with some interesting stuff. Fosset House, for example. It's been a ruin for about fifty years, and before that it was empty back to Dr. Creighton's time.'

'Any clue why he buried the Nondescript?' asked Carol.

'Perhaps there was another hot summer and the water fell,' said Mum. 'Though that doesn't explain why.'

'Probably to get rid of the thing!' said Carol.

Dad changed the subject and went on with his tea, but he looked thoughtful. 'Bob gone out?' he enquired casually.

'Yes,' said Carol. 'He was looking at the map—said something about Fosset Pool.'

Dad looked startled and seemed about to speak, but changed his mind. He finished his tea rather quickly and said idly that he was going for a walk.

Once out of sight of the house, he walked faster, heading for Fosset Pool. There were three things he hadn't mentioned at the tea table, not wanting to worry anybody. First, the eccentric Dr. Creighton had died by drowning, in the Pool, in strange circumstances; second, Thurston Bayliss had drowned a year later *in the same pool*; third, Dad remembered that some animals, like turtles, spent periods hibernating in the mud at the bottom of a pond. He quickened his pace further.

Bob, at that moment, was not walking. He was standing on the bank of the Pool, gazing across the water with mingled fear and curiosity. Although he had not worked it out logically, he knew he had not been dreaming the other night. The Nondescript *had* come to life. It had torn its fake replica to pieces and escaped through the window. He wouldn't have thought it could move well on land, but then a seal, although clumsy, can still get around so perhaps a Nondescript could too.

The creature had made straight for home, for the Pool. Bob wondered where its real home was. Some far-off land, whence Dr. Creighton had unwisely bought it. On its way to the Pool, it had spent a night each in two goldfish ponds, feasting on the inhabitants. Bob preferred not to speculate about Mr. Maybrick's death. Steve must be right—except that it wasn't a cat the old man caught attacking his pets.

And now the beast was home. Somewhere in these murky depths the weird creature lurked, and Bob wanted to see it once more, then he'd leave it alone. And hope that *it* would leave others alone.

There! Bob started violently and stared. His long wait had been rewarded at last. In the middle of the Pool a grotesque head emerged, dripping, from the dark water. As Bob stared, fascinated, forgetting to be frightened, the beast reared its torso above the surface, turning its head about as if looking for something... or someone.

It saw him!

Despite the distance Bob could hear its savage hiss as it fastened its pale eyes on him. Instantly he knew he had been wrong to come here, and equally he knew he could not run. Those eyes...

Just as they had that night in his room, the Nondescript's eyes seemed to swell, glowing with their own internal light, until they were the only things in the whole world. There was just Bob, and those eyes. The beast was swimming slowly, smoothly towards him, though he was hardly aware of it; he knew only that the eyes were, impossibly, growing bigger still.

They stopped moving.

They seemed to shrink a little, though they were brighter than ever, then they began to pulse. Their cold light throbbed like some evil signal, and now Bob heard the voice. It wasn't a real voice, not real words, and it was somehow coming from inside his own head, but he knew what it said.

It was calling him to the Pool.

Like an absurd dummy Bob stepped, swaying, across the mud towards the deep, dark water where the small hissing monster waited, grinning in triumph and beckoning with crooked claws. His feet reached the water's edge, passed beyond it, and even in the warm summer evening a chill entered his bones. But he did not notice, because the eyes held him, and the voice called.

The water was at his knees.

'Bob!'

Somebody else called, somewhere far off, too far for him to care, but the eyes wavered, just for an instant, and the hateful voice faltered.

'Bob!'

This time he did respond, or he tried to, but the eyes pulsed with a fiercer light, and the voice swelled to a summons he could not fight.

The water was at his waist, and his wet clothes were pulling him down.

'BOB! *Close your eyes!*'

Pain lanced suddenly into his arm, and the spell almost broke. Bob shook his head and grasped his bruised arm, and in that instant he saw, not only the glowing eyes, but the beast behind them. The Nondescript chattered with age, trying to bring Bob under its spell again, but he closed his eyes and put his hands over his ears, and stumbled out of the water. He tripped on the ridged mud and fell, hurting his knee, but the pain brought him back to himself. He opened his eyes to see his father running towards him, his head held oddly to one side.

'Don't look at it, Bob! Don't look at its eyes. It nearly had me, too...'

'Look out!' shouted Bob, and his father spun round, but the beast was too quick. Shooting through the water in fury, it leapt like a salmon, six feet in the air, straight for Dad's throat.

Bob's father fell backwards, taken by surprise, but he managed to get an arm in the way and the Nondescript fastened claws and fangs in it, instead of his throat. Bob, forgetting his own bruises, rushed to help, and grabbed the stringy neck. Dad got his other hand to the thrashing tail and with a mighty effort dragged the beast off him. With a great sweep of his arm he swung the thing like a whip, to thud on the hard ground.

The Nondescript lay still.

Bob and his father sat down, breathing heavily, and neither spoke for some time.

'Sorry about your arm,' said Dad. 'I threw a stone—I had to wake you up, but I couldn't get too close, or that brute would have hypnotized me too.' He looked at his torn sleeve and bleeding arm. 'I think... we'd better say we were attacked by a dog, and this beast, well, we'll never mention it to anybody.'

Bob nodded agreement.

'It's dead now, after however many years. I don't want to see any more of it,' said Dad.

Making a face, he picked up the Nondescript and studied the limp form. There was no sign of life, no breathing or heartbeat. He flung it in a long arc across the Pool, and with a final splash it sank from sight.

Bob and his father turned and limped away across the fields. Bob took a last look over his shoulder at the peaceful waters of the Pool, purged now of their monstrous occupant.

Did he see, at the deepest part, the merest hint of the flick of a scaly tail?

WHAT WE WERE LOOKING FOR IN HORROR

M. R. JAMES ONCE WROTE that the reader of a ghost story must be put into the position of saying to himself, "If I'm not very careful something of this kind may happen to me". Therein lies the effectiveness of most ghost and horror fiction, certainly that of M. R. James himself who always took painstaking trouble to set his marvels amidst the most mundane of realistically detailed settings. Fantasy of course is quite distinct from this. Here there is no attempt to involve the reader—or viewer—directly. While a perfectly legitimate branch of literature and the cinema, the observer has no chance to live vicariously through the central protagonist; he is merely presented with a deliberately stylised and mannered sequence of events, with all the formalism of poetry, which should at its best and most successful arouse in him a feeling of awe. He is taken out of his everyday surroundings. while the kind of macabre story we are concerned with, as was Mr James, should involve him deeper, making him almost super conscious of his own environment. If he is no longer aware of the tapping outside his window he won't worry about what is making it.

Fantasy, even if it were permissible within the context of our TV series, is almost impossible to put over convincingly on TV because of this one-remove aspect in which the viewer watches it. TV to succeed must be immediate. Therefore all the stories we have chosen rely for their effectiveness on unlikely happenings in unlikely, everyday surroundings—even if it's the surroundings of the Victorian era.

The Cinema too has recognised this difficulty. There have been few genuine fantasy films. Instead for the most part what we term the horror film—even the superior horror films—has relied for its effects on mechanical contrivances which nullify objectives. Familiarity with cliché has certainly bred contempt there. Cliché, in effect, in atmosphere, in character delineation, even in the fact that the same actors are used over and over again, has been employed here more than in any other genre of the Cinema because the horror film has evolved from the cheap Gothic novel of the nineteenth century which used just such mechanical contrivances to cover the vacuity of genuine emotion. SF absorbed elements of horror and to a certain extent liberated the genre from the entrapping folds of cliché, but too often vampirically, it has become absorbed itself into the conventional format.

In this TV series, the first the BBC has ever done, discounting *Quatermass*, we have tried to divorce the macabre from the cliché-ridden treatment under which it has been almost stifled. We've had to do this in sheer self-defence, if for no other reason because we've only got 25 minutes to tell a story and we can't waste too much tine tracking down endless corridors. Or too much money on too many guttering candles. We do have candles which gutter, but only in one of the stories and only as I hope you'll agree for a very dramatic reason not for Corman-esque effect (I'm *not* knocking Corman).The stories all concentrate on plot, pure and simple, with no conscious striving for atmosphere—though atmosphere will, we trust, grow out of the plot. Horror means more than it says: thus in this form of fiction, more than in any other, viewer and reader write their own story. Good horror is implied but not stated. How many films have collapsed into anti-climactic giggles when the monster is revealed as being motivated by wire and rollers? How much more effective if he had stayed hidden behind the door, or even invisible altogether, as in *Forbidden Planet*.

Because as kids—and very often grownups—we fantasise around the traditional race-memory concepts of evil and diabolism, night and the dark are sure-fire aids to unease. But too often, as I said above, in literature Gothic symbols were used as facile replacements for genuine chills, feelings and atmosphere. Films have inherited this fatal flaw and in a sense one can only blame the baneful influence of Poe, too often in whose stories this facile exploitation of stock effects has stood in for genuine imaginative and creative power.

I was at a disadvantage because my producer only wanted to use published stories for the series, not originals. We are doing six only initially: if the series is successful we may be allowed to do some more next year. It is the first regular series to be made in colour, though it probably won't be the first to be shown. We hope to sell it abroad, but we don't even have a transmission date yet. By the time this article appears you may know all about it, but at the time of writing we can only look forward to a vague date in January. How-ever back to my point about originals. I've got some very good ones which will have to wait. The format for a possible second series may be more flexible. It is, I think, a short-sighted policy to only use published stuff. Finding published stories which are suitable for a 25 minute dramatization is not as easy an assign-ment as it sounds. Apart from the various copyright difficulties which often prove insuperable—a story I wanted to use was Aga-tha Christie's 'The Last Seance', just about the only story in the genre she's written, and very very nasty, but it was unavailable—there are other important considerations. You can't use a story which takes place over a vast period of time: it is too diffuse and the impact, divorced from its narrative environment is dissipated. You've got to find something which builds up its action to a crescendo over a very short period; ideally a matter of hours only. Like John Burke's 'Party Games' or Robert Aikman's 'Ringing the Changes'—both ideal subjects. Rules are of course to be broken, and there is the case of Lady Sannox, if you'll pardon the pun. The action of the adaptation, not the original story, does take place over a period of weeks and the scenes are deliberately short and sketchy so that the impact of the denouement is that much greater. However this is the exception and apart from Diane Cilento's lovely performance I'm afraid this may be the least successful.

Ideally in the short teleplay, as in the best short story, it is the last shot which should be the most crucial. Summing up and emphasizing, or counterpointing what has gone before. A good example is the final close-up of Michele Dotrice in 'Ringing the Changes'. Has she really emerged as unscathed from her terrible experience as she pretends! Those of you who know the story will know the answer. It is the last shot, like the last sentence which should induce chilling realisation, or recognition, in the viewer— or the reader, stretching the parallel to near breaking point. Algernon Blackwood gives us one of the best illustrations of this, in one of those stories he told over the air shortly before his death, and a superbly visual example it is too. A man has been told particularly not to go near a certain stretch of woodland at night. It is very terribly haunted by a species of ghoul whose facial characteristics are missing. To meet one can mean death. Well of course he does visit the place: after a particularly Blackwoodian atmospheric build up he sees ahead of him one of the creatures. Frozen with horror he sees the thing turn round. Where the face should be is only a white blob. Then he begins to run and run and run. Only when he sees the lights of the town approaching can he afford to relax. If only he could meet a fellow living creature, anyone in whom to confide. Then ahead of him he sees a man walking. At last a companion. He taps him on the shoulder. Blackwood ends: "Only when he turned round did Jack notice that he too had no face." What I call the rule of the man with no face is one we have tried to following the series. So be warned, don't switch off before the end.

Another problem which presented itself was the fact that the more suitable a story was for adaptation, the more similar was its plot, or theme, to one we had already. It is true that there are only a limited number of basic plots available to any writer: how much more applicable is this to stories in this' particular genre. With stories specially written for TV this can be taken into account; but not so with works written for another medium.

Also there were vast numbers of stories which revolved round one single character, all the action occurring inside his head. Some of the most chillingly effective stories ever written revolved round the onset of madness: Charlotte Perkins Gilman's 'The Yellow Wallpaper', or Conrad Aicken's 'Silent Snow, Secret Snow' are examples. If you don't know them you should. But try doing 'em on telly. (I'll shoot the first man who tells me the French have made a version of De Maupassant's 'The Horla'. Yes dears, I know. But we have one day's filming and one day in the studio. That's yer lot.) Then there's the story that begins: "Well, we went to this haunted house—" The resulting phenomena while effective in print would too often be merely laughable visually, if indeed they were practicable anyway. Marching off smartly at a tangent, if the makers of *The Shuttered Room* had stuck to the original Lovecraft story, how would they have shown the nasty fishy things without looking like Disney?

I did lay down one or two strict dicta. Madness as an evil in itself was out. It's okay for a character to do something *therefore* he's mad; but one mustn't allow him to do it *because* he's mad. A subtle point I know but I think a valid one. Stories about sinister nursing homes and hospitals were out too. Whatever one might think about the merits or demerits of *Emergency Ward 10* one cannot deny that it reduced drastically the fear and ignorance about going into hospital. It's not up to us, within the context of a purely enter-tainment series—and I stress this point—to run the risk of undoing any of this good work. We do have a story set in a hospital, but the hospital itself is very far from being sinister as you will see. The same goes for the treatment of lunatic asylums as places of evil in themselves. (Let's leave Sam Fuller out of it.) One story was sent to me which attempted to do just this and was sent back very smartly. One doesn't want to pander, God forbid, to Mrs. Whitehouse, or others of her ilk, but one must remember that there are a mixed bag of viewers watching.

But more than anything else, stories about concentration camps or places of real life horror were out. I needn't elaborate on this. But although John Campbell may not agree with this, I maintain that we're still playing a game with the viewer, a game which must be played like most games within certain boundaries, and if we attempt to cross those boundaries, it ceases to be a game. The object of the game is to chill his blood and this we will do to the best of our ability, but not to antagonise him. I hasten to add that I'm not against treating all aspects of human behaviour on TV, the bad as well as the good. Nothing should be allowed to remain under the carpet and fester, to mix metaphors. But I must stress the "right context" bit.

In case you think I'm overly squeamish, let me repeat what I said in an interview with the *Shepherds Bush Gazette*—who seemed interested. We aim to hit the viewers hard. We aim to freeze their blood, and because the plays will go out late at night when the kiddies should be in bed we're not putting on the soft peddle.

This isn't the place to go into the difficulties of colour, even if I were technically qualified to discuss them intelligently. We've had plenty. Green leaks, believe it or not. So you have to cut down on showing too much greenery. Yellow tends to come out looking very sick and it's hard to match up an exterior shot with an interior shot. So if a girl wearing a yellow dress walks from a street (film) into a room (studio) the dress is apt to change colour. So you have to write a line into the script intimating that she was wearing a—preferably neutral coloured—mackintosh. However for horror fans the fact that the first drama series to be recorded in colour is for you constitutes a major breakthrough. I hope when you see the shows early in 1968 you will feel that it's been worth it.

AN INTERVIEW WITH RICHARD DAVIS

CONDUCTED BY DAVID A. SUTTON, with new annotations
(Published in Shadow Fantasy Literature Review 8, Oct-Nov 1969)

THE INTERVIEW TOOK PLACE on Easter Saturday (1969) when I met Richard Davis for the first time. We had a drink and a chat, and the conversation wound round to the interview I had suggested earlier by letter. During the three short hours I spent with Richard I found out that he is a modest young man who has done a great deal in the genre, both in the visual medium and in literature.

Mr. Davis is perhaps best known for his work on the BBC series *Late Night Horror*, but he has also worked on *Out of the Unknown*, made a film, edited a Tandem anthology of horror stories and has another in preparation and has had himself a number of stories anthologised.

We met at the London Pavilion Cinema in Piccadilly, and immediately retired to a bar where we spent the lunch hours in vivid conversation.

DS. *What are your opinions of horror stories?*

RD. I hate the term "horror", which implies revulsion, and gruesomeness of the purely physical kind. I agree with Karloff's idea of using the word terror. I like tales which heighten the limits of imagination, which make the reader more perceptive of underlying truths in the same way that poetry does. Blackwood's stories do this. I think really stories like 'The Man Whom the Trees Loved', 'Ancient Sorceries', 'The Willows' and 'The Wendigo' are my all time favourites. Blackwood always saw beauty in horror—

the threat of the elemental world, which though it is hostile to mankind, in nevertheless a more perfect unity. Arthur Machen achieves this. Lovecraft, though influenced by Machen, very rarely does.

DS. *Any other favourite stories or novels?*

RD. No particular favourite. 'Ringing the Changes' by Robert Aickman and 'The Beckoning Fair One' by Oliver Onions. Stoker's *Dracula*. I think Robert Aickman is the best living ghost story writer.

DS. *And films?*

RD. *Invasion of the Body Snatchers* and *Dead of Night*.

DS. *What fanzines do you like?*

RD. They vary. I like *Shadow*[1]. It's the only one which concentrates on books rather than films, a praiseworthy job. I would like to see you expand the scope to factual stories and experiences of the supernatural. The best magazine is *Twylight*[2], but I haven't seen a great many.

DS. *And* Supernatural[3] *magazine?*

RD. I like it. The articles are of a high standard. I think it should embrace all aspects of the supernatural and not pigeonhole subjects.

DS. *Can you tell us about your film* Viola?

RD. It is in colour and is based on my own story 'The Female of the Species'. It was shown at the Trieste Film Festival and the music is to be published by World Pacific Records this year. It was not only composed by Ravi Shankar, but recorded by him and also Alla Rakha on table, and Les Structures Sonores[4].

DS. *The* Late Night Horror *series?*

RD. *Late Night Horror* went out last May (1968), I was story editor, chose the stories and worked closely with the adaptors on the scripts. There were six plays based on fiction by Richard Matheson, John Burke, Roald Dahl, Conan Doyle, Robert Aickman and H. Russell Wakefield [5]. They starred Diane Cilento, Claire Bloom, Donald Sinden, Roy Dotrice, Michele Dotrice, Brenda Bruce and Andrew Keir.

DS. *And* Out of the Unknown *and* Thirteen Against Fate?

RD. In *Out of the Unknown* and *Thirteen Against Fate* (stories by Simenon) I was assistant story editor – but *Late Night Horror* was virtually my own show [6].

DS. *What about your interest in* The Twilight Zone *series, which hasn't been fully shown in this country?*

RD. Yes, agitate for its revival. It was the best television series ever made!

DS. *Would you like to see H. P. Lovecraft's work on television?*

RD. I don't think there'd be any point in attempting to televise Lovecraft, although we talked about it last year. His storylines aren't all that strong and his stories are essentially literary. The disastrous Blackwood series is an indication of how this type of material can go completely wrong [7]. I'd like to see a really good film done though, with a film's greater resources. Perhaps the new *Dunwich Horror* from AIP might prove a breakthrough— I believe Matheson has written it. Wouldn't it be marvellous if Welles or a giant of that calibre could be persuaded to make a Lovecraft subject?

DS. *What are your feelings as editor of Tandem anthologies? How do you react to fiction sent to you and what do you like to see in stories?*

RD. Just send me good stories! My reaction then will be one of satisfaction. I don't want lurid strip-cartoon stories with little adult appeal, and I don't want stories over-written! This is a basic mistake horror story writers tend to make. Too many "forbidden horrors" merely bore the readers. Good horror must imply more than it says! My introduction to *Tandem Horror 2* is my gospel.

DS. *Finally, what are your ambitions? I know that you want to start a publishing house.*

RD. Yes, this is a big thing with me. Ideally it would be along the lines of Arkham House. I should like to publish August Derleth's Lovecraft biography and John Campbell's *The Inhabitant of the Lake* as a start. Original stuff and so far unobtainable (in UK editions, ed.). I also want to write novels, produce and script movies... you name it!

REFERENCES

1. Shadow: Fantasy Literature Review, edited by David A. Sutton. 21 issues published 1968-1972.

2. Twylight, edited by Michael J. Harris. Two issues published 1967-1968.

4. Les Structures Sonores. A French avant-garde instrumental group using shaped metal and plastic, bars and sheets played with a bow, drumsticks or by hand.

5. *Late Night Horror*. Six plays broadcast by the BBC in 1968. The stories were 'No Such Thing as a Vampire' (Richard Matheson), 'William and Mary' (Roald Dahl), 'The Corpse Can't Play' (an adaptation of John Burke's story 'Party Games'), 'The Triumph of Death' (H. Russell Wakefield), 'The Bells of Hell' (an adaptation of Robert Aickman's 'Ringing the Changes'), and 'The Kiss of Blood' (Sir Arthur Conan Doyle).

6. *Out of the Unknown* and 13 *Against Fate*. *Out of the Unknown* was created by Irene Shubik and 49 episodes were aired on BBC2 from 1965-1971. *13 Against Fate* featured adaptations of five (non-Maigret) Georges Simenon stories, broadcast by BBC1 in 1966.

7. *Tales of Mystery*. Aired by ITV in three seasons between 1961-1963. Adaptations of Algernon Blackwood stories, with actor John Laurie as the host "Algernon Blackwood".

HORROR IN FICTION

I WANT TO SAY a few words about horror in fiction generally, and then make a few statements which might reasonably form the basis for our discussion afterwards. "Horror" as applied to fiction means in the majority of cases "the supernatural", so that most of what I say will apply to that. To a certain extent this type of story is a mass substitute for poetry, dealing as it does with wonders and marvels outside the narrow range of the purely physical.

Thus firstly let's begin by defining what the term literary "horror" is *not*. It's not the facile relation of gruesome physical events: or the painstakingly accurate and detailed descriptions of corpses in various stages of decomposition. It's certainly not the portrayal of sadistic practices for their own sake. This kind of story, relying for its effects on the ability to inspire the maximum of disgust and revulsion in the reader, or in turn if the reader is in any way perverted enough to respond with pleasure to these descriptions, to grant him a correspondingly vivid sexual thrill, is now turning up more and more between the covers of paperbacks and in some cases hardbacks too. With the growing influence of the so-called permissive society and the correspondingly greater freedom of expression literature can now utilise, the good and liberating effects may be counter-balanced by evil ones, if we're not careful: and "horror for its own sake", using a titillating mixture of sexual perversion and violence, could usurp and take over the genre completely. It's all too easy to write this type of material. Whereas the business of the author is to elicit reader response and reaction by his own skills, in this case half his job is done for him already. No one can help being moved by descriptions of physical horror, whether the reader be thrilled, titillated or just plain nauseated. If the horror is revolting enough, the effect will stay with him long after he's put down the book, and of course if he's sufficiently sensitive, it will stay with him forever. If he has been misled into believing that this type of spurious effect is the primary business of the "horror story", he will believe that the story has been a good one. It will either put him off the genre for good, or, as I say, if his inclinations lie along—shall we say—unusual channels, he will become addicted to horror stories for the wrong reasons. This type of pervert material is not what we should mean by a horror story, and just because very often it is a facile substitute for literary skill in creating genuinely terrifying, chilling tales, it has done the genre as a whole a very great deal of harm. Not least perhaps because today it seems to be the easiest type of story to get published.

With all due respect to Mr. Lee, who in fact I know agrees with me over this, the film industry hasn't helped here either. More and more, what in nominally labelled a "horror" movie, is becoming merely an excuse for the maximum amount of sexual titillation and violence.

In any case "horror" in this context always has been a misnomer. Boris Karloff preferred the term "terror" in describing one's reactions. I certainly think that if "terror" were more widely used as a definition, we wouldn't feel quite so guilty about admitting that we enjoy these stories. Who of us feels entirely at ease and not the slightest bit apologetic when we admit a liking for "horror stories"? And yet what on earth is there in common between one's enjoyment and appreciation of the exquisitely subtle and chilling tales of cosmic horror by, say, Algernon Blackwood and the squalors and morbidities of your average Sunday tabloid case-history? And yet they are all described by the blanket term "horror".

The terms have always been confused. Different practitioners have had different definitions. Dennis Wheatley maintains that "terror" describes one in the face of physical danger only while "horror" conveys fear of the supernatural. Alfred Hitchcock's position tallies with Karloff's. H. P. Lovecraft, one of the genres greatest assets, maintains that only the term "horror" is applicable. But Karloff summed it up best when he said that "horror" is awakened by gruesome physical realities, whereas "terror" is the feeling we experience in the presence of the Unknown. 'The terms,' he said, 'are literally poles apart in their meaning'.

H. P. Lovecraft, in his essay *Supernatural Horror in Literature*, says, 'The oldest and strongest kind of fear is fear of the Unknown'. That is why most genuine horror tales—we must continue to use the term for convenience—are about the Unknown, hence the supernatural.

But fear isn't necessarily a pleasant emotion. Why do we need to encourage it? One of the most obvious answers is Man's temperamental and emotional need for something beyond the boundaries of the purely physical and the purely realistic, as perceived by his five senses. Something outside himself. Freud spoke about repressed infantile complexes needing to be channelled into harmless outlets. We all have nameless fears and dreads, though in most of our well-adjusted cases they remain subconscious. If they can be captured and held within the confines of a work of fiction, perhaps they can be shut between the pages of the book when we close it. In this sense horror in fiction shares with the horror movie the function of a cathartic agent. We give concrete form to something which otherwise might remain vague and fester inside us.

Going off at a tangent for a minute, it's significant to observe that in the genuine horror tale there is very little excess violence, certainly never violence for its own sake, unlike the crime story, and human life is *always* sacrosanct. Death is treated as a *tremendous* event, and never, except in the case of black comedy which is a completely separate genre, treated as a casual ingredient. The repercussions of death can continue eternally. That is why those who condemn horror movies for contributing towards teenage violence couldn't be more wrong. Westerns have much more to answer for. I say that for the *genuine* horror story. This ruling certainly applied in the days of Browning and Lewton for instance, at the old Universal Studios. Unfortunately today many "horror" movies aren't *genuine* horror, in this sense, because they're made for the wrong reasons.

We were talking just now about the 'subconscious need for "horror"', or rather fear. There is an extension to the theory of repressed infantile complexes. This places the fascination most of us feel for the vicarious experience of fear in the existence of the subconscious race-memories: some sort of vast universal pool which we can tap and extract what emotionally suits us best. Thus primitive man, fearing the Unknown, which could afford perils and dangers which were only too real, peopled it additionally with demons and monsters and all kinds of supernatural Beings. Thus he invented the first Mythology.

In fact the earliest stories were concerned almost exclusively with supernatural beings. In keeping alive the ghost story we are in fact carrying on the oldest tradition of all. Probably ghost stories were written even before kings or rulers thought to ask the priests to record their glorious deeds in writing.

We have to remember too the changing nature of readers. *Now*, the great art of the convincing ghost story is in atmosphere build-up, the ability to knock down the reader's natural reaction against accepting the incredible. But the story of the Witch of Endor, for example, was taken as nothing more than a record of facts, a truthful revelation questioned by none. Some of the earliest written examples of the supernatural appeared in Petronius. Later Chaucer was to use the supernatural in 'The Nun's Priest's Tale'.

Until the great era of the English short story in the 19th century, it came to be the property exclusively of the drama of Elizabethan days, and later the Gothic novel. This was because audiences still didn't need to be convinced of the objective truth of this world of parallel gods, demons and ghosts. They knew it existed, and thus it could take its place in the longer form without undue emphasis. The drama wasn't essentially a drama of the supernatural, nor the Gothic novel essentially a ghostly romance. Shakespeare didn't need to convince his audiences that Hamlet's father's ghost could walk the battlements, nor that Macbeth's witches could foretell the future. They lived cheek by jowl with such omens and portents, which thus were nothing remarkable.

It needed an age of Materialism for the supernatural to really come into its own. After the paraphernalia of the Gothic novel with its haunted castles, secret passages, trap-doors, vaults and cemeteries, readers' impatience and disbelief continued to grown and materialistic thought was spreading. Weird fiction had to change its methods. It left the newly-conquered domain of the novel and returned to the primitive and most logical form, the short story. The public wouldn't accept any longer ghosts and goblins for hundreds of pages. It had to be taken by surprise in a short tale. Thus 19th and 20th century weird fiction did what the Gothic novels hadn't done—it gave us the tale wholly and unique-ly devoted to the supernatural to the exclusion of all other dra-matic effects: and it took pains to build up the kind of atmosphere which would attempt to convince the new, rather self-conscious sceptics.

M. R. James, still one of the greatest ghost story writers who ever lived, defined the genre thus: 'Let us then be introduced to the actors in a placid way: let us see them going about their ordinary business undisturbed by forebodings, pleased with their surround-ings: and into this calm environment let the ominous "thing" put out its head, unobtrusively at first, and then more insistently, until it holds the stage. It is not amiss sometimes to let the loophole be so narrow as not to be quite practicable...'

This, it seems to me, is the great secret of the effective ghost sto-ry, or the tale of horror even if it isn't a ghost story. The willing suspension of disbelief, to coin a cliché, isn't easily won. It is a precious victory for a writer to win at all, and once gained is too easily lost. The abnormality at the core of the story should be seen in isolation. It is *vitally* important that the backcloth against which it is painted should be as un-sensational as it's possible for the writer to create, and a great deal is gained through reticence and understatement. If you start describing your monsters in intricate detail, you run the great risk of being laughed out of countenance. Just as in the cinema, what you don't see is always more effective than what you do see, to quote Christopher Lee. As the creaking door opens, suspense is much more effectively maintained if you cut to a reaction shot of the heroine's face, to quote an obvious example. So in fiction, the effective chiller is the story that *hints* the most successfully. Thus the functions of the sheer tale of fantasy or the fairy story are quite different, and it is not their business to convince the reader that in certain cases the events in the story he is reading about might actually happen to *him*.

This was very much M. R. James' precept, and he stuck to it brilliantly. Other writers who have earned themselves respectable places in the history of the genre had different aims, of course. Dickens and R. L. Stevenson used the supernatural to lend weight and authority to their moral teaching. Conrad, Aitken, W. F. Harvey and Henry James had the psychologist's interest in the illusions of the "haunted" man and de la Mare added to this interest the poet's love of the Marvellous. My personal favourite, Algernon Blackwood, had visions of Nature's hidden forces which might be based on truths deeper that mere imagination could reach.

Because Blackwood's themes were more diffuse than most

writers in the genre, he was able to use them, with varying degrees of success, in his novels. *The Centaur* and *The Education of Uncle Paul* for example, work extremely well in parts, and have passages of great beauty, even if they *are* uneven. With the current renewal of interest in mysticism, and what he called 'the opening of the inner door', I feel that a renewal of interest in Blackwood's lesser known work is overdue. Perhaps like the recent H. P. Lovecraft cult, he'll also become a cult figure as soon as his novels are rediscovered. On the whole though, novels of the supernatural, and plays too, have never worked very well. I discount here the Gothic romances mentioned earlier which used the supernatural as one of a series of other events centering round plots of melodramatic contrivance.

No, I mean the novel centering exclusively round a supernatural visitation. Bram Stoker's *Dracula* stands head and shoulders above any other example, but Stoker never wrote anything else to compare with it, and certainly his other novels are a very poor lot. Also of course *Dracula* is chockfull of Gothic romantic influence. Offhand I can think of only one other novel which manages to sustain throughout its length the requisite atmosphere of credibility, and that's Dorothy McArdle's *The Uninvited*. This was made into a fair enough film, but it's rare indeed for the cinema to tackle the supernatural on any serious level.

A favourite theme of writers in the genre has been the creation of a complete mythology, with its attendant gods and demons, providing a usefully fruitful supply of cosmic menace to mankind. H. P. Lovecraft, with his Cthulhu Mythos, is an example. He wrote, 'All my stories, unconnected as they may be, are based on the fundamental lore or legend that this world was inhabited by another race who, in practicing Black Magic, lost their foothold and were expelled, yet live on outside, ever ready to take possession of this earth again'.

Many writers have used this since: in fact Lovecraft himself encouraged this friendly plagiarism, and August Derleth, who was himself almost completely responsible for the rediscovery of this Rhode Island recluse, started a publishing house, Arkham House, named after the mythical town which figured so largely in Lovecraft's stories, but which was in reality the town of Providence. Arkham House is devoted solely to the publishing of weird stories or biographies of writers of weird stories, and among their most popular authors are names like Clark Ashton Smith, Manly Wade Wellman, Robert E. Howard, William Hope Hodgson and H. Russell Wakefield. The Cthulhu Mythos is still being freely drawn upon, by young English writers like John Ramsey Campbell and Brian Lumley, both of whom have books on the Arkham House list. Even Colin Wilson has used the mythos in two of his novels. Blackwood once observed that it was a great shame that we don't have the equivalent of Arkham House in this country—a point of view with which I heartily concur.

Lovecraft had many influences in his work, including inevitably Edgar Allan Poe—of whom there is very little left to say—and Arthur Machen, who also used the theme of the elder, hostile race. In Machen's stories this race was equated with the "little people", the fairies, whom in self-defence we identify with children's nursery imagery, but who in reality are evil, stunted, hideous and terribly hostile. Banished from the haunts of men, they live on in remote places, ever scheming to return to power, to throw out the Human Race, the usurper. A short story of his, 'The Novel of the Black Seal'—which *was* a short story not a novel, although it originally *appeared* in a novel—dealt pretty typically with this theme.

Lastly, in connection with the Cthulhu Mythos, I must mention the author who is perhaps the top American writer in this field alive today, Robert Bloch. He is incredibly prolific, churning out a never ending supply of material for magazines and anthologies, on all subjects and in all styles. He began his career as a member of the

"Lovecraft Circle", writing Cthulhu stories very much in the Lovecraftian precise, academic style, but now prefers the modern, laconic, staccato approach. He has also written many screenplays both for cinema and television... and this leads me to a consideration of horror on TV.

About three years ago I edited a series for BBC television called *Late Night Horror*. A great title! While not entirely successful, the series was fairly well received, and we used adaptations from writers as varied as Conan Doyle through Roald Dahl to Robert Aickman—in my opinion, incidentally, the finest and most polished writer of supernatural stories alive today, certainly in this country. I strove to obey the principles of "reticence" mentioned earlier, although physical horror was certainly used. I think it worked because in the context of the series it came as the climax—in true short story technique, the effect wasn't vitiated by horror piled on horror over-balancing into absurdity: the horrific incident was given its due importance and emphasis. So that the viewers' capacity for appreciating its subtler chills wasn't blunted. Admittedly our stories each lasted only twenty-five minutes—in the average feature length movie, this sort of structure is invalid: that's why the old Gothic ingredients are reworked so often in the movies.

Choosing subject-matter for horror on TV is a dodgy business, though perhaps one is freer now than even three years ago. One has to tread somewhat warily over viewers' susceptibilities, not forgetting the greater impact of visuals in the home. For example horror in a setting which will cause pain to people because it's too real—when I was sifting through scripts someone sent one in with the background of a German concentration camp. Well, this was quite impermissible within the context of a fictional entertainment series whose motive was basically frivolous. Whereas of course in a serious documentary one could explore this area pretty thoroughly.

Then too the question of insanity as an object of horror per se, is in my opinion immoral. This is just as true for a piece of written fiction. Some of the greatest uncanny tales ever written have dealt with insanity brilliantly, but they have done so with compassion. One thinks particularly of Conrad Aitken's 'Silent Snow, Secret Snow' and Charlotte Perkins Gilman's 'The Yellow Wallpaper', both of which describe with horrifying conviction, cases of schizophrenic obsession. The all-important distinction, as I see it, in using insanity in a horror story is that the reader—or viewer— must be able to say, "He does this *therefore* he is mad", not "he does this *because* he's mad". This isn't as hair-splitting as you may think when I throw it to you like that.

In my opinion, Tod Browning's famous film *Freaks* is guilty of not making this distinction. And that's why I, personally, can't take it. Despite what has been written about this film by its admirers—and there's no denying it's a remarkable piece of work—and the apologists who maintain that the freaks are treated sympathetically, until the end when the girl deserves all she gets at their hands, the fact remains that the ending does choose to show the freaks as objects of horror in themselves. I've seen the film twice and each time the last reel comes up, I've felt uncomfortable watching it, and for no reason connected with the plot. It seems to be a betrayal of everything that's gone before. Browning seems to be saying "You see they *are* really monsters after all. If you upset them, they revert to savagery..." His use of *real* freaks in this movie adds immeasurably to one's unease.

Compassion then is all-important in the horror tale. Mary Shelley knew this well, when she wrote *Frankenstein*—which is really Gothically inspired Science Fiction. SF also deals with extensions to the known world, and because so many SF writers wrote straight horror tales the two categories have become entangled. *Now*, it seems to me that the line which attempts to divide SF from the straight horror/supernatural tale is a false one.

SF is no longer a specific term in which to describe literary works. Many publishers have dropped it as a definition from the covers of their books, in which authors normally associated with SF appear. In any case the best SF has nothing to do with science—it's much more concerned with sociological questions, most often used to point a sociological moral, or cautionary lesson.

But unlike horror, SF is a generalised term. Its various forms are more and more a microcosm of the "mainstream" novel or short story, embracing all moods, forms and styles. To say "this is an SF anthology" and "this is a horror anthology" seems to me an artificial and contrived distinction. The term SF will become less and less meaningful as literature comes to concern itself more and more with the pressing problems of the next few years.

I want to end by quoting Dr. Peter Penzoldt in his excellent *Supernatural in Fiction*. 'The short story of the supernatural is a fine and dignified form of literature, and well worth critical attention'. Long may it remain so. Please don't let's cheapen the coin.

(This is the complete text of Richard Davis' speech at the Bedford Square "Book Bang" in London, June 5th 1971. On the panel, entitled "Two Hundred Years of Horror Fiction", with him were Christopher Lee, Philip Strick of the BFI and Mary Danby).

BIBLIOGRAPHY

HORROR ANTHOLOGIES
Tandem Horror 2, Tandem Books 1968
Tandem Horror 3, Tandem Books 1969
The Year's Best Horror Stories 1, Sphere Books 1971
The Year's Best Horror 2, Sphere Books 1972
The Year's Best Horror 3, Sphere Books 1973
The Year's Best Horror Stories: Series I, DAW Books 1971
The Year's Best Horror Stories: Series II, DAW Books 1974
The Year's Best Horror Stories: Series III, DAW Books 1975) *

* NOTE: DAW Series I is a reprint of the Sphere no. 1. Series II
is a selection from the Sphere no. 2, and 3. Series III is original,
and was published in the U.K. the following year as *The First
Orbit Book of Horror*, Orbit 1976 *

HORROR & SF ANTHOLOGIES FOR YOUNGER
READERS
Spectre 1 Abelard Schuman 1974
Spectre 2 Abelard Schuman 1975
Spectre 3 Abelard Schuman 1976
Spectre 4 Abelard Schuman 1977

Space 1, Abelard-Schuman 1973
Space 2, Abelard-Schuman 1974
Space 3, Abelard-Schuman 1977
Space 4, Abelard-Schuman 1977

Space 5, Hutchinson 1979
Space 6, Hutchinson 1980
Space 7, Hutchinson 1981
Space 8, Hutchinson 1983
Space 9, Hutchinson 1985

Armada Sci-Fi 1, Armada Books 1975
Armada Sci-Fi 2, Armada Books 1975
Armada Sci-Fi 3, Armada Books 1976
Armada SF 4, Armada Books 1977

OTHER ANTHOLOGIES
The First Orbit Book of Horror Stories, Orbit Books 1976 *
Vincent Price Presents: The Price of Fear, Everest Books 1976
The Jon Pertwee Book of Monsters, Methuen 1978, Magnet paperback 1979
Animal Ghosts, Hutchinson Junior Books 1980, Granada Books 1982

NON-FICTION
I've Seen a Ghost: True Stories From Show Business, Hutchinson 1979, Dragon paperback 1981
Spies: The True Story, Hutchinson 1982
The Encyclopaedia of Horror, Octopus Books 1981, Hamlyn paperback 1987
Real Life Monsters, Macmillan/Nelson Thornes Ltd 1988
Endangered Species, Macmillan 1989
Prodigies: Exceptional Childhoods and Supernormal Powers, Aquarian Press 1992

WORK FOR TELEVISION AND FILM

Out of the Unknown, Assistant Story Editor. Broadcast 1965-1971
Thirteen Against Fate, Assistant Story Editor. Broadcast 1966
Late Night Horror, Story Editor. Broadcast 1968
Viola. Producer/Writer. Made in 1968
The Price of Fear Contributed his story 'Guy Fawkes Night' to the BBC Radio series, which episode aired in 1973.

SHORT FICTION

Guy Fawkes Night, The Fourth Pan Book of Horror Stories, Edited by Herbert van Thal, Pan Books 1963, Vincent Price Presents: The Price of Fear, edited by Richard Davis, Everest Books 1976.
A Nice Cut off the Joint, No Such Thing as a Vampire, Edited by Frederick Pickersgill, Corgi Books 1964
The Female of the Species, And Graves Give up Their Dead, edited by Frederick Pickersgill, Corgi Books 1964
The Inmate, The Sixth Pan Book of Horror Stories, edited by Herbert van Thal, Pan Books 1965, Horror 7, edited by Frederick Pickersgill, Corgi Books 1965.
The Lady by the Stream, Tandem Horror 2, edited by Richard Davis, Tandem Books 1968
A Day Out, The Fifth Ghost Book, edited by Rosemary Timperley, Barrie & Rockliff 1969, Pan Books 1971, The 19th Fontana Books of Great Ghost Stories, edited by R. Chetwynd-Hayes, Fontana Books 1983.
The Sick Room, Tandem Horror 3, edited by Richard Davis, Tandem Books 1959
Elsie and Agnes, The Sixth Ghost Book, edited by Rosemary Timperley, Barrie & Rockliff 1970, Pan Books 1972

The Time of Waiting, New Writings in Horror & The Supernatural 1, edited by David A. Sutton,
The Clump, A Chill to the Sunlight, edited by Rick Ferreira, William Kimber, 1978
The Nondescript **, The Jon Pertwee Book of Monsters, Methuen 1978, Magnet Books 1979. Skylark Ghost & Monster Stories, edited by Jill Bennett, Book Club Associates, 1980

** NOTE. In the Jon Pertwee Book of Monsters, the author for *The Nondescript* is shown as 'Philip Welby'. However it is unlikely that the editor of the Skylark anthology ascribed the wrong author to this story in both the contents list and acknowledgements, which leaves the very real possibility that 'Philip Welby' is a pseudonym used by Richard Davis. Which then leaves the intriguing possibility that the short story *Buffy*, which appears in both the 11th Fontana Book of Ghost Stories (Fontana 1978) and 65 Great Tales of Terror (Octopus Books 1981), under the by-line of Philip Welby, and the novel *The Pleasure Domes of Sigma 93* (Robert Hale 1978) also by Philip Welby, may indeed be the work of Richard Davis. However, without further material evidence this will remain conjecture.

Also available from
Shadow Publishing

Phantoms of Venice
Selected by David A. Sutton
ISBN 0-9539032-1-4

The Satyr's Head: Tales of Terror
Selected by David A. Sutton
ISBN 978-0-9539032-3-8

The Female of the Species And Other Terror Tales
By Richard Davis
ISBN 978-0-9539032-4-5

Frightfully Cosy And Mild Stories For Nervous Types
By Johnny Mains
ISBN 978-0-9539032-5-2

Horror! Under the Tombstone: Stories from the Deathly
Realm
Selected by David A. Sutton
ISBN 978-0-9539032-6-9

The Whispering Horror
By Eddy C. Bertin
ISBN: 978-0-9539032-7-6

The Lurkers in the Abyss and Other Tales of Terror
By David A. Riley
ISBN: 978-0-9539032-9-0

Worse Things Than Spiders and Other Stories
By Samantha Lee
ISBN: 978-0-9539032-8-3

Tales of the Grotesque: A Collection of Uneasy Tales
By L. A. Lewis
ISBN: 978-0-9572962-0-6

Horror on the High Seas
Selected by David A. Sutton
ISBN 978-0-9572962-1-3

Creeping Crawlers
Edited by Allen Ashley
ISBN 978-0-9572962-2-0

Haunts of Horror
Edited by David A. Sutton
ISBN 978-0-9572962-3-7

Death After Death
By Edmund Glasby
ISBN 978-0-9572962-4-4

The Spirit of the Place & Other Strange Tales
By Elizabeth Walter
ISBN 978-0-9572962-5-1